TURBULENCE

SCREENPLAY AWARDS

Turbulence*: Awards
 Semi-Finalist – Creative Screenwriting Unique Voices, 2021
 Semi-Finalist – Chicago Screenplay Awards, 2021
 Semi-Finalist – Rhode Island Film Festival, 2021
 Quarter-Finalist – Screen Craft Competition, TV Pilot, 2021
 Honorable Mention Wiki – The World's Fastest Screenplay
  Contest, 2021
 Quarter Finalist – People's Pilot, 2019
 Favorable Review on The Blacklist, 2015

Mr. Zak: Awards
 Burbank International Film Festival, 2021
 Santa Barbara Film Festival, 2021
 People's Pilot, Finalist, 2019

Mission to Indochina
 Second Rounder – International Screenwriters Awards, 2021

Whistleblower
 Second Rounder – Austin Film Festival, 2015

Magnum P. I.
 Best Original Spec Script for Classic TV show, 2011
 Table Read in 2016 Wild Sound Film Festival

Jury – Script Reader
 New York International Screenwriters Awards, 2027 and 2019

---

*History of Turbulence
Turbulence originated as a television script written in 2013 by Lew Ritter. In 2019, it developed into a television series concept compete with Pilot Script and Series Bible with five seasons of character arcs and episode ideas. It dealt with the political and social movements of the time.

Each season would represent one year in the lives of the students in the series from 1970-1974. It had potential to continue till the end of the 1970's and explore issues of inflation, gas crisis, Jimmy Carter, disco and the rise of Ronald Reagan.

Story by Lew Ritter | Teleplay by Lew Ritter and Joe Rosario

TURBULENCE

Dispatches from the Student Protest Movement

Rutgers 1970

Lewis Kenneth Ritter

Wild
ginger
Press

Turbulence: Dispatches from the Student Protest Movement, Rutgers 1970
© 2022 Lewis Kenneth Ritter

ISBN: (print) 978-1-943190-30-0
        (eversion) 978-1-943190-31-7

Front cover protest photo by Ken Hawkins / Alamy Stock Photo.

Publisher's Cataloging-in-Publication data

Names: Ritter, Lewis Kenneth, author.
Title: Turbulence : dispatches from the student protest movement , Rutgers 1970 / Lewis Kenneth Ritter.
Description: Yachats, OR: Wild Ginger Press, 2022.
Identifiers: LCCN 2021922116 | ISBN 978-1-943190-30-0 (print) | 978-1-943190-31-7 (ebook)
Subjects: LCSH Rutgers University--History--Fiction. | Rutgers University--Students--History--Fiction. | Student movements--United States--History--20th century--Fiction. | Friendship--Fiction. | BISAC FICTION / Biographical | FICTION / Friendship | FICTION / Historical
Classification: LCC PS3618.I778 T87 2022 | DDC 813.6--dc23

Wild Ginger Press
www.wildgingerpress.com
Book & Cover Design by Bobbi Benson

To my wife Bonnie
who never stopped believing in me

Contents

1

Rutgers: Autumn 1970

There are many unpleasant moments in life that you cannot avoid and must confront head on despite your fears. For Danny Watkins, late teens, lanky, with long brown hair, granny glasses and a worldly expression, this was a moment that he truly dreaded. He trudged up the stairs towards the office of the *Daily Targum*, the student newspaper. He took a deep breath and proceeded up the stairs. He hesitated before entering, certain that no matter what he did, Morris, the editor of the paper, would find fault with his story. Jim Morris, in his twenties, was a large, ill-tempered man with a full beard and a gut from drinking too much beer. Morris was a brutal taskmaster who demanded much from his young staff.

Danny had suffered from a bad relationship with the mercurial editor. It was the height of the Vietnam War protests on campuses around the country. Rutgers and many other college campuses were being rocked daily by large-scale protests opposing the war in Vietnam.

Danny wanted to cover these protests, but Morris kept giving him stories that Danny considered trivial or uninteresting.

Danny entered the newsroom and spotted one of his fellow reporters sitting at his desk. He eyed Danny as he entered but turned away and refused to make eye contact. Danny knew what was coming and it was clear that this other reporter did not want to be in Zeus's line of fire when he hurled his thunderbolts.

"Is that Danny? Tell him to get his ass in here!" Morris roared from his office.

Danny suspected that the meeting would not be pleasant given the events that transpired that night at the board meeting. He knew that he was entering the lion's den and that he would be the next meal. As he entered, Morris slammed the door behind him.

"I just got a phone call from the Dean," thundered Morris with a totally 'if looks could kill' expression on his face. His mouth twisted into a demonic grimace.

"Where are your notes on the building fund?" Morris hissed. The questions were in rapid fire order. Danny had no time to pause and think of what to say. He handed him his notebook.

Morris scoured the notes with a look of acrid distaste. They were gibberish. "Where is the stuff about the Dean's decision on the endowment fund?"

Danny sputtered. He knew that his ticket had been punched. "I did them in a hurry."

Morris shook his head, eyeing the notebook again of indecipherable gibberish and then he ripped them into shreds, tossed them into the nearby garbage can. "Danny, I gave you an important assignment to cover the Board of Governor's meeting. You fucked it up," he said, shaking his head.

Danny bowed his head. He felt a wave of nausea strike him. It was getting worse.

Morris stared at him with a bitter, cold expression full of disdain. Not an ounce of remorse; it was his job to punish Danny for his misdeeds. "You represent us, the paper," thundered Morris.

"I understand," said Danny, his voice weak and face filled with doubt.

"Do you? Do you really understand?" Morris ranted as he paced around the floor.

Danny knew that his job was on the line. It was possible that he could lose his scholarship and be forced to leave school. Many students who dropped out of school lost their student deferment and risked a fate worse than death by being drafted into the Army.

Danny felt his facade crumble. "I'll call and explain that it was my fault." Danny hoped to mollify Morris and deflect any errors that he had committed.

Danny was wrong. Morris was not in a conciliatory mood. He rose out of his seat, face beet-red with anger and confronted Danny. "There isn't going to be a next time," he bellowed at the young defenseless reporter.

Danny was riveted to his spot. The words echoed through Danny's brain. All he could hear were the words 'no next time.'

"We'll print an apology. Do not bother to sign out. Now get out!"

Hunched over, Danny exited the building, red-faced and embarrassed. Danny's world had just collapsed. He contemplated his future and it seemed bleak. He could barely carry himself. He trudged back to his dormitory. Even though it was a short distance away, the distance back to the dormitory seemed never-ending. He had no idea what he would do to redeem himself or his career.

2

Student Advisory Meeting

Several Days Earlier...

Danny walked out of Scott Hall, the large lecture hall on the campus. He had finished his classes for the day. He wandered back into Tinsley, a modest, three-story, faded red-brick dormitory. It was in the center of the campus surrounded by a few patches of withered grass. He was eager to relax and watch television before resuming his duties as a student advisor.

Tinsley was adjacent to several other smaller, working-class dorms. Tinsley was one of the first dormitories on the campus to house female students, or 'co-eds', at the school. During its long and distinguished history, Rutgers had been a male-only college. It had recently followed the national trend to becoming a co-ed college. Across town in another section of New Brunswick was Douglass College. It was the all-female counterpart to Rutgers and would remain a women-only college for many years to come.

Most dorm rooms housed two students. As the student advisor,

Danny was entitled to live in a single room. Danny's job was to mentor the incoming freshmen students. He realized that freshman year could be a huge adjustment for many kids. Being student advisor meant guiding newbies: it was part taskmaster and part social worker. Everyone thought of him as their worldly older brother. His sympathetic manner and eagerness to help made Danny a respectable choice for student advisor. Many of the freshmen sought Danny's advice on school or personal matters and he could be helpful to others but, at the same time, he was blind to his own issues.

Danny's room was a typical student's dwelling with clothing and books scattered around the space. Strewn around the room were piles of dirty clothing destined for a date with the laundromat. He wandered around the room, picking up empty soda cans and placing his laundry into a bag for the laundromat. On his desk were a small American flag and a picture of a younger Danny wearing his Eagle Scout uniform. In those days, Eagle Scout was the highest rank in the Boy Scout organization. He admired the grainy, black-and-white photo of his younger self. It was a tremendous accomplishment at a young age. A local paper had even written a story about him. He had it framed and displayed it on a prominent shelf in the room.

On another part of the wall, Danny stared at the autographed pictures of Western stars from the popular TV show, *Bonanza*. He was a big television buff and would sit in front of his television set every Sunday night to catch another episode of the Cartwright family conquering the Old West. *Bonanza* was one of the longest-running television series of the era. It was always in the top ten most popular shows of the week according to the Nielsen ratings, which measured the size of the audience watching a show during the week. On Danny's wall was a photo of John Wayne as a Green Beret soldier. In the corner of the room was another treasured object: his guitar. He loved to sing along with some of his favorite rock and country western artists, and he played the local entertainment venues around the campus with his friend, Ryan Marshott. On the desk was a pile of hard-bound textbooks. Several notebooks filled with class lecture notes were scattered about on the linoleum floor. Danny tried hard but was not a model of neatness.

On Danny's desk sat a photo of Kenny, his older brother. Danny stared at the photo and a warm smile came to his lips. Kenny was a handsome lad with a wholesome All-American smile. As a young boy, Danny recalled playing army with Kenny and his friends. One of his childhood memories would be playing army soldiers. They would march into the local park near their home. Their objective would be to attack an old crumbling cement structure. The structure was where the park service launched fireworks on the Fourth of July. They pretended that it was an enemy fort. Their mission was to capture the fort even though the enemy soldiers were all invisible figments of their imagination. No one ever died in those fake army wargames. Everyone took turns being wounded but there were no fatalities.

Kenny was among the first high school graduates enlisted in the real army. He was now a real soldier in the jungles of Vietnam. Danny grew dejected at the thought of his older brother trekking through the lush, humid jungles of Vietnam, thousands of miles from home. A tear rolled down his cheek as Danny recalled saying goodbye to Kenny on the day that he left for boot camp.

Kenny had grown up knowing that he would someday inherit the family farm, but he had gotten caught up in the initial patriotic fervor over the war in Vietnam. He volunteered for military service, feeling that it was his patriotic duty to serve. Matthew, their father, had been a sergeant in the Marines during the Korean War and had won several medals for bravery. Matthew was proud of his older son and disappointed when Danny expressed reluctance about joining. For Danny, his older brother was a hero and confidant. He couldn't care less about Danny's reluctance. They were tight and that is all that mattered. They had grown up playing touch football in the front yard of the house. Danny was never impressive as an athlete, but Kenny never cared, he just enjoyed playing. He also listened to Danny's complaints about their father. Matthew often berated young Danny about some real or imagined shortcoming. When Danny ran into trouble with the bullies at school, Kenny taught him how to fight and defend himself.

Danny sadly turned away from the picture of Kenny, finished his reminiscences and placed the photo back on his desk. He stared at the walls of his room. They were decorated with posters from early 70's rock-and-roll bands such as the *Grateful Dead* and the *Moody Blues.* On the stereo, Danny listened to the song, *Wooden Ships*, from a folk-rock group called *Crosby Stills & Nash,* an immensely popular 70's pop-rock group.

Danny started singing as a freshman named Barry Lipkin entered the room. He was reed-thin, with straight black hair and a tie-dye shirt with a peace symbol on it. He handed Danny a provocative anti-war pamphlet.

"Barry, I got no time for politics!" Danny sighed.

Danny liked Barry but felt that he had to remain neutral in his politics with the incoming freshmen. His upbringing had been in the rural part of Pennsylvania where politics were rarely discussed. National politics seemed removed from everyday life, except every four years during the presidential campaigns. The obsession with politics was something new and alien to him. Politics seemed secondary to his interest in day-to-day living. He was surprised when he reached the college campus and discovered that political discussions had become commonplace and even more loud and passionate.

Barry nodded and stared at the photo of John Wayne posing as a Green Beret soldier on the wall. He broke into an off–key rendition of the lyrics from the popular 60's song, *Ballad of the Green Berets.* "Fighting soldiers from the skies. Fearless men who jump and die. Men who mean what they say. The brave men of the Green Beret."

"You can't carry a tune in a fucking wheelbarrow," Danny huffed.

Barry stopped singing and squinted at Danny. Danny took a deep breath and heaved his shoulders. He tried to be impartial even though he knew of Barry's hard-left position on the student movement and the war.

"There is a big bad war going on, my man," announced Barry.

Danny drew in a breath. "Save it for your anti-war buddies," he sighed.

"I know you haven't made up your mind," countered Barry.

"I'm not taking sides just yet," Danny countered. "Besides, we have a meeting in a few minutes." Barry nodded and exited the room. Danny leaned out of doorway and shouted out to him. "Remember not to bring up politics at the meeting!" Danny said, wagging his finger and eyeing the freshman sternly.

Danny brushed his teeth and changed his shirt. He combed his hair and barreled down the marble stairwell into the dorm's front lobby. It was furnished with a few hand-me-down couches and a patch of time-worn grey carpeting. Most of the students sat on the cold black-and-white checkered linoleum floor.

The room was crowded with eager, fresh-faced freshmen students. Danny waded through the crowd, but the students chattered amongst themselves. Seeing they would not stop talking, Danny blasted a *Led Zeppelin* heavy metal song on a FM radio station. The sound reverberated around the room. The students immediately froze in mid-sentence and turned their attention to Danny.

"Now that I have your undivided attention, I want to begin today's meeting."

As he spoke, Alexandra Doherty and several other girls from the upper floors of the dorm entered the room. Alexandra, better known by her nickname 'Alex,' was a stunning redhead with pearl-green eyes who made a lasting impression simply by showing up. Even in faded jeans she was a showstopper. Many of the male students swiveled their heads to ogle her as she paraded past them. Danny found her attractive but felt that he had to avoid any romantic involvement to prevent any possible conflict of interest.

Barry joined some of his radical friends hanging out in the back of the lobby to argue the latest political controversies. "I told you Nixon was a dirt bag," screamed one of the radicals. Barry was about to respond with his own verbal blast, but he saw the look of disapproval on Danny's face, smiled and suddenly stopped.

Danny cleared his throat and tried to concentrate despite the disruptions. Talking for any length of time was not Danny's forte, but he struggled to make it look effortless. He rustled through several pages of hastily handwritten scrawl on note cards. He shuffled them as he tried to decipher his handwritten notes. His normal set of glasses were thin-framed granny glasses, but for the meeting he preferred his older, thick black glasses to indicate a scholarly image. "Point number one, be aware that there will be a big protest on the field tomorrow."

A deafening cheer rang out from Barry Lipkin and his comrades sitting in the back of the crowded room. "Stop the war, stop the war," they chanted. This lasted for a few seconds until Danny frowned and motioned to become silent.

Danny continued his talk. "Point number two, I know that many of you enjoy having a bottle of beer in your room, but the janitors are complaining that they find too many empty bottles in the waste basket."

He struggled to conceal a huge grin on his face. He had consumed more than his share of alcohol as a freshman. However, as the student advisor, he chose the higher ground. "Cut them some slack, those folks work hard to keep this place neat." A smile danced on his lips. He knew that chugging large amounts of beer was a rite of passage for many of the young male and female students. Several of the male students cracked up with laughter at that last remark. It had become a friendly competition to see which section of the dorm consumed the most bottles of beer.

Danny slid his glasses down his nose to indicate the gravity of the next topic. "Some of the girls are complaining about lack of privacy late at night. I'm asking the guys to refrain from too many late-night visits." The faces of the boys grew downcast. Danny impishly grinned. "Unless of course you're invited."

Having a co-ed dorm was a new experience for many of the students. It provided a way for the boys and girls to mingle in a more natural manner than the traditional college dances. Danny flipped to the final page. He caught his breath and scratched his head. He seemed relieved to be nearing the end of the meeting. "Okay, those are the things I wanted to tell you, any questions?"

The student's expressions grew penetrating as they searched their minds for a question that they could ask without embarrassment. The first volunteer was Pamela Winters, a plump, oval-faced young woman with curly hair who raised her hand, trembling. She pushed her hair back and cleared her throat to speak. Her voice cracked, indicating her nervousness. Her eyes darted back and forth as she evaluated the potential reaction from her fellow students.

"It's only the second month, but I'm kind of nervous about college," she said, with a wide-eyed expression. She stopped at that point. She grew red-faced at the agonizing admission. Danny nodded, encouraging her. "Everything's so new. I'm overwhelmed," said Pamela continuing, her mouth getting dry as she finished her sentence.

Danny offered her a reassuring smile. "You're getting the same feeling every freshman gets, asking themselves, 'can I handle it? Am I in over my head?'"

He looked around the room and spotted the bobbing heads and the knowing smiles of the students. "Everyone feels it, even if they are afraid to admit it to anyone, including themselves." Laughter and recognition filled the room, as the students murmured to each other.

Fred Turner, a preppy-looking African American student, raised his hand and stood up to face the crowd. He smiled at his fellow classmates, painfully self-conscious at being the only black student in the room. He had made attempts to befriend the other students on his floor, but there was always the nagging thought in the back of Fred's mind that his skin color made him a perennial outsider. Fred had requested a change in roommates during the first weeks of school, as his roommate had made it clear that he was not happy having a black roommate. Danny had offered to have Barry Lipkin become his new roommate.

"Hello, my name is Fred Turner and I want to make a confession.... I'm Black." Everyone giggled at his obvious mild attempt at humor. Danny smiled and offered him a thumbs-up gesture.

"My parents are putting a lot of pressure on me to be the first college graduate in the family," continued Fred. Everyone was sympathetic to Fred for being brave and stating what many of the kids in the room felt. They recognized the universal pressure from their parents to succeed at the college. Some of them appeared cool. However, most students were, deep-down, scared children questioning their life choices. Most of them had gone to college because their parents insisted. Others felt an education improved their chances of a better life. Unfortunately, it was also a way to avoid the draft. The draft was the selection of students aged 18 and over to serve in the Army. College-age students were offered a deferment and avoided the possibility of having to ship out to remote war zones like Vietnam.

Barry had a mischievous grin on his face and reached into his shirt pocket. He triumphantly whipped out a large 'blunt' (marijuana joint) from his shirt pocket and waved it high up in the air for everyone to see. He had a shit-eating grin on his face. "Tell them to relax. Offer them a doobie."

The students exploded into raucous laughter and the tension in the room lifted.

Danny pointed to several students. "Look around, talk to each other, share your fears. Many of you will make lifelong friendships with the people here. Some of you may even wind up married to each other."

The kids laughed. He offered his encouragement in the form of a thumbs-up gesture. From the end of the hallway, a student called out to him. "Danny, you got a call on the phone in the hall."

Danny was in no mood to take a phone call. The meeting was just about over, and he wanted to get back to studying or head off to the local bar to play pinball.

"Tell them I'll call them back," he yelled out to the unseen student.

"It's your dad!" the boy shouted back.

Danny froze at the mention of his father's name; the muscles of his upper body tightened as he inhaled and took a deep breath. He did not want to speak to his father. It was the last thing he wanted to do tonight.

"Tell him I'll call him back," he snapped again, then he paused, reconsidering the situation. He dreaded having to deal with his harsh father but realized that sooner or later he would have to take the call. If not tonight, then perhaps another time.

"No, screw that. I'll take it," he yelled again. He looked at his audience of freshmen and joked, "Go have fun and stay out of trouble!"

Danny bounded down the hallway, a determined look in his eyes. Thoughts of gloom and doom swam inside his head. His eyes were focused downward on the tattered pink carpeting. Was there a way out of the phone call? he wondered to himself. Maybe the connection will go dead? After all, Jersey Shore, Pennsylvania, was a tiny town in the middle of nowhere. Maybe he could say that he was going to the hospital. He inhaled a deep breath, approached the open phone booth and seeing the receiver dangling, put the phone to his ear. It was dead.

"Your dad had an emergency; said he'll call back later this afternoon or evening." The kid who had answered it called from down the hall. Danny breathed a loud, audible sigh of relief. He hung up the phone and slid the door of the phone booth closed, then stormed back towards his room. The look on his face betrayed his angry feelings. Damn the old man, Danny thought to himself. His father could turn a sunny day into a blizzard with his frosty attitude. Back in his room, he slammed the door shut and collapsed onto the bed. A pleasant day had been ruined just by the call from his father.

3

Ryan Marshott

After a few minutes, the anger about his father's call had subsided. Danny felt relieved. He sat in his favorite chair and looked around his room. He seized his beloved guitar, hidden under a pile of dirty clothing. He grew calmer as he strummed a folk song written by Bob Dylan, a popular singer/songwriter of the day. He did not agree with Bob Dylan's left-wing politics, but he wanted to play contemporary material that was in demand and the melodies were soothing.

"The answer my friend, is blowing in the wind, the answer is blowing in the wind," he sang.

Danny reached for the sheet music inside his guitar case. He spotted a faded black-and-white photo of himself and Ryan performing at the local coffee house. The two had become a hot commodity at the shows on campus. He had no driving musical ambition, but he enjoyed playing at the local coffee houses. Coffee houses were informal gatherings where students could listen to up-and-coming folksingers practice their craft.

Coffee houses were also a less pressured way of meeting the opposite sex. It was more relaxed than suffering the anxiety of trying to meet at the giant social mixers, with their swirling strobe lights and blaring music pouring out of the bulky, giant loudspeakers. Besides, Danny had two left feet. He could fake it but he was not a graceful dancer. Sitting in his dorm room, Danny poured his heart and soul into the song. His fingers raced across the strings.

"For the times, they are a-changing!" he sang with gusto.

He was singing so loudly that, for a moment, he could not hear the thundering sound of banging on the door. It grew more intense, and the door began to visibly shake.

"Go away," he shouted. "I'm armed and dangerous!"

He kept singing and doing his best to ignore the pounding on the door. He continued strumming his guitar but the knocking continued unabated. Finally, Danny stopped, put down his guitar and opened the door. There in the doorway stood his friend Ryan Marshott, late teens, boyishly handsome. He was slender, with short-cropped blond hair and a winning smile that melted the hearts of many young women. Even dressed in worn blue jeans and a faded army jacket, he appeared as if he were stepping out of a Sears' catalogue for stylish young men.

They had become fast friends during their freshman year, bonding over many things—especially having to deal with demanding fathers. Danny was gratified when Ryan was nominated to become the student advisor at the other freshman dorm down the road.

Ryan leaned on the door frame, his eyes sparking with a wicked grin. "Hey, stud!" Ryan joked.

Danny chuckled; it was rumored Ryan had a girlfriend in every dorm. That might not be true, but many people were willing to bet serious money that he had. In those days, 'stud' was a sobriquet of pride. It denoted someone who got laid by the opposite sex on a regular basis. Danny was not sure if this was the case with Ryan, but Ryan had all the mojo he needed regardless. Danny admired Ryan's charm and breezy manner.

Danny stared at Ryan's patched army jacket. He recalled that Ryan's father was a retired army officer and wealthy businessman. Ryan had a disarming disposition and people were attracted to him. His father made no bones about his expectations for the young man. He had also been voted 'Most Likely to Succeed' at his high school.

Ryan strongly felt that someday he would take over the reins of the family business. It was a paper and printing empire, begun during the first half of the twentieth century, and it guaranteed that Ryan would be set for life.

"I've been practicing our set. You are not going to do a Tony on me if you find a better partner?" questioned Danny.

"Of course not, you're a better singer than he was," joked Ryan.

Danny smirked as he recalled the fate of one of Ryan's friends from grammar school. Unfortunately, Ryan could also be a fair-weather friend. He had once confessed this dark secret to Danny after consuming a few too many bottles of Budweiser beer. In grammar school, he had been close friends with Tony, a young boy who lived two houses down from him. They had played together and formed a tightly knit bond of friendship. As Ryan matured into his early teens, he began to drift away from his childhood friend. Ryan, who was a popular kid, began running with the school's 'in-crowd.' He abandoned Tony because he was neither as handsome, nor as socially adept as Ryan. Ryan disregarded his friend's pleading. He had been nasty and told the young boy that he had found other 'cooler' friends. Tony was crushed by Ryan's cruel abandonment. Ryan disregarded his childhood friend as one might disregard an old toy that had outgrown its usefulness.

Ryan had confided to Danny how sorry he felt about the whole situation. During a session at the local bar, Ryan had also shared the story of how his life had taken a difficult turn after his mother was caught cheating on his father with a man she had met at their country club. It was the classic story of the neglected wife. She felt that her husband had become married to his business instead of her. Ryan's father refused to admit his feeling and become increasingly remote. The divorce was swift and brutal, following several months of shouting and recriminations. Ryan's father seemed determined to avoid any sort of future romantic entanglement. He offered similar advice to his strapping young son.

Ryan was now suspicious of women. Afraid that he would be hurt like his father, he always found fault with even the most desirable girls in his school. Despite his good looks, rumors of his lack of commitment made it evident. In high school, this did not make much of a difference. In college, when young men and women dated frequently, they evaluated each relationship for its long-term marriage potential. A long-term relationship was not something that he wanted. Like most young men, he just wanted to date around with no commitments and have fun.

"Did I disturb you?" said Ryan, strutting into Danny's room, seemingly ready to hit the town.

"No, but a few more minutes of that pounding on my door and I'd go insane."

"Pretty short trip for you." Ryan shook his head.

Danny bristled. "So, what's the big fucking deal?"

"Morris called an emergency meeting. He's probably going to want the photographers at the meeting," said Ryan.

"Got things on my mind," replied Danny. He was not happy to hear that. Danny slumped back into his favorite chair.

"Whatever it is, you can tell me," Ryan offered, sitting on Danny's bed.

"Not in the mood," Danny mumbled.

"C'mon, something's eating at you. And it's gotten indigestion."

Danny frowned. He did not want to talk about it. He rose from the chair and walked out of the room. "Maybe later, let's go." Danny put on a fresh shirt and the two headed out the door.

They made their way down the main street of the campus. They walked at a brisk pace toward the Student Center, a modern concrete and glass structure situated along College Avenue, the tree-lined thoroughfare of the campus. They passed several students huddled inside the glass bus shelter. They were waiting for the campus buses to take them to classes at different locations on the vast Rutgers campus.

"Morris doesn't like me," Danny groaned.

"Whatever you do, don't piss off Morris again," said Ryan pointedly.

16

Danny stared innocently at his friend. "I don't do it intentionally. Our relationship is sort of like North and South Vietnam."

Ryan shook his head; his eyes bore directly into Danny's psyche. "Your scholarship depends on making nice with Morris. Don't forget that. " He probed Danny as if he were a prosecuting attorney. "What's the deal with you two anyway?"

"I think he overheard my criticism of one of the front-page stories. I tried to apologize but no dice. He likes that kid Kevin who always calls me 'Hayseed Watkins'. Gives him better stories."

Within a few minutes they reached the Student Center. Ryan snickered. "There is your destiny, my son." Danny took a deep breath. Ryan snickered again. "Just don't fuck it up." They continued up the stairs to the floor containing the school paper.

Danny hesitated; he felt a sense of impending doom having to face the hostile editor of the school newspaper.

"Oh, for god's sake, don't be a baby," said Ryan.

"He likes you for some unknown reason," countered Danny.

"I'm a good photographer. End of story."

The two men continued their journey. Danny was lost in thought. He was uncertain what manner of cruel fate would befall him upon entering the lion's den. They continued up the stairs to the second floor, containing the offices of the student newspaper. Whatever it was, it was not going to be pleasant or painless.

4

The College Newspaper

A few minutes later, as Danny and Ryan walked to the top of the stairs, they spotted a large set of doors occupying most of the rear of the second floor. They observed a frosted glass door with a sign imprinted in bold letters that proclaimed, *The Daily Targum*. The *Daily Targum* was the campus newspaper. Ryan dabbled in being a photographer but for Danny it would be his passion and the center of his universe during his time at college.

Danny's first exposure to journalism had been on a school field trip to a major daily newspaper in Philadelphia. He had been intrigued at the sight of many people typing stories, the hum of the newsroom and the looming presses printing hundreds of copies of the paper. The amount of work needed to put out one daily paper was fascinating to Danny. He worked for a time at his high school newspaper and even volunteered at the local town newspaper.

He had decided long ago that working on the family farm was not what he wanted to do with his life. The farm had been owned by his family for decades. It was his father's proudest accomplishment and he intended to hand over the reins to his sons when it was their time. Danny knew that his father would never accept Danny's decision. Working the family farm was his father's obsession. He wanted it to be Danny's obsession too, but already he held a grudge against Danny for not showing any passion about following in his father's footsteps.

At the top of the stairs, Danny hesitated before the frosted doors.

"What are you waiting for, an invitation from the Pope?" Ryan joked. "Get going, Morris won't bite... Well, maybe he will." Ryan smirked.

The two men entered the complex of rooms. It was a maelstrom of activity. A thick cloud of billowing cigarette smoke wafted into the room's air. Pictures of famous staffers hung on the back wall. Rows of metal cabinets full of supplies lined the wall. The staffers sat at metal tables scattered around the room. A staffer hovered in the corner over the teletype machine hooked to a phone line. It printed out national and local news from a news service. They would pluck the story 'hot off the wire' and hand it to the news editor for consideration in the next day's paper.

Some of the staffers listened to their sources on their rotary telephones. Sometimes a reporter recorded an interview using an ultra-compact portable tape recorder. They would play back the recording to assure the quality of their quotes. Others furiously pounded away on their small metallic Smith Corona typewriters. Many of the staffers bragged of their ability to type 60 words per minute without mistakes. Other staffers scurried from location to location gathering piles of materials for the day's edition. Some staffers sat at adjoining desks and conferred with their fellow journalists. Many of the young student journalists chain-smoked cigarettes or cigars and had ashtrays piled high with cigarette ashes. They wore fedoras tilted back in the style of Hildy Johnson, the hero of the Ben Hecht journalist comedic masterpiece, *The Front Page*.

The Assignment Editor sat in a corner with a pile of stories on his desk, working at a traditional U-shaped copy desk. He either assigned a copy reader to go over the story or proofed the story himself. A good copy desk was a crucial part of the editorial quality control process. He examined the stories to make certain it covered all the desired angles and was of suitable length. Once the story was accepted, it was sent to the back of the office for typesetting. Typesetting made a mock-up of a printed version of the story. A page editor then added the story to a dummy of the page, estimating its length according to a traditional formula.

Danny and Ryan observed the frenzied atmosphere in the room. "Something's definitely on," Danny muttered.

"Where's the Big Kahuna?" Ryan asked, referring to Jim Morris.

At that moment, an office door suddenly flew open. Jim Morris, editor, sporting a two-day scraggy beard and wrinkled clothing, marched into the room clutching several sheets of paper. He took a drag from his cigarette, dropping ashes on the floor as he bounded along the beige carpeting. He was the Big Kahuna, the major-domo of the newspaper. It was his kingdom. Everyone else were merely his loyal servants.

Morris came from a long line of newspaper journalists. His relatives had been in the news business for decades. Even though he admired the greats, like Edward R. Murrow and Walter Cronkite, he felt that the best work was being done by the beat reporter from the local newspapers. Morris had tremendous savvy, but his personal bedside manner left much to be desired. He could be volatile and had no patience for rank beginners. He had a chart pinned to the wall listing the names of all the reporters and their importance. If a story was good, the status marker of the reporter would move up a spot. If the story did not meet Morris's standards, it would move down a spot. It was sort of a pecking order that allowed Morris to keep track of his favorites. Reporters knew where they stood in the Morris favoritism food chain.

"Listen up, everyone. We need to be organized," barked Morris.

Morris sauntered around the room handing out assignment sheets to everyone except Danny. Morris fired his directives like a rapid salvo of torpedoes. His eyes lit up as he envisioned the day's activities. He stared up at his wall chart. It listed the names of all the reporters. "Here are your assignments. The protest is going to be a lot bigger than we thought. Dave, I want you and Ryan getting some crowd shots." His eyes studied Kevin, a pudgy, round-faced reporter, staring at his assignment sheet. He moved closer to the young reporter and jabbed his finger in Kevin's chubby stomach. "Kevin, I want good, solid interviews. As many protest leaders as you can."

Morris passed out the last of the sheets and turned to the room. "Soon as it is over, I want everyone back and working. A little luck and this story goes national." His eyes twinkled when he uttered the word 'national.' If he smiled, many feared that his face might crack. One of his missions was to raise the level of awareness for the tiny newspaper. He envisioned himself working for a large circulation daily paper upon graduation. Making the *Daily Targum* a nationally recognized college newspaper guaranteed him a plum job at one of those papers upon graduation. The staffers all returned, engrossed, to their work. Ryan checked his sheet. He was to snap a few photos of the crowd on the field.

Danny waited for his assignment sheet. A look of curiosity mixed with dread crossed his face. "You forget someone?" he inquired. The words slipped out like someone using caution to avoid notice.

Morris paused and turned to Danny. A deep sigh and a look of discouragement crossed his face. As if he were talking to the missing-in-action, Morris handed Danny his assignment sheet. It was folded in half. Danny unraveled it and read it. His facial expression took a tumble. He struggled hard to camouflage his disappointment. He had expected the worst and had gotten it. His worst nightmare had come true.

"Reporting on menu choices in the middle of the biggest protest of the year?" Danny protested in a loud voice. The entire room gawked at Danny for a second before ducking their heads back to their assignments.

Morris raised his hand to stop Danny from uttering another word. He concealed a smirk. "The cafeteria insisted that they had a newsworthy story. They have been begging me to send someone to talk to their head chef. Do you want it or not?"

21

Disheartened, Danny sat down at the table. Morris disappeared into his office and slammed the door. Danny looked at Ryan, the misery in his eyes suddenly replaced by a look of mischief.

"I always get the shit stories," muttered Danny.

"Not so loud," replied Ryan.

"I'll find a way to make the story interesting," Danny whispered to Ryan.

"Danny, don't do anything you might regret," Ryan responded.

Danny seemed determined to cover the story his way. He was clearly not listening. "Don't you worry, buddy. I will cover it and then some," Danny stated with conviction.

Ryan just shook his head and sighed as the two of them exited the room.

"I have to do it my way," said Danny.

"You're going to antagonize him. Just watch your ass," hissed Ryan. Ryan shook his head.

"Danny, don't even think about screwing up the assignment," said Ryan.

Danny shook his head. He was determined to make a big story out of it regardless of the newsworthiness.

"You're a problem, bro."

Danny was not the reckless type but Ryan worried that he might do something he would regret in order to get his story. He had that look in his eyes that spelled trouble. He had crossed the Rubicon and was determined to take fate into his own hands.

5

Before The Protest

After leaving the newspaper, Ryan invited Danny to join him for a late-night beer at the DKE fraternity house. The two men walked down several blocks on College Avenue to the fraternity house. Many other fraternities on campus were older houses that defied the city inspection codes for habitation. DKE, on the other hand, was a magnificent brick structure with white pillars worthy of the pages of Architect's Digest.

Inside the frat house they were welcomed by several frat brothers, including Jeff Tomlinson, Ryan's old friend from high school. The group trotted down the stairs into the finished basement to play pool and sip some ice-cold beers. The pungent smell of cheap beer and wine filled the air.

"Don't forget the big party next Saturday night, and don't forget to bring some hot girls," chortled Tomlinson. He turned to Ryan; his expression serious. "You're not going to that stupid protest tomorrow?" inquired Tomlinson.

Ryan grimaced at the thought. "Listening to a bunch of boring speeches, bad-mouthing America. I have to take a few quick photos for the paper but then I'll split."

"Fucking hippies, need a bath and a haircut," interjected Grillo, another fraternity brother. Everyone laughed at the crude stereotype.

Danny piped up, "In my town we didn't protest, we had parades honoring our soldiers and our country. Some of the veterans would make speeches and toss out the first ball at the annual baseball game. That is how I was brought up. We didn't question patriotism," he added.

"I grew up watching John Wayne movies. The Duke single-handedly charging up the beaches of Iwo Jima. Everyone wanted to be him. He was our hero," Danny concluded. Everyone raised their glasses in salute. "To John Wayne, a tough motherfucker."

Tomlinson nodded but interjected, "Yeah, but you live in a small town in Podunk Pennsylvania. Small Town USA, it's a different world."

Sadly, Danny shook his head in agreement. "Some of the people in my town would have a tough time on this campus." In the back of his mind, he identified his father among the select group. His father had drilled the glories of serving his country into Danny's head at an early age. He had no idea of the challenge to his homegrown ideas until he arrived at Rutgers.

"Bunch of fucking Commies, if you ask me," interjected Grillo.

"Lots of bad feelings. Stuff is really dividing our campus," said Danny. He reflected on the divergent opinions of the students. Hippies were on one side and 'straights' were on the other side of the political divide. One of the frat brothers moved closer; Danny saw that he had a swollen black eye but tried not to stare. The guy could sense it.

"We were coming back from lunch and stopped by one of the tables that these protesters had set up in front of the Commons," he started to explain. "All I said was that I didn't like one of the fliers that he had on the table. It was titled *American War Crimes*." The frat brother shook his fist in rage. "The SOB got into my face and began threatening me. I had no choice, but to deck him. Took three of my frat brothers to pull the SOB off me."

Danny reflected, "I wasn't political my first year. I was too busy with my studies to pay much attention. This year I have a few freshmen who are already intensely into politics."

Ryan interjected, "You're talking about that hippie douchebag, Barry Lipkin?"

Danny laughed. "Yeah, he's always bugging me to read some of his radical newspapers or fliers. He's determined to convert me."

"You turn them down, of course?" said a defiant Ryan.

"Of course, I'm always willing to listen. He's an interesting character but man, he's like a broken record."

Ryan suggested that it was becoming unwise to offer an opinion counter to the growing radical movements on campus.

"You're just being paranoid," stated Danny.

"Am I?" responded Ryan, "How about I scream 'USA, USA' in the middle of the upcoming protest?" Danny conceded that it did not seem to be a particularly good idea.

"I wonder what Barry's up to tonight. He's probably smoking weed and getting fired up for the rally tomorrow," mused Ryan.

He was on the money. Across the campus in the Student Center, another group frantically prepared for the next day's protest and Barry Lipkin was one of them. Members of the SDS (Students for a Democratic Society), a radical leftist organization, frantically huddled over the mimeo machine, creating crude fliers. They sat at separate tables, printing signs with provocative slogans on their cardboard posters. They screamed inflammatory anti-war slogans. The slogans ran the rhetorical gamut from 'End the War' to 'End US Imperialism.'

The room contained several other offshoots of the protest movement. They included Progressive Labor, a militant offshoot, and the Yippies. The Yippies (Youth International Party) were free-wheeling anarchists who often had trouble explaining their anti-establishment positions. Whatever their ideological differences, the members overlooked them for the purposes of presenting a unified front.

In the front of the room, Tom Klonsky, the volunteer leader of the SDS, wandered around overseeing the work of the protesters. He was a large, florid-faced man with a face pitted with acne scars. He wore his long hair pulled back in a ponytail. Bennett Andrews was the most charismatic and visible protest leader on the campus. Klonsky was known as Bennett Andrew's hatchet man. Some even labeled him Bennett Andrew's political commissar or enforcer. Klonsky walked past the tables examining the content on the wooden placards. He squinted as he examined the material for its volatile content. "I want to feel the anger pulsating out of the sign!" he said. He appeared deadly serious about his analysis. Some of the volunteers smirked but quickly doused the smile when Klonsky passed by their workstations. He glared at them with no signs of amusement or indication of the remark being tongue-in-cheek.

"We have to get people to the protest," he roared. "Not angry enough!" he continued with his rant. He was more like a humorless drill sergeant than a protest leader. He walked around the room scowling and intimidating the volunteers.

Barry Lipkin appeared unhappy printing the fliers. He wore his straight, long black hair down to his shoulders and a shirt with a dove carrying an olive branch. His goal was to eventually become a leader of the protest movement. He had been a powerful voice for student rights at his old high school. He was very articulate and could talk himself out of any tough situation.

The son of a divorced mother, he had been forced to move with her from a comfortable middle-class house to living in a cheap, barely furnished apartment on the wrong side of the tracks. He resented her divorce and their loss of social standing, but the move helped shape his view of society's inequities. The turning point for Barry was enrolling at a Quaker high school in Philadelphia. The Quakers took a pacifist, anti-war view of society. He quickly adopted the philosophy as his own. It fueled his desire to join the growing anti-war movement.

A disgruntled Barry looked up. "I came here to be a leader, not print fliers," he said, as another flier flew off the mimeo machine onto the floor. The other volunteers stared at him with amused smiles on their faces. "I told Bennett that I should lead the protests," he uttered proudly.

"You're part of a larger movement," sneered one volunteer. "Isn't that enough?"

Barry felt a severe heaviness in his body. A pained expression crossed his face. He would not back down. It was not in his nature.

Klonsky had overheard the discussion and approached Barry. "You haven't proved yourself!" Klonsky roared. Klonsky inched closer to Barry.

The two men stood face-to-face, but Barry was not intimidated, even as the other volunteers laughed and nodded their heads in cruel agreement. Barry envisioned himself doing great deeds and would not be satisfied with playing second violin to anyone. He would be the leader of the orchestra.

At the same time, across the campus in a small nondescript brick building, Campus Patrol also prepared for the upcoming protest. Many of the men were middle-aged and overweight and would not have been selected for active duty on the city police force. However, for the limited role of the campus security they filled the bill. Their uniform was a greenish grey, topped off with Smokey the Bear hats. Their main job was to hand out parking tickets and direct traffic. However, if the event arose that they were facing a potential riot or large-scale disturbance, they would be ill-equipped to handle it.

In the center of the room stood the imposing sergeant's booking desk and the dispatch section. The Campus Patrol officers stood in a solid line as Jorgenson, the commanding officer, walked up and down the line to inspect his men. He saluted the men, as if they were a military force about to face a serious battle.

"Remember, our first job is to maintain order," said Jorgensen.

"What if they provoke us?" said one of the patrolmen, who cleared his throat as he spoke. He raised the point that all the others in the room felt but were reluctant to offer. "We are only there to direct students in and out of the field. What happens if the students get out of control?"

"Yeah, what about Kent State?" remarked another officer.

Jorgensen's face grew beet-red. "This will not happen on my watch." Kent State University was an aberration, a bitter reminder for the officers. It had started off as a simple protest. It quickly escalated into a deadly shooting of several students by untrained National Guard troops. It would become a rallying point for the protesters.

As if to answer that question, Jorgenson popped open a nearby locker and grabbed riot gear, consisting of a helmet with a visor and a protective vest, and plunked them onto the nearby metallic table. "In your locker, you have riot gear with a visor and baton. This is a last resort, gentlemen." He bowed his head in silence for a moment emphasizing his point.

"We have been told that the students intend to mobilize hundreds of people. Some of you will be handed your riot gear, if you are assigned to watch the protests on the fields." He bit his lip and strutted up and down the line. Sweat poured off his face, grim with determination. "We aren't anticipating any sort of trouble but if trouble comes looking for you, we will be prepared!" The Campus Patrol Officers whispered among themselves for a few minutes until Jorgenson's scowling face led to an end of the discussion. "That will be all, ladies. Be here at 0700 hours sharp," he barked. Everyone nodded in agreement and then returned to their assigned duties.

At the same time, across campus was Dean Mansbach's office, located in Sproul Hall. Inside the freshly painted administrative offices sat the numerous strait-laced, well-dressed male administrators of the college. They sat at their desks and completed their daily assignment. They arranged paperwork and were the paper-pushers, indeed, the bureaucratic heart and soul of the college. Several of the administrators stared out at the empty field. They admired the beauty and vastness of the field and realized that within 24 hours it would be inundated with noisy, chanting demonstrators.

The Assistant Dean strolled in and noticed the staff peering at the empty field. "You may or may not be called in to help with the protest. We will determine the best ways to handle it as the situation develops," he stated.

"Should we help the students in or out of the field?" inquired one of the administrators.

"You are not to be involved in the protest itself unless I direct you," a voice thundered from the back of the room. Everyone turned to locate the source of the voice.

The administrators turned around to observe the formidable Dean

Arthur Mansbach, early fifties, flinty, enter the room. It was a command from God and the administrators nodded meekly as Mansbach headed into his office without a follow-up comment. Mansbach wore his familiar English tailored suit, hand-sewn in Hong Kong. It was topped off with a red power tie. His shoes were spit-shine perfect. Arthur Mansbach was not a man who shirked a fight. In fact, he relished the thought of overwhelming his opponent with his eloquence and indomitable presence. He entered his room and slammed the door behind him. He stared out of his office window at the field. He had a difficult week ahead of him, but he relished the fight. He would devour his opponents as a four-course meal.

6

The Big Protest

The next day, the warm sun beat down on the paved streets of the campus. The crowds had begun to swarm onto the field. Some were hardcore activists, but most were curious onlookers. Danny and Ryan exited the Commons, the school cafeteria, and walked down the street. Both had consumed a large, calorie-rich breakfast in preparation for the day's intensive festivities. Ryan walked at a quick pace toward the field. He had his camera strapped to his neck. He probed his friend's anticipated feelings toward the upcoming protest with a puzzled expression on his face.

"You're really going to ditch Morris's assignment for the menu and try to get some interviews with the protest leaders?" asked Ryan, his face laden with doubt. Danny said nothing, just kept walking.

"I mean, you're going to antagonize his majesty like that?" Ryan continued his inquisition. Danny shrugged, avoided Ryan's penetrating gaze and sighed. "Yeah, I know it's Kevin's gig," Danny stated with a resolute expression.

"Suicide mission, if you ask me," Ryan scoffed as they continued their journey.

"If I can just get some good quotes…" Danny did not finish the thought.

Ryan turned his head and took a deep breath. "Anything you do will antagonize Morris."

"Hey, it's my shot," Danny said with a straight face. "I'll take the chance."

"Hell, it's your career," Ryan shot back, without a moment's reflection.

The two men strode down the street. For the moment, the lush green trees and relaxing atmosphere of College Avenue were the picture-perfect vision of a modern college campus.

They passed a small, wooden, makeshift booth manned by several hippie volunteers from the Students for a Democratic Society (SDS) group. The volunteers wore long hair, tie-dyed tee-shirts emblazoned with a prominent protest symbol, and bell-bottom jeans typical of the era. They passed out fliers to busy students announcing the latest student demonstration. One of the most prominent volunteers was Barry Lipkin. He dashed over to Danny and pressed a flier into his hands.

"Hey, Danny, protest is starting soon. Can we count on your support?" he shouted in his typical boisterous manner. Ryan rolled his eyes.

"How about you, Ryan?" Barry teased. He knew the answer and chuckled.

"When hell freezes over," replied Ryan.

Ryan was a Cadet in the ROTC (Reserve Officer Training Corps). He bristled at the sight of Barry handing out fliers. Ryan was a staunch conservative and found this new form of radicalism distasteful. He wondered if it were some sort of fad that would dissipate upon graduation. He shuddered to think that this form of political protest and expression might carry on in later years. However, Ryan forced himself to be relatively congenial.

"Yet another protest?" said Ryan, with an ounce of derision. "How fucking quaint."

"Going to be the biggest protest so far," Barry puffed with pride.

"Man, you seen one, they're all the same," Ryan replied, shaking his head and displaying his monumental disinterest.

"I'll be there," Danny volunteered.

"I'm taking some pictures and then I'm out of there," added Ryan in a huff. "It's just an assignment for me, nothing more."

Barry stared disdainfully at Ryan. Danny grabbed the fliers from Barry's hands and then the duo continued on their way. The two men examined the message printed on the flier as they continued down the street. In bold handwriting, it screamed information about the big protest that would occur near the statue of Henry Rutgers, school founder. Flamboyant colors and boldface type proclaimed, 'US out of Asia.'

"Same stuff, different day," snorted Ryan with ever-mounting disdain.

Ryan squinted at the flyer and appeared stung by the strident messaging. "How about my cause? They would cut ROTC off the campus in a New York minute. They are not just anti-war, they are anti-establishment. They want to destroy everything we stand for," Ryan continued. "I'll take a few pictures, but then I'm gone."

Danny refused to absorb Ryan's political rant. Despite growing up in a deeply patriotic farm area, he struggled to understand both sides of the political debate. He'd been forced to become aware of differing points of view when he arrived on the campus. It was an eye-opener for Danny, having grown up in a culturally isolated rural town. Danny felt compelled to be open-minded about new ideas even if they clashed with his old established ones. It was his nature to be open-minded.

In his youth, he had been taught as a Boy Scout not to be judgmental. He tried to see both sides of an argument and often mediated disputes between friends.

Ryan crumpled it into a wad of paper and tossed it into the nearby circular trash bin. "I mean, what about your brother?" said Ryan, his face bursting with anger. "Don't you think he's dead right to fight for our values?"

"My brother made up his own mind. I'll make up mine," Danny

asserted. Ryan looked disgusted. The two friends often discussed music, but politics was not open to discussion. The two men headed toward the protest. Danny spotted several Volkswagen minibuses, vividly decorated with peace signs painted along the doors, lined up along College Avenue. Traffic had backed up to a standstill along the main street of the campus. The huge volume of students crossing the street to join the protest seemed like a river that had overflowed its banks.

7

Trip to the Heights

Not all the students looked forward to cutting classes to attend the rally. Many of these students were enrolled in programs such as Pharmacy and Pre-Med. They were brutal curriculums that required total dedication and an insane amount of studying. One of those freshmen was Pamela Winters. She would spend most of her time in classes or in the library. As the protest was getting underway, she found herself racing to catch a bus to a class at the University Heights. The Heights was a remote section of the campus containing the Pre-Med and Pharmacy departments. They were a distance from the main campus and could only be reached by car or campus bus.

Pamela was a brilliant student who didn't care about politics as she trudged across the street, carrying a heavy knapsack full of books. Pamela preferred plain jeans and a simple plaid cotton top. She wore minimal makeup and jewelry. Many of her relatives had been refugees from Russia or Eastern Europe. Pamela came from a family of doctors.

From the time she was a little girl, it was understood that she would go to medical school and join the family practice. She understood that her place in life had been pre-determined by her family. She was not going to let them down.

She spotted the campus bus marked University Heights and raced toward it. Panting and out of breath, Pamela charged into the empty bus, looked around and noticed that the bus was empty. "What's the rush, dear?" questioned the bus driver as he stared at his young charge.

She peered at him with an expression of intellectual curiosity. "I'm late for class."

The bus driver shrugged. "Can't help you. We're being held at the Student Center. I got a call from my dispatcher that the protesters are blocking the road down the street."

A reluctant Pamela dropped her heavy backpack on the seat of the empty bus. She shook her head in silent frustration. "My biology quiz is this afternoon. I must pass it and get a great grade."

The bus driver nodded amiably. "I'm sure your professor will understand."

Pamela snapped back, "My professor won't understand. He's a tough grader."

"Might as well join the protest. Maybe you will find some nice boy," smiled the befuddled driver.

"Protests don't help me get into medical school," she said in a serious voice. She decided to make the best of her time by staying on the bus and studying for the quiz. Pamela was a dedicated student but she feared the wrath of her family more than the student protesters.

8

Bennett Makes a Speech

cross the campus, a large, unruly crowd of students had already gathered at the campus green opposite the statue of Henry Rutgers. The field was teeming with wall-to-wall students. They waved large wooden placards with signs reading: 'End the War' and 'US Out of Vietnam.'

The protesters had placed a wooden platform besides it. A pudgy, balding, school administrator emerged from a nearby administration building and walked over to confront the hostile crowd. He stared nervously at them. He had been the unlucky administrator selected to be point-man in the protest. He raised his hands and struggled to calm everyone, waving his arms in frustration. He grew hoarse and shouted at the students. "Listen, we don't want this to get out of control." His pleadings fell on deaf ears as the students continued to mingle, talk, and generally ignore him.

Several patrol cars sat parked on the nearby street. The Campus

Patrol officers emerged from the vehicles wearing their riot gear. They exited the patrol cars and strode onto the open field. They clasped wooden batons in their hands. The sergeant motioned for his fellow officers to stand their ground and remain calm. Above all, he reminded them, the main mission would be to avoid provocation. They stood silently as they stared down the hostile crowd directly in front of them. The students raised their fists and jeered at them from across the street, "Off the campus!" or "Pigs, go home!"

The officers adjusted their visors and shields, trying to appear calm. The Campus Patrol sergeant turned to his men and shouted, "Hold your ground."

Ryan and Danny weaved their way through the boisterous crowd. Ryan snapped a few shots of the crowd and the speaker's stand. Danny moved into the crowd, attempting to take notes or get interviews with the skittish participants. This promised to be the biggest turnout of the year. He was astonished by the intensity and energy of the crowd. He waded through the large crowd. Danny built up his courage and approached a young protester standing alone. Danny was building up his courage by asking this lone protester a question.

"Can I ask you a question?" he started off slowly with his reluctant participant.

The young protester turned his back on Danny and ignored him. He began waving his arms and shouting slogans in his most provocative voice. "US out of Vietnam," he shrieked in his loudest, most heated voice.

Danny repeated the question, but the student kept ignoring him. Finally, Danny gave up and began searching for a more willing participant.

As he waded through the crowd, the crowd took on a life of their own. The students started to lose control. They began hurling chairs and sticks at the podium. The administrator panicked and motioned to the Campus Patrol, who raised their batons. Danny tensed as he watched the officers advance on the crowd. Would it devolve into a violent confrontation with tear gas and numerous arrests? It was exciting, but Danny did not relish being part of any violent protest.

He watched as out of the crowd, like a self-appointed Moses, Bennett Andrews, a burly, bearded man in his early twenties, suddenly projected himself in front of the crowd. He wore a vibrantly colorful tie-dye shirt. He pumped his fist into the air, the symbol from the Black Power movement. He raised his arms and then signaled for everyone to calm down. Bennett was flamboyant if a bit arrogant. If there was one thing that he was good at, it was crowd control. Crowds were a moth to Bennett's flame. Bennett had a commanding presence, with a powerful voice that captured the crowd's attention. He could be charming when the situation required it. He could also be a ruthless adversary when he was opposed.

In the distance, a television camera truck carrying a crew of reporters from the CBS evening news could be seen setting up their cameras. A reporter could be seen preparing notes for his on-camera report on the protest. It was unusual for Rutgers to make a spot on the evening news. However, news of the protest had caught the attention of the broadcast news stations.

The reporter stood in front of the camera and recited a brief background of the conflict to his unseen anchorman. The reporter recounted how the United States had blundered into a guerilla war in Southeast Asia during the early 1960's. They were certain that they were fighting the spread of Communism in Asia. However, as the war dragged on, many grew opposed to the intervention. Some even managed to declare the US at fault or simply on the wrong side of the conflict. He reminded his audience that it had become a very divisive issue that rocked the campuses all over the US, including Rutgers. Several of the students preened and flashed the peace sign at the amused television crew.

Others calmly passed around marijuana cigarettes, called 'joints' or 'doobies,' from student to student. They did not fear arrest as the police would not risk a confrontation over the smoking of the drug. Drug use had become broadly ignored by authorities.

The atmosphere was one of serious protest and party. Bennett Andrews bounded up the wooden stairs of the makeshift speaker's platform. A Viet Cong flag flapped gently in the cool autumn breeze. Bennett called out to the crowd. His voice echoed in the morning air.

"This morning, we had a near-riot. I do not want a repeat of that. The University will not take us seriously. At some point, I will meet with Dean Mansbach and his staff." His expression was blunt, his voice was composed of righteous anger. He grabbed the students' attention with his no-holds-barred manner. The students murmured their approval. Bennett stared out at the large crowd, his eyes blazing, soaking up their energy.

"Now for the business at hand. We demand that the University cut its ties with the Pentagon. The government says we are fighting the spread of Communism in Asia. Stopping the North Vietnamese from spreading the invisible 'Red Menace.' I say the North Vietnamese are nationalists fighting for their country. They defeated the French, who tried to recolonize them after World War Two. I say, leave them alone." The crowd shot to their feet and cheered. Strong words from Bennett Andrews were precisely why they were there.

"Stop supporting the war!" he roared. "Demand that the University stop supporting the war effort. Say 'NO' to military recruiters on campus. No to the ROTC," he demanded with a passionate tone in his voice.

The energy generated by Bennett and the crowd grew more incendiary. Ryan and an additional photographer from the *Daily Targum* weaved through the large and boisterous crowd. They snapped photos of the crowd with their Polaroid cameras. One of the young photographers motioned toward Ryan.

"Move toward the left, Morris will want some photos of the crowd."

The other photographer wound his way through the crowd taking pictures with his bulky Nikon SLR camera and began making notes about who or what the picture represented. The crowd cheered wildly as Danny wandered through the crowd. He stared at the students shouting and thought to himself that this would be a career-building story. He took a deep breath and approached another student.

"What's your opinion of the war?" he asked in his best journalistic voice.

The student stared blankly at Danny, as if he had not thought about the subject deeply, just chanted along with his friends. He shrugged and did his best to squirm away and distance himself from Danny but not before Kevin, the overbearing chubby reporter for the *Daily Targum*, observed Danny in the distance trying to take notes. Now fuming, he marched up to Danny. "What the fuck do you think you are doing?" The question was more accusatory than anything else. Kevin and Danny had never hit it off. Even from day one, the two had feuded over their status at the paper.

Kevin was a kid from the Bronx. He made it clear that anyone who was not born and raised in New York City was a hick. Kevin made fun of Danny's occasional farm-hand drawl. He laughed at the name of Danny's hometown. He made disparaging remarks about Danny's rural background. He liked to zing him with the disparaging nick name of 'Hayseed Watkins.' Morris had taken a favorable view of Kevin from the beginning. He was soon getting many of the best stories. Danny was envious of Kevin. A rivalry had been established.

"Trying to get a couple of interviews for the paper," Danny stated with a hint of embarrassment.

"This is my story. Morris gave it to me. Butt the fuck out," he snarled.

"This is a free country," Danny stated defensively, his face red with anger and embarrassment.

Kevin snarled at him. "Morris asked me to remind you if you tried to do any interviews that your interview was with the Cafeteria Chef." Kevin turned and walked away. Danny was speechless.

At the same moment, on the fringes of the crowd were several African American students, including Fred Turner, one of Danny's freshmen from Danny's dorm. He was with Timmy, another African American student. They stayed a few minutes before feeling out of place, being outnumbered by the predominantly white student crowd.

"Not many brothers here today," said Timmy.

"You ever get the feeling that we are outnumbered?" said Fred.

"What gave you the first hint?" joked Timmy.

"I was just curious that's all," smirked Fred.

"I don't think that they are interested in our issues."

Fred Turner shrugged. "Hey, I got a better idea. I want to show you my record collection."

Timmy smiled. "Sounds like the best idea you had all day."

"Let's get a sandwich from the Greasy Truck and then compare collections."

"How's your white boy roommate?" asked Timmy.

"Just another white kid, but he's sort of okay."

Fred and Timmy trudged off the field and walked back to their dorm. In the distance, Fred spotted Danny, but he could see that Danny was preoccupied and did not feel like having any sort of discussion about the protest. Danny was still suffering from the embarrassment of his run-in with Kevin and was not in the mod to talk to anyone from the dorm.

At the same time, Bennett continued his stump speech. "Every day, more innocent Vietnamese are killed. More villages are destroyed," he stated. "We demand the US withdraw its troops. End the needless bloodshed. Leave Vietnam to the Vietnamese."

The crowd roared in response. "Stop the war!"

"We will keep protesting until our voices are heard. Let us hear it."

He stared out at the massive crowd. The crowd rose and cheered wildly. They raised their arms upright, fists clenched in the Black Power salute. Bennett stared out at the vast crowd, clearly loving the power trip. He held the students in the palm of his hand as he continued his speech.

"Dean Mansbach, can you hear us?" he shouted." We demand that you listen to our demands. Meet with us."

The crowd roared their approval. They stood up on their feet and cheered as Bennett raised his clenched fist and departed the stage. Tom Klonsky, the other speaker, mounted the stage but his speech had little of the eloquence or passion of Bennett's speech. He droned on.

"The United States is guilty of war crimes against the Vietnamese people. We, the citizens of the United States, must protest this unjust war." Klonsky waved his arms and exhorted his crowd.

Danny spent the remainder of the morning standing on the edge of the crowd. He was absorbed, thinking about his disastrous encounter with Kevin. He attempted to remind himself that at least he had his upcoming interview with the chief of dining services. He hoped that

Kevin would not mention it to his arch-nemesis, Morris. However, he doubted that Kevin would be so magnanimous. He felt a sense of anger at himself for not taking Ryan's warnings to heart. After a short period of time, he decided that he had witnessed enough protest for the day. He trudged back toward his dorm. He had acted rashly and was afraid that he might suffer the consequences from the volcanic Morris.

9

Dean Mansbach

The morning of the protest, Dean Mansbach was at his desk promptly at 7:30 in the morning. He felt that there was a lot of work to finish before the start of the protests. The Dean's office was in Sproul Hall. It was in the center of the campus and in the center of campus life. The office was magnificently decorated with luxurious, leather-upholstered furniture and oil paintings of former Deans.

Dean Arthur Mansbach was a distinguished flinty man in his fifties, who could instill fear in even the toughest campus administrator with just a look. He sat at his desk with a pile of folders stacked in front of him. He was absorbed in the details of various projects at the school. He made notes in the margin or marked the pages with a bright yellow marker. He was obsessive about minute details. It had served him well, as the demands of his job made him responsible for many campus-related issues.

For most of America, the 1950's were a time of enormous prosperity and patriotism. No one questioned that America was the greatest country in the world. The death of President Kennedy brought into play forces that would change America forever. Arthur Mansbach grew up in that same quaint America. In the middle 1960's, he detected the beginnings of change. At the beginning of 1964, Dean Mansbach believed the student protest movement would be a short-lived phenomenon or restricted to ultra-liberal bastions like Berkeley. However, the student movement had spread and would rapidly become a dominant force on many campuses. After the students occupied the Administration Building at Columbia University, Mansbach realized that it was no longer a small movement but a nationwide movement. He recognized that Bennett Andrews and his SDS chapter were a force to be reckoned with. He was unhappy that the students were disrupting his university. He hated the polarization of the University into the different factions. A generally pro-American view had splintered into different political views from the America of his youth.

He kept photos of himself as a young man standing with teammates in several sports, including soccer and crew. He was as proud of his athletic accomplishments as he was of his impressive career. He loved to play sports and had won medals in such sports as soccer and as captain of his crew team. He loved to display his medals and talk sports with the various members of college teams. He hung photos of the various teams on the walls of the office alongside the portraits of the former presidents.

Arthur Mansbach came from a family of writers and poets. His grandfather had been a famous writer of non-fiction books on topics such as military history. He had earned his PhD degree in the sociology department. Eventually, he rose to the position of department chairman, where he terrorized the professors and reorganized the curriculum. His blunt style and forceful manner made him many enemies in his department. However, his ability to speak and make his point elevated the young Arthur into positions of authority at an early age. Everyone called him Arthur. He never tolerated being called 'Artie.'

He had served as an officer in the Korean War and rose to the rank of captain. He had been wounded and captured by the Chinese during their offensive down the Korean Peninsula. He and several other soldiers spirited away a bolt-cutter and escaped by cutting the barbed wire in the pre-dawn morning. They were rescued by advancing American units from the Twenty-Eighth Infantry Division just hours before the Armistice that ended the war in 1953.

He felt a special kinship with the military. His direct style and bearing made him a perfect fit to become an officer. He served with distinction and retired after serving a distinguished career. He had a sharp sense of patriotism and was not ashamed of wearing an American flag pin on his lapel. He had married his high school sweetheart. As a young man, he had been invited to teach at Cambridge University for a semester. He had been a popular visiting professor but returned to America when a position opened at his alma mater.

Mansbach stared at a picture of a younger Arthur volunteering at a voters' rally in the South. He admired the picture. He was shaking hands with Dr. King and several other leaders. He had volunteered for the voting rights campaign of the Freedom Summer of 1964. His army training had made him a formidable speaker and leader. It was dangerous work as the white population of the South was hostile to Yankee interlopers who volunteered to help the negro population. He had several near-fatal encounters with hostile crowds. However, he was a stalwart man who stood his ground. He won the respect of his comrades in the civil rights movement.

He had two children with his first wife, Mary. She had contracted cancer and died at an early age. A distraught Arthur was always at his wife's bedside until the very end. He would take weekly trips to the hospital, bringing her books and family gossip. Following the funeral of his beloved wife, Arthur was determined to remain a widower, but soon fell in love with Sarah, an administrator at another college. He had promised himself that he would remain a widower, but soon felt the need for female companionship.

His son, David, was an officer in the military. He had served one tour in Vietnam with distinction with the Air Cavalry division in the Central Highlands. He had been wounded but seemed to recover from the wounds. He had volunteered for the Army and Arthur was proud of his son. David had married and had two children. Arthur was the doting grandfather.

Mansbach was lost in thought as he analyzed a thick folder brimming with materials for an upcoming Board of Governors meeting. The phone rang and he answered it.

"Yes, I reviewed your proposal. I think we can discuss it at an upcoming meeting."

"I think the new project should take priority, Arthur," said the voice on the other end.

"I think that the money could be better spent on other projects, but I need to concentrate on the upcoming protest event," explained Mansbach. "The protest is another attempt to intimidate us, but I am not easily intimidated, as you well know." He was relentless in uncovering wasteful spending. He had the reputation of being a fearless warrior for his pet causes. On the other hand, anyone on the receiving end of a tirade by Mansbach would be left cowering in the corner.

As the minutes passed, however, the staff gathered in the front office. They gazed out the window at the spectacle of the crowd started gathering on the field. From the front office, the administrators stared out at the large crowds, gasping wide-eyed at the enormous size of the crowd.

"This crowd goes all the way back to Brooklyn," chuckled one administrator. The other administrator shook his head and laughed at the preposterous image.

"Should we disturb the Dean?" one of the office workers pondered.

Everyone realized that one did not bother the Dean with trivial matters. Not unless you stopped valuing your job or wanted to lose the Dean's respect. The others looked away. This was the common feeling about him. He could be a tiger in your corner, but if not precise in your work, you could wind up as his next meal.

"I think the Dean should see this," mentioned the brave administrator.

The other administrators shrugged. They were not going to be the brave ones. Better not poke the tiger if you valued your limbs. One did not disturb the great Dean Mansbach with trivial matters. The administrator slowly tiptoed into the great man's office. The look on his face was one of caution as he approached the desk. Mansbach heard the man's footsteps on the carpeting and looked up.

"I think you should come see this," cautioned the administrator.

Mansbach peered up from his desk. His fierce bulldog expression indicated his annoyance.

"It's the students, sir."

Mansbach glowered. "Yes, I'm aware of the student protest today. I shall handle it as necessary," he continued. "They will not intimidate me."

The administrator bowed his head. He seemed embarrassed to mention it. "I think you should see it. It's all the way back to old Henry himself."

Mansbach remained unamused with the administrator's attempted humor. He scowled and the pudgy administrator beat a hasty retreat. He emerged from behind his baronial desk and the two men exited the Dean's office. They joined the other administrators in the main office, perched up against the front plate-glass window. Everyone moved away and gave the Dean a little extra space at the window. He peered out at the overflowing crowd gathered in the field in front of their building. He had a look of distinct displeasure on his face. He stared out at the demonstrators with a look of frosty disdain. Mansbach murmured loud enough for all the staff to hear.

"Do they really think that we will bow to their pressure?" he said in his loud, unbending voice.

"They are making demands," said the administrator with caution in his voice. "It will be tough to ignore when they bring this many people."

Mansbach said nothing and continued to peer out the window. Perhaps he was counting the number of students in the field or determining the vastness of this new development.

"Nonsense," snapped Mansbach, in a defiant mood. He paced around the room, leaving his impression on the carpeting and the administrators. "I refuse to be intimidated by their bombastic rhetoric," he continued, unbowed. Mansbach stared off into the crowd. If Bennett thought they could intimidate the old master with sheer numbers, he was mistaken. Mansbach was more than ready for them. He was a thoughtful man, but he disliked the disruptive aspect of the protest that interfered with the smooth operation of his beloved university. He was eager to join the fight and knock down anyone who opposed his vision of Rutgers University.

10

Ryan Views the Protest

Ryan had been assigned to take pictures of the protest, so he circulated through the crowd snapping candid shots of the protesters. He regarded the protest with a heavy dose of disdain. However, he enjoyed his photography assignments for the paper and dutifully wandered around snapping pictures of the crowd.

After completing his assignment, Ryan turned in his film to be processed at the newspaper. After that, he headed a few blocks down College Avenue to the small wooden framed building that housed the ROTC (Reserve Officer Training Corps). He was descended from a solidly Republican family. The family had been Republican since the late 1920's. His grandfather had been a mayor of New Milford, a small town in Bergen County. They had vehemently opposed FDR and his New Deal. They were 'Old Money,' meaning that they had developed wealth through family businesses going back several decades. They resented many of the ideas that Roosevelt espoused. Ryan was not very political, but the frequently heated political discussion around the dining room table had made an impression on him. He had not been exposed to many different political points of view until he had come to Rutgers.

"Just give me the facts. Argue with facts, not emotion," was his talking point. He felt that the overriding emotion of the protest sometimes overrode the complexity of the arguments. Others might have had some curiosity about the political drama erupting on their campus.

Ryan had a deep distrust of the egotistic Bennett Andrews. He was a good judge of character. He decided that Bennett was a pompous, ego-driven man. He was more interested in personal gain than passionate about his politics. He was not interested in the stormy rhetoric pouring out of the oratory. However, he gave Bennett credit for his skill in manipulating crowds and emotions.

After leaving the protest, Ryan wandered over to the ROTC building. It was an unpretentious wooden building in a secluded portion of the campus. It seemed to be undisturbed by the vast wave of protest engulfing it. In past decades, ROTC had enjoyed a more favorable opinion on campus. Now, the recent and unpopular Vietnam War had spilled over into hatred for anything connected to the American military. ROTC members were proud of the unit but most of the cadets kept a low profile on campus. Many of the cadets would not appear in uniform except on days when they had classes in the building or the occasional field parade drill. Ryan had a strong desire to serve as an officer in the military; he felt that it would help him train and learn the skills necessary for military leadership. It required a commitment of a few hours a week and would earn him a commission in the Army upon graduation.

It was business as usual inside the building. Ryan spotted several cadets sitting at their desks typing reports or sorting mail. Ryan walked up to one of his friends.

The cadet looked up. "Was it the same old speeches?"

Ryan's eyes glazed over. "Does a bear shit in the woods and is the Pope Catholic?"

"Aren't these guys anti-American?" said the cadet glumly.

Ryan stood for a moment to gather his thoughts. "Bingo!" he shouted.

The cadet bristled. He was undoubtedly a pro-military young man, who probably hoped to be sent to lead men into battle against the Vietnamese Communists, a/k/a the Viet Cong.

Ryan had no doubts that the war effort in South Vietnam was a just cause. He was unbending in his beliefs. He had argued with some of the students in his dorm but realized that most of them had built stone walls to keep out disturbing world views. No amount of raucous argument would change their rigid, unbending minds. It was chic for everyone to pretend to be a hard-core radical on campus. Conservative views had to be carefully soft-pedaled or even camouflaged. Views that had been the norm even five years earlier were under siege throughout the country.

When Ryan entered the main office, it was as if he had entered another world. An American flag was proudly draped from the rafters of the office. It had the smell of freshly painted walls. It was a junior version of the Pentagon. Everyone wore crisp, form-fitting uniforms with cuffed, short-sleeve shirts, emblazoned with their military rank on their sleeves, and grey or black pants. Their hair was trimmed, and their faces had no facial hair. Everything about the unit seemed to be out of place at the school. It was indeed a throwback to earlier times, as if the Vietnam War had never taken place. Duty, Honor and Country were not mere slogans but a way of life. They were not questioned. The officers of the ROTC were dedicated students eager to become officers in the United States Army and future leaders of the Army protecting the country.

He walked past row after row of stainless-steel lockers until he reached his own and grabbed his freshly laundered ROTC uniform. After putting it on, he stared at his image in the mirror as he adjusted his soft field cap. He was handsome and could probably serve as the front-cover model for a recruiting brochure or spokesman on a television commercial that endorsed the war.

Ryan walked into the orderly office of Timothy McNeil, the commanding officer. McNeil was a fastidious man, with everything artfully arranged in organized piles and crisp folders on his desk. He could locate a document within moments. He saluted McNeil, who was sitting at the desk. The colonel was ramrod straight and wore a crisp, blue dress uniform and thick, horn-rimmed black glasses.

He offered a gleaming, toothy smile as Ryan entered the office. Then he saluted the young cadet. "At ease, Cadet Marshott," said the Colonel.

Ryan stood at attention as the colonel spoke. The colonel made no bones that Ryan might go far as an officer in the armed forces. The fact that McNeil tried to know him personally made Ryan feel a sense of pride and renewed dedication to the group.

"I read your report, very thorough," said the Colonel, nodding at his favorite cadet with an admiring tone.

"Thank you, sir. I tried to get the facts straight," said Ryan.

"I wish I had a dozen more like you, Marshott," barked the Colonel.

They exchanged a few more pleasantries before the issue of protests arose between them.

"Sometimes I feel like I have a target on my back," said Colonel McNeil, admitting his discomfort walking around campus in uniform. He felt safer in the little building. It was his fortress of solitude. At least he was not in the line of fire near the scenes of the protests.

"Very unfortunate, sir," replied Ryan.

"Did you hear any rumors about threats of violence?" questioned the Colonel.

Ryan shrugged. "Nothing special to report. Same shit, another day. They should just record it and repeat it," concluded Ryan.

Colonel McNeil chuckled at the remark. He made a mental note to use it himself. "Good, I would hate to think all this rhetoric might be leading to some sort of violence against us," sighed McNeil.

"Just a lot of hot air," replied Ryan. He smiled at his remark.

The Colonel absorbed the information and went back to his work. Ryan saluted him and went to his desk. His job was to open and sort the mail. He opened a package of newly minted Army training manuals. He smelled the ink wafting off the pages, then squinted at the cover.

Danny entered the building and walked over to Ryan's desk. Ryan looked up in surprise to see Danny.

"I wanted to remind you that we have an invitation to sing at the Mine Street Coffee House at the end of the week. I'd forgotten all about it."

"Did you get your story at the protest?" Ryan smiled.

Danny grew red-faced with embarrassment. "Seen one protest, you've seen 'em all," said Danny.

"I guess you ran into Kevin," Ryan smirked in response.

Danny's jaw tightened and he shifted his stance. Ryan could tell that Danny was embarrassed by his encounter with Kevin.

Another cadet who had overheard bits and pieces of the conversation chimed in. "So, you attended the Commie protest?"

Danny did not want to get involved in a deep discussion. He had been intimidated by his strong-willed and opinionated father regarding political matters. Matthew was a strong patriotic individual who would not tolerate a difference of opinion on political issues. In particular, he had drilled into Danny the fear of the 'Communist menace.' There was no discussion on these matters. As a result, Danny was reluctant to get involved in any heated discussion.

"Yeah, there were some interesting speeches." Danny was reflective. "I was surprised at how well-organized and well-behaved the crowd was." Danny was surprised that he was learning about his ability to speak thoughtfully on controversial topics.

"Bunch of anti-war bullshit," the cadet snorted as he pounded the table in disgust. "Did they tell you how the Viet Cong likes to enter a neutral village and chop off the ears of the village chief if they don't cooperate?"

Ryan chimed in. "We have to stop Communism. They want to take over Asia. Stop them here or they will take over the entire continent."

Danny appeared flustered. "Bennett said the North Vietnamese were nationalist."

"Don't listen to that stuff," Ryan continued. He shook his head in disbelief.

Danny remained non-committal. He was about to continue the discussion when an officer entered the room.

"You men are late for class!" the officer declared with an air of martial authority. "Get to it," he demanded. All the cadets saluted, packed their gear and raced out of the office. Outside the building, Ryan stared at the cadets marching around the field. They marched in lockstep out of the building. Danny excused himself and took off down the street.

Danny checked his watch and realized that he had to put time aside for studying and told Ryan that he would meet him later for dinner. He walked back to the dorm to get in some study time. Everything seemed peaceful but Danny sensed that this peaceful moment would be short-lived.

11

After the Protest

The morning wore on; speaker after speaker got their chance to speak but protest fatigue had begun to settle in and the crowd eventually began to thin out and disperse. The Campus Patrol officers were happy to leave the field without any confrontations. They could stand down and return to their normal peaceful status. Everyone breathed a sigh of relief that the protest had been peaceful. However, no one assumed that this would be the end of the protests or that the anti-war movement had run its course. It was merely a brief armistice in the war between the hippies and the administration.

Danny decided to take a few final minutes to check out the protest. Now, the field was almost empty. He was disappointed that his dream of getting a great story on the protest had been thwarted. Within a half an hour the field would be emptied, and the protest would be part of the history books. Danny's mood darkened. He had failed to be a real part of it. Danny glanced up at old Henry Rutgers standing alone on the field. His only company was the flock of birds resting on his metallic shoulders and the janitorial staff cleaning up the litter left by the exuberant crowds.

Danny glanced at them sadly as he headed back to the dorm. Even hard-core protesters and their sympathizers were going back to being normal college kids again. Danny sat in his room studying but felt drowsy. While Danny took a nap, the students refocused their energies on enjoying campus life beyond politics. Some of them adjourned to play darts at the neighborhood bar or play pinball at the Student Center. The clanging sound of the primitive pinball games resonated through the basement of the Student Center. Other students headed for a graduate students' lounge to watch *Dark Shadows,* a spooky, supernatural soap opera featuring Jonathan Frid, everyone's favorite vampire.

The adrenaline rush of the big protest was wearing off like a beer buzz at a frat party. Students realized that they had to return to the day-to-day grind of succeeding at college. For some, the war and the protests were serious business. For others, it was a diversion from the grind of the day's events. Even Bennett Andrews and his stalwart group took a short break from their anti-war activities.

After a few minutes, Fred and Timmy had left the protest. They met with a contingent of African American students in the Student Center. The room was decorated with posters of prominent African American civil rights leaders. The purpose of the meeting was about planning social events.

"We need to have some dances for our black brothers and sisters." The group nodded in agreement.

Fred Turner and Timmy Ford were both black men from Newark, a predominantly African American city in New Jersey. Fred appeared clean-cut in jeans and a sweater. Timmy wore a dashiki, a colorful flowing shirt of African origin. His hair was curled in a large bushy Afro style. Fred and Timmy were freshmen at different dorms on the campus. They had become fast friends despite being different in appearance and values. Timmy was a veteran of the rough scrabble neighborhood of Newark. He had grown up in a housing development in the Central Ward. Fred had grown up in a one-family home in a moderately integrated section of Newark called Ironbound.

Both men were proud of their native Newark, even though it was undergoing difficult times. In the 1950's, Newark, New Jersey, had been a prosperous bustling metropolis filled with family-owned businesses and large department stores like Bamberger's and Klein's. Many sections of the city were composed of large Jewish or Italian populations. Many mom-and-pop stores lined Bergen Avenue, a main thoroughfare of commerce in the city. However, in 1967 Newark erupted in riots after a black cab driver was arrested by the police. The National Guard were called in to quell the violence. At the end of the week, several people were dead or wounded. The image of Newark would be tarnished for many years. Many sections of the Central Ward had burned to the ground. Many buildings would remain abandoned years after the riots had ended. Some stores and burnt-out buildings would be bulldozed and turned into green areas or overrun with vegetation. The racially charged riots had left the city devastated. After the riots, the city fell into a deep decline and became a landmark of urban decay that many claimed would never recover. Newark would become synonymous with urban decay.

After conferring for a few minutes, one of the black students began discussing the day's protest.

"I went to the big protest. How come so few of us Black students attended?" asked one of the students.

"We have different issues to deal with than the white boys," said Timmy.

"Can we stick to the issues? We came here to organize social events," protested Fred. "We have to organize our students to have fun on this campus," Fred continued. He did not want to get dragged into the political discussion. "We have important decisions to make," declared Fred.

"Yeah, whose record collection is greater," snickered Timmy.

Fred and Timmy could see that no one was interested and headed off to the dormitory.

That afternoon, the Greasy Truck that sold cheese-steak sandwiches to the kids did a booming business. At one point, the crowd in front of the boldly colored truck snaked halfway down the block. The steak sandwiches were piled high with onions and most students requested 'extra grease.' The term originated from the residue of cooked oil and onions left on the grill. It was not a healthy request, but health was not on the mind of most of the students.

At the same time, Dean Mansbach sat at his desk, pondering how to make a formal report to the Board of Regents, who were the real power behind the throne at the university.

"What are your plans regarding how to handle the student's demands, Dean Mansbach?" questioned a member of the Regents.

"We will not let them force any unrealistic demands on us, I can assure you."

"Very well, we will await further developments," demanded the Regent. "Please send us a detailed report." The phone went dead and Mansbach jotted down some notes to himself. He pinned them on his calendar.

Later that morning, Danny was now back at the dorm with Ryan, where they sat on the bench in front of Tinsley. They had put their political views aside for more important issues—a football game that was about to begin.

"So, we agree that this game will be for bragging rights as the best team on campus," said Ryan.

Danny sneered at his friend. "You guys are a bunch of wussies. We'll mop the field with you." They bumped fists to seal the deal. "Losing team buys beers for the winning team," demanded Ryan.

"You're on. And we do not accept the watered-down Rolling Rock beer. It's Budweiser or Heineken," demanded Danny.

The scrimmage began a few minutes later. Spectators from both dorms gathered to watch the grudge match. Among the crowd was Alexandra Doherty, or by her nickname of Alex, the Irish rose with flaming red hair. She stood outside her dormitory with several of the female co-eds, wearing a multi-colored blouse with hip-hugger pants and a pale lipstick. Although Alex was the type of young woman that a boy would proudly introduce to his parents, she was no shrinking violet about expressing her thoughts and feelings.

"I can't walk down the hall without some guy staring at me," she said without an ounce of egotism to the other girls. To her, beauty could be somewhat of a curse. It came all too easily and naturally to her. The girls stared at her and shook their heads. They watched the young men start the game. They were happy to be the subject of attention from the handsome young men in the crowd.

"Being the first co-ed class at Rutgers has its advantages," one of Alex's friends said, watching the guys play on the field.

"Yeah, we get the pick of the litter," another agreed.

"I like that puppy over there," the first one said, pointing to Ryan. The other girls nodded as Alex sighed, bored by the conversation.

"It would be nice to be taken seriously." She sighed again, annoyed.

"Please, no complaining, Alex, you don't have to chase the boys," pouted another girl.

"Yeah, they come looking for you," sniffed the other co-ed. There was a hint of jealousy at Alex's effortless beauty. Everyone turned their attention back to the game.

"We should all have your problems, Alex," added the third co-ed. Alex smiled and absorbed the comments. She was used to this reaction from other girls. It did not faze her.

The women stared as the muscular boys from the two rival dorms marched onto the field. The boys wore grey tee-shirts adorned with the Rutgers logo, khaki shorts, and white sneakers. Some of the boys waved back at the young girls. It would be a mutual admiration society on both ends of the spectrum. Maybe it was just the raging hormones of normal growing young men and woman or more bluntly, horniness. Either way, it would be a burgeoning normal human desire for sex.

On the field, the guys played a rough and tumble take-no-prisoners sort of game. The quarterback from Tinsley threw a pass to one of his teammates. The ball was intercepted by Ryan, who made a great show of capturing the ball. He showboated as he floated downfield with the football and triumphantly scored a touchdown. He rushed toward the other side of the field, where all the girls were gathered.

He charged up to them carrying the ball. He was wall-to-wall smiles and shouted, "I'm recruiting for the Sexual Revolution, any volunteers?"

The co-eds giggled and a few brave souls raised their hands. Ryan smirked and then noticed Alex standing aloof from the rest of the co-eds. Encountering her up close left Ryan suddenly tongue-tied. This was uncharacteristic of Ryan. It was as if there were a force-field pulsating around her. He could not pinpoint the reason. He just felt differently about her. He just stared at her with a blank expression for a few minutes. The words remained frozen in his mind. He blushed to hide his embarrassment. The other co-eds noticed the sudden change in Ryan and giggled at his being at a loss for words.

When Ryan returned to the group of guys, they crowded around him and slapped him on the back of his shirt. The game was soon over, and the group moved over to a cooler loaded with frosty, chilled cans of beer. They popped open the cans and consumed the cold, refreshing liquid inside. Ryan drank his beer but stood quietly transfixed, staring in Alex's direction.

"Hey, Ryan, you going to take out that cute redhead?" prompted one of the students.

Ryan held up his beer to confirm as he quickly retrieved his game-face. "Of course, all I have to do is ask and she's putty in my hands," he crowed.

"Bullshit artist," retorted another student. His voice was a sarcastic challenge that could not be ignored.

Ryan chewed on his lip as he contemplated his course of action. He poured his can of Budweiser on the student's head. No one dared challenge him again. He had made his point and had a look of satisfaction.

Before he could approach her again, Alex and the other girls had left the playing field to head to their afternoon classes. Ryan was intrigued and made a mental note to ask her out as soon as he could. It was not easy to find a girl who appealed to him as much as Alex.

Alex was a mystery to some of her dorm mates. A passionate art student, she could talk a blue streak when she spoke about a favorite subject. At other times she could be quiet, absorbed in her own thoughts. Many male suitors found that she could be demur but suddenly discover that she was a wildcat with controversial opinions. Sometimes the

60

young men enjoyed her candor; others sought a painless escape route. If it bothered her, she rarely let anyone know.

Tammy, her mother, had seen how impressionable Alex was and attempted to empower her to express herself and enjoy what the world offered. Derrick, her father, had abandoned the family when Alex was a young girl. It soured her vision of marriage and made her question whether a lasting relationship between the sexes was even possible. She remained hopeful, as any girl her age would feel about potential relationships. However, the events had clouded her views and she remained skeptical if such an event could occur. Many of the girls in the dorm had formed quick opinions about the Alex. You were either entranced by her intense independence or grew annoyed by her. She left little room in the way of middle ground.

Despite his bravado, she sensed that beneath his flirty nature was a man worth knowing. She hoped to encounter him later and make sure her intuition was right.

12

Fred and the Music Collection

After leaving the Student Center, Fred Turner spent the afternoon talking record collections with Timmy. The two young men had a friendly wager as to who had the larger record collection. Fred invited Timmy to his room to inspect his vast collection. Fred boasted that his record collection was the biggest and his friend Timmy decided to check it out. Later that afternoon, the two men walked down the hallway.

As they entered Fred's dorm room, he hauled a weighty chest out of his closet containing his vast record collection. He yanked a vinyl disc out of the dust jacket and inserted a *Miles Davis* jazz record on the turntable of his record player. The disc would spin, and the listener would place the spindle into the grooves of the song they wanted to listen to. It was Fred's favorite album entitled *In a Silent Way*. The two young men placed headphones on their heads and soaked up the sound of the jazz master. The music of the jazz great engulfed the four corners of the room. As they listened, there was a knock and then Danny popped his head in, smiling at the freshmen.

"Just following up to see how you and Barry were getting long?" questioned Danny.

Fred was absorbed in listening to the music. He seized his headphones off his head to address Danny. "He's a little flaky. Likes to smoke a lot of dope," Fred lamented.

Danny chuckled and made a mental note to himself. "I'll talk to him. There was a big turnout at the protest. Did you guys attend?" said Danny.

"We've got some issues the white boys don't want to handle," interjected Timmy.

Danny was a little surprised by Timmy's outburst but decided not to make an issue of it. He smiled and nodded understanding.

Fred elbowed his friend. He was not interested in discussing politics now. Danny smiled again awkwardly and left quickly.

"Do you want to want to talk politics, or just listen to music?" demanded Fred.

"Certain things we can't avoid, my brother," hissed Timmy.

"Danny's okay for a white dude," whispered Fred with an air of confidence.

Fred felt disappointed that he could no longer dodge the issue. He grabbed a group of family photos from his desk. One photo showed his father standing in front of a sporting goods store. Fred's father had a business in the Ironbound section of Newark. It had escaped the worst of the riots. He maintained a healthy relationship with many of the residents and enjoyed a thriving business. "My dad's really proud of that store. He always wanted me to be the first college graduate in our family," Fred said, with his chest puffed up with pride.

Timmy was suitably impressed.

Fred grabbed another photo of his mother Cecilia standing in front of a class of young students. "She taught for over twenty years at the local elementary school."

Timmy grabbed another photo from the desk and examined a photo of Fred playing golf with his white high school teammates. Timmy snickered. "Hey, golf is a white boy's game," chuckled Timmy.

Fred's eyes narrowed. "You expected me to play basketball, just because I'm Black?" Fred sniffed indignantly.

"Only white boys play golf," replied Timmy with a provocative smirk.

"It's my sport and I'm damn good at it," Fred asserted.

Timmy just shook his head, then stopped in his tracks on seeing photos of white relatives.

"Yeah, my family's integrated. So is my high school," Fred declared, now on the offensive. "You got something to say?" Fred glared at his friend daring him to continue the conversation.

Timmy shrugged. "Just wondering if you're ready to join the movement?"

Fred brooded and shook his head. He felt antagonized by Timmy's remarks. He could not believe that his friend was asking these questions and challenging him. "I came here for an education. Politics isn't important," Fred huffed.

Timmy snorted derisively and shook his head. "We'll see in a month."

Down the hall in his room, Danny was wondering if he had done the right thing with quickly ending the discussion with Fred and Timmy. Only time would tell if the marriage between Barry and Fred was a good one.

Danny began to study but he flipped open his appointment book. He noted that he had an evening appointment to interview the head of Dining Services. He began to panic; it had slipped his mind. It was slated for ten minutes from now. He grabbed his notepad and rushed out the door. He was not enthusiastic about his assignment, but he was resigned to doing his best. He just hoped the story went without a hitch. He felt that Morris had given him the assignment on purpose. It was his way of handling lower-level reporters. Danny was determined to make the story relevant and impress Morris. It would elevate his standing at the newspaper. Any problems with the story could jeopardize his budding career as well as his scholarship. He was aware that his tenure as a student depended upon maintaining his scholarship. Without it, he would be forced to leave school. He did not plan to ruffle any feathers, but he was not going to take Morris's damned assignment lying down. Danny was determined to make the second-hand story something that he could be proud of. Even if it killed him.

13

Interview with the Head of Dining Services

Later that night, Danny breathlessly entered the offices of the school cafeteria known as the Commons. It was the slow time between meals where the staff washed dishes or prepared the vegetables and meats for the evening meal. He wandered through the labyrinth kitchen toward the cubicles containing the office of Victor Frangione, the head of Dining Services. He was a large, oval-faced man, with thinning hair and a large bulging stomach. He wore a dingy white frockcoat and apron. Danny followed the signs in the office and found himself standing in front of Frangione just in time. The chef offered him a seat and a freshly brewed cup of coffee.

Danny declined as he was not a big coffee drinker, save when pulling the infamous all-nighters before a major test. Frangione's desk was strewn with thick, bulging files and papers. He shuffled them and selected a folder marked 'Meal Plans.'

"So, you're thinking of adding new meal plans for students with difficult schedules?" Danny leaned forward and struggled to appear interested.

"I'm so proud of our meal plans," Frangione declared. "We have taken a lot of time to make the plans flexible for commuters. We have options for commuters and those staying on the campus," said the director in rapid fashion. He droned on for a few minutes and grew more enthusiastic with every chart that he plucked from a thick file. Danny struggled to keep up with the details. He felt his point of information-overload had been reached and was bored beyond rescue.

"Make sure you also point out the extra menu options we're offering," demanded Frangione. Danny dutifully scribbled notes in his pad, smiling as forcefully as he could.

"I've been told that there were rumors of one of the staff being dismissed for juggling the books. Is there any truth to the rumors?" Danny questioned in a journalistic, inquiring tone.

Frangione scowled at Danny, his face contorted with a mixture of contempt and anger. He grabbed Danny's notebook and flipping it closed. "That has very little relevance for this interview," he snapped, with eyes squinting and a clenched jaw.

Danny realized that his question had been out of line. He looked down, unable to meet the Dining Services Director's eyes.

"Are we writing for the *Targum* or the *National Enquirer?*" said the disgruntled Director.

Danny realized his mistake and fidgeted in his chair. "Of course, I just want to clarify the rumor and get the facts right for the story. Make it interesting for my readers."

Frangione was unamused and ushered Danny out of the office. "I have to get to work on tonight's menu, if you'll excuse me."

Danny shuffled into the main cafeteria area. Cafeteria workers were still rushing around preparing the dining hall for the next meal. The workers scrubbed down the tables, loaded cartons of milk into the dispensers and shined the silver. They had the radio on, blaring music through the empty dining room. As he mounted the stairs, he gave one last look. Danny crossed the street to the Student Center. He trudged up the stairs to the *Targum* office.

Shortly thereafter, Morris received a disturbing phone call from the Director. The phone rang and he listened to the Director rant about Danny's performance. His face contorted with anger. He thanked the Director and hung up the phone. Morris sat with his legs crossed at his desk, chain-smoking cigarettes and barely finishing one cigarette before lighting another one.

A few minutes later, Danny entered the office. Morris was waiting for him, his face contorted, and arms crossed as he spoke to Danny. He felt his facial muscles tightening. "What did I send you out to do?"

"Get the story on the cafeteria choice?" said Danny defensively.

Morris examined him from head to toe like a zebra about to be devoured by a leopard on the hunt. Danny tried to pretend the problem was minor. He was usually skilled at diplomacy. but apparently, he was unsuccessful with Morris. Morris clenched his jaw and offered, "Damn straight, there's a problem," his vitriol unleashed.

Danny steeled himself for the prospect of being dismembered. "Problems with my interview?" Danny asked.

Morris drummed the top of the table. "Your job was to get facts, not launch fishing expeditions about unsubstantiated rumors and above all, not to piss off the Director."

"You're always giving me soft stories like this," Danny whined. "Why can't I do important stores like you give Kevin? Kevin gets to interview protest leaders; all I do is articles that no one cares about."

Morris smacked the table. "If you want to stay on my paper, you'll apologize to Frangione and write the story the way I asked."

Danny was trapped and he knew it. Danny's scholarship was riding on this moment, and he had almost bet the house. Morris picked up the phone and spoke to the Director for a few seconds. Then he handed the phone over to Danny.

Danny stuttered as he picked up the phone. "I am sorry for the questions that I asked. I'll write a great piece that will highlight the new menus." Danny listened, then sighed, "thank you" and hung up.

"Type up the correct story and drop it in the basket," Morris demanded. He stared at Danny and then stubbed out his cigarette.

A tired Danny nodded and made his way to an empty desk. He

yawned as he typed. It had been a long, frustrating day. He spotted Alex sitting in a rear cubicle. She was a speedy typist and freelanced on some of the graphic design projects and the typesetting machine. She waved to him, but he ignored the gesture. He was not in any mood to exchange pleasantries. He rushed through typing the article on his shiny Smith Corona and ripped it out of the typewriter, then dropped it in the 'to be edited' basket and headed back down the stairs to the dorm. Danny hoped to escape into his bed, but his evening had only just begun. He was about to face another unpleasant experience.

14

The Ex-Girlfriend

Danny wandered through the winding halls of the Student Center in search of the exit, hoping to avoid anyone and get a good, silent sleep. He was angry at himself for nearly risking his college education. He felt that he had been walking on thin ice and only a quick apology had saved his journalistic career.

He was not interested in any more confrontations. He simply wanted to collapse in his bed. When he got to the bottom of the stairs, he spotted a long line of students waiting for an event at the Center. At the end of the line, he spotted Tracy, his ex-girlfriend. Danny had dated her several times, but he felt that they were not communicating very well. She had long legs and long brown hair with expressive, flirty, blue eyes. She wore a buckskin jacket with fringes and calf-high boots. She wore a heavy dose of perfume that could be detected from a distance. She was sexy in a college girl sort of way. He had met Tracy at a college social and he liked her, but he always felt that she was overly critical of him or was looking for some quality that he did not possess. He had not handled his last communication with her very well.

She gazed uncomfortably as Danny approached, and turned away, red-faced with anger.

"Hey, how's it going?" he said.

"For real? You stood me up the last time I checked," she countered.

"I had an emergency Student Advisor meeting that night." Danny tried to explain, but Tracy appeared cold, distant—she was not buying it. "My girlfriend saw you with some blond chick later that night."

An annoyed Danny shook his head. "She's an advisor for the River Dorms," he insisted.

"Please just go away." She turned her back to him. Several students turned their heads to listen to the confrontation.

At that moment, Storzillo, a large, muscular jock student, emerged from the crowd but seemed oblivious to what had happened. He was tall and impressive in a dumb jock sort of way. His tight blue tee-shirt displayed his rippling muscles. He wore a shirt emblazoned with the name of his fraternity. He handed her a ticket and a bag of popcorn.

"Something the matter?" said Storzillo.

"No, he was just leaving, weren't you, Danny?" She giggled, ignoring Danny completely, and placed Storzillo's oversized arm around her shoulder. He led her away. They disappeared into the crowd around the corner and out of sight. She appeared to be relieved that she had ended her numbing encounter with Danny.

Danny slinked away and walked up the stairs to the exit for the Student Center. He bowed his head and walked out of the building and headed for the dorm. As Danny neared the dormitory, he decided to park himself in front of the Greasy Truck for a late-night snack. The owner appeared bored as he leaned out of the window of the truck, taking orders. Tonight, the line in front of the truck was short. Danny did not have long to wait for service. This was good because Danny's patience was thin. The owner recognized Danny and perked up as Danny approached the truck. The smell of the ripe odor of the greasy stove lingered in the air like a bad dream.

"The usual cheese steak, hold the onions?" said the owner. Danny nodded. He stood there and felt no compulsion to make conversation. The owner nodded to his co-worker standing in front of the grease-stained hot grill. "How's it going? The kids giving you problems?" quizzed the owner.

Danny shrugged unhappily, then stood silently.

"I usually get some good juicy gossip out of you," the owner gushed. "tell me about that girl, Alex. She's sexy."

"Not tonight. Okay?" Danny grumbled. The owner could see that Danny was pre-occupied and did not press the issue. The co-worker slapped the food onto the grill. It sizzled and cooked for a few minutes. When finished, the cook handed it to the owner of the truck.

Danny grabbed his wallet and slid a few crumpled dollars onto the counter. He snatched up the sandwich and drowned it with ketchup. Normally, he savored every morsel; however, tonight he devoured only a few bites of the cheese steak before it lost its appeal. It was like eating cardboard. He walked a few feet and chucked the remainder of the sandwich in the trash. He had lost his appetite.

As soon as he reached the dorm, he headed down the hallway toward his room. The sound of laughter and the smell of cigarette smoke filled the air. A loud din indicated the nightly poker game was in progress in the lounge. Several freshmen sat hunched around the table, analyzing the cards and monitoring their pile of poker chips. They swilled a few bottles of beer, smoking joints or cigarettes to make themselves appear sophisticated. The trash basket was filled with empty beer bottles. Normally Danny would get upset, but tonight he was not in the mood to grouse at the slovenly freshmen.

"Shouldn't you guys be studying?" said Danny, as he walked toward the lobby. It was a rhetorical question. The students shrugged their shoulders and turned their concentration back to their life-and-death card game. Several empty bottles and crumpled bags of chips and snacks indicated that the game had been going on for the better part of the evening.

"Any of you guys at the protest?" said Danny, making his way across the room.

The students snickered. "Same old boring speeches," laughed one of them. One of the players offered Danny an empty chair. "Want to play?"

Danny was flattered by the offer, but he declined. His eyelids heavy and face drained of color, he appeared both mentally and physically drained. "Not tonight," Danny mumbled quietly.

"Hey, we want your money," joked one of the players.

Danny yawned and motioned that he was too tired to play and headed for his room.

"So, who's in?" Danny recognized that it was Barry sitting at the head of the table, concealed beneath the dealer's cap. He nodded towards his friend but felt no interest in having a conversation about his disastrous evening.

The raucous laughter of the card players echoed through the corridors as Danny made his way down the hallway. On some nights, the games could go well into the overnight hours. It was extremely easy to lose track of time. Many students enjoyed their newly found freedom of college, away from the demands of their parents. Kids partied well into the night with their friends and without a care in the world.

As he passed by several other rooms, he noticed a few students pounding the books, hard at work studying. Many of these students would be either in the Pre-Med or Pharmacy programs. They were intensive, merciless programs that demanded relentless sacrifices. He admired their singular dedication.

One of the students he observed was Pamela. She noticed Danny and got up to speak with him. "Can I speak to you?" she said.

"Kind of tired," he replied. "Try me tomorrow." His tone was gentle so as not to hurt her feelings. She nodded and returned to her desk.

Danny popped open the door to his room. He intended to watch an episode of *Gunsmoke* on television but could barely hold his eyes open. He slumped into bed. He was too tired to even remove his clothing and he passed out, fully clothed, on his mattress.

Within the hour there was a loud, relentless knocking on the door. Danny bolted upright, roused from his deep sleep. He appeared groggy, but awake.

"Go away or I'll have to shoot you," he thundered.

The knocking continued, despite Danny's warnings.

"I'm armed and dangerous," Danny said in a sleepy voice.

"It's long distance," intoned an unfamiliar student voice.

"Tell them to go away." His voice grew louder, more insistent.

"It's from the Jersey Shore or something," said the student voice.

At first, Danny thought he was hallucinating that someone was shouting his name. Maybe it was a bad dream. Slowly, he realized that the call was real and that he was not dreaming. A groggy Danny bounced out of bed. He barely acknowledged the student and padded down the hallway in his bare feet. He spotted the brown phone booth at the end of the hall. The phone sat on its cradle, waiting for Danny to answer it. Danny perched on the bench of the phone booth. "Hello?" He listened for a long time without speaking, growing upset as Matthew, his father spoke.

"We may need you to come home. We may not be able to pay your tuition," Mattthew, his father concluded.

"We've had this conversation over and over, Dad," said a weary Danny. Danny leaned forward with a large dose of frustration in his voice. "I need to stay at school. I want to be a journalist."

"Danny, I'm getting older. I had an accident this morning."

Danny leaned into the phone. His manner changed; his voice filled with concern. "You okay, Dad?"

There was a long pause at the other end. "Yes, but it scared your mother and me."

Danny sighed. He felt intimidated by the ominous sound of his father's voice.

"It's not as easy as it used to be to run the farm. It needs a younger man," stated Matthew.

"Kenny can run things," said an exhausted Danny.

"He's not available," his father lamented at the other end. "He's serving his country. Unlike certain people."

It was a hideous rebuke that hit Danny at his core. Danny was a very sensitive person. He had survived enough verbal abuse from his father; it made him very sensitive to criticism.

"He'll be home in a few months," said a weary Danny. Danny stared up at the ceiling of the phone booth as he prayed for a bolt of lightning to hit it, or for the phone call to end. His mind raced to find some way to gracefully end the conversation.

"You're not one of those professional agitators?" demanded his father.

"No, sir," Danny corrected him.

"Good, they're a bunch of fucking Communists."

Danny was not in any mood to discuss this sore point between the two. Danny was not political but living on the campus had opened his eyes to many new viewpoints. Viewpoints that his father certainly detested with every fiber of his body.

"Dad, I have to study for a test tomorrow." He slid the phone down to the floor. A long pause ensued. Was he buying it?

"This conversation is far from over, young man," bellowed his father's voice over the phone.

There was a click and then a loud dial tone permeated the other end of the phone. It was over, at least for the moment. With a sigh of relief, Danny hung the phone back in its cradle and exited the booth.

His father, Matthew, was a proud and demanding man. As a veteran of the Marine Corps in the Korean War, he had won several bronze stars for bravery. He felt that Danny never took things seriously and gave up too easily. Danny recalled that despite his best efforts, his father would always berate him. Danny tried to be a star athlete like his father, but either it was too hard or Danny found the competition too fierce. Matthew often yelled at Danny that he had never met his expectations. "You never finish anything, or you're never good enough." It was demoralizing for Danny, who was more a scholar and musician. These were qualities that his rough-and-tumble father did not appreciate. Matthew was proud of Danny for achieving Eagle Scout status and he hoped that it might inspire him to begin a career in the military. However, Danny had clearly indicated a lack of interest.

Danny was shy by nature and his father's attempts to denigrate him caused him much pain. Danny sometimes gave up the things that mattered to him. He was more of a thinker or dreamer than a fighter by nature. Danny walked back down the hallway to his room, passing Barry, who held winnings from the poker game jangling in his hat. He fanned the dollar bills in Danny's direction. Danny did not react. Barry had only to look at Danny's sour expression to realize what was going on. Barry did not have to work too hard to figure out the deep freeze in his expression.

"Your dad finally called?" asked Barry.

Danny growled his disgust and made no attempt to explain further.

"You want a cheese steak or something? I'm buying," Barry bragged as he jangled his ill-gotten gains. Danny shook his head and kept on walking. "Hey man, none of my business, but if you want my advice?"

"Fuck off. I don't need to spell it out to you," Danny blurted out, without hesitation.

Danny's bitter defensiveness caught Barry off-guard. Danny stalked off in the opposite direction leaving his puzzled friend in his wake. He could not have made his anger more visible than if he had painted a big bold sign on the door. As he entered his room, he slammed the door shut. It had been a difficult day for him, and he prayed that sleep would somehow deliver him to a better place.

15

Curtis's Class

The next morning, Ryan knocked on Danny's door. No response. Ryan knocked again on the door. Still no response. "You alive in there?" He waited for a few seconds. Still no response from Danny. "Answer me, goddamn it!" He began pounding on the door.

Slowly the door opened, and Danny peered through the crack in the door. He looked haggard. "I'm okay," he muttered slowly.

"We're going to be late for class," insisted Ryan.

"I'll be out in a minute."

Ryan leaned against the wall. A few minutes later, Danny emerged from the room. He still appeared cranky.

"You want to talk about it?" Ryan muttered.

Danny remained silent. His features hardened. Ryan gave up the inquisition. A wall of silence separated the two men as they exited the dorm.

The pair walked a few blocks to the classroom. Ryan and Danny entered the doors to the marbled Scott Hall building. They mounted the stairs to the second floor. It consisted of a series of smaller, more compact classrooms. Downstairs, the enormous lecture halls held several hundred students. The smaller upstairs classes handled twenty to twenty-five students.

The morning class was led by Professor Peter Curtis. He was in his early thirties, short, with a Napoleon complex and a tall opinion of himself. He sat at his desk and flipped open his briefcase. Curtis was young compared to most of the professors, but he had experienced much in his life. Curtis had been an army officer, after which he attended Columbia College. This had given him a front row seat to the burgeoning student protest movement.

He attempted to relate to his students and keep his lectures lively. He was aware that many of the older tenured professors were on autopilot. They stood behind their lecterns and bombarded the students with tons of facts. The students had to learn how to take notes as fast as the professor spoke. It was like Moses handing down wisdom from the mountain. They would offer their knowledge, then disappear after the lecture.

Curtis tried to keep an open channel of communication to his young charges. He normally started off each class by going through a list of projects and deadlines for the students. He was aware that young students had limited attention spans and needed to be reminded of deadlines and projects on a regular basis. He did not resent having to spoon-feed them. He felt that as a young, vibrant member of the faculty, it was his job to inspire the students. When he became an old tenured professor, he could afford to be distant and non-responsive to the needs of his students.

"How many of you attended yesterday's protest?" he asked. "Show of hands." Most of the hands in the room shot up. He nodded with interest, noting that Ryan was almost alone in not raising his hand.

"Don't forget that we are starting a new research paper for the next few weeks. I'll have the syllabus for you in the next class." The students groaned, but in a respectful way. They knew that Curtis was supportive. He popped open his briefcase and dredged out a handful of term papers.

He called out the name of each of the students as he walked around passing back papers.

"Nice job, Mr. Tucker."

Tucker smiled as he spotted the large A-grade pasted on the front page of the term paper.

"Mr. Zabriskie, come see me during office hours." A young student had an unhappy look as he stared at the grade. He folded the paper in half as if to conceal the bad news and headed for his seat.

Curtis headed over to Danny's seat and handed back Danny and Ryan's paper. Ryan had a B on the paper. Danny's term paper had a C+ grade on it. Danny moaned slightly and then tucked the paper back in his notebook without examining any of the professor's other comments. Ryan studied his friend, aware that Danny was still very agitated.

"I want to talk a bit about the Cold War," he stated. "How many of you know we are living in a Cold War?" A few students raised their hands, but most sat and gave no visible response. They were living in dangerous times but seemed oblivious to the world outside the campus. Curtis continued, "We are going to start with the Yalta Summit at the end of WWII. Did Stalin promise not to invade Eastern Europe? These are big questions that we need to discuss."

Danny raised his hand. "Professor, the Feinberg book is sold out in the college bookstore."

Curtis adjusted his glasses. "I have several copies on reserve at Errol's Bookstore downtown, Mr. Watkins. He always keeps a few on hold for my students." Danny jotted down the information in his notebook.

"So, again let's talk a bit about the Cold War," said Curtis. Curtis lowered his glasses, studying the class as they listened or took notes. Curtis leaned forward on his lectern. "Does everyone agree that the US was responsible for starting the Cold War?" questioned Curtis.

Ryan tentatively raised his hand. He was not sure he wanted to commit to answering the question. Sometimes the atmosphere of the class did not welcome opposing viewpoints.

"Mr. Marshott, you had a comment?" The professor's eyes shot over to Ryan's desk.

Ryan struggled to contain himself. His face reddened. He appeared ready to explode, but quickly stifled his anger. "No sir," was his curt, almost defiant response. Curtis smiled at Ryan nodding him to continue. Ryan hesitated for a moment, and then blasted loose his opinion.

"I think the Russians are the aggressors. Stalin promised to promote democracy in Europe after the war. Instead, he dispatched the Red Army, who took over Eastern Europe. Set up border walls like the Berlin Wall." Ryan's opinions had been shaped by an uncle who had been a diplomat during the Truman administration. He'd grown furious when Stalin, the Soviet dictator, had promised free elections in post-World War II Eastern Europe. Shortly after the war ended, he had installed Communist dictatorships in all the countries controlled by the Red Army.

This remark was greeted with a series of loud boos from some of the students in the back of the class. Some of the others offered the thumbs-down gesture behind his back.

"I read a book by I.F. Stone called *The Hidden History of the Cold War*. He felt that many of the world's problems were the result of US imperialism," declared one of the students.

"Stone is a Communist. He has a history of writing substandard history and intellectual garbage," argued Ryan. Some more boos and loud farting noises greeted his remarks.

"Go on, Mr. Marshott. I encourage critical thinking and different viewpoints in my class. I applaud Mr. Marshott's viewpoint. He is entitled to his point of view. If you disagree, you can express this through debate, not shaming," said Curtis.

Ryan could sense the growing hostility to his comments. He had wandered into a minefield of disapproval, yet he bravely held his ground. He was cool under fire. He would not yield or give in to negativity in the room. Ryan heaved a sigh of relief. He felt relieved to be able to speak his mind and not be condemned for it. He felt encouraged and went further. Almost despite himself.

"I also support the war in Vietnam," he declared. Almost without thinking, Ryan had stepped on a landmine with that remark. His remarks were received with hostile stares from the other students. One of the students in the back of the room shot a wad of paper at Ryan's head. They offered thumbs down in disagreement. More loud hissing and booing erupted from the peanut gallery. Many of the most visible students held anti-war viewpoints; conservative viewpoints were not heard very often.

"ROTC asshole," hissed one of the students in the back of the room. Curtis waved his arms. "We'll have none of this, not in my class. Please continue," sniffed Curtis.

Ryan's infamy as a ROTC cadet had followed him into the classroom. Ryan fired off a defiant glance at the student. The other student backed off. "I think we are over there defending South Vietnam from the Communists," Ryan retorted. More loud groans. Ryan retained his composure and would not back down.

Curtis smiled; it was a lively discussion. He waved his arms to bring order back to the classroom. "This is a university. Everyone has a right to express his opinion," said Curtis. "He's very brave for standing against the majority view. I commend him for that." He turned and nodded his approval to Ryan. Ryan offered him a smallish smile but shifted restlessly as his classmates continued to offer discouraging sound effects.

Behind his back, Danny watched Ryan with admiration as his friend braved sniper fire from their classmates and refused to duck for cover. Curtis dismissed the class and headed for the door.

"That was very brave. Took a lot of balls," Danny said.

"Why didn't you support me? Leaving me hanging out there," said Ryan.

Danny was embarrassed and at a loss for words. He just stared at his friend. "I just felt that you were doing a great job on your own," he declared.

"Sometimes you have to face the incoming fire and stand for what you believe in," retorted Ryan.

Danny shrugged. He thought that he would try to learn to disregard other people's opinions, especially if they clashed with his opinion. "I'll catch you later. I have to find Errol's bookstore."

"Go ahead, pussy," muttered Ryan.

Danny walked alone. He had thought that he was secure in his political viewpoints. He had learned many viewpoints that consisted of a patriotic view of America as a youth in his hometown. However, after observing the many protests on campus, he began to have doubts. He was impressed with the orderliness and enthusiasm of the protest. For many weeks, he had done his best to ignore Barry's urgent desire to debate. However, he began to sense that perhaps the political viewpoint that he held so fervently had begun to change. He was not expecting his journey to the bookstore to be anything more than a small chore. It would bring an unexpected turn.

16

Errol's Bookstore

L ater that day, Danny departed the campus and hiked into the heart of the downtown business district of New Brunswick in search of Errol's bookstore. He needed to purchase the book for Curtis's class. New Brunswick, like many urban areas of the time, had begun to slide into urban decay. Many of the neighborhoods were considered crime-ridden and were to be avoided after dark. Many of the shops were empty or boarded up. The main street in the town was George Street. It connected the Rutgers and Douglass college campuses. The main attractions on George Street were fast food restaurants and a porno theater called New Arts Cinema. It showed a mixture of recent movies and porno films such as *Sexual Freedom in Denmark*.

The Rutgers and Douglass campuses were separated by two miles of the downtown area. Students generally passed through the town on their way to the other campus for classes. It was not a place for a solitary walk after dark.

Soon, Danny spotted a gritty storefront bookstore located at the end of the street. Errol's Bookstore and Café was a seedy storefront crammed with books piled on unpainted wooden shelves. It was in the unfashionable center of town. Like many urban areas of the time, many businesses had fled following the riots of 1968. Only the foolhardy or the desperate kept their stores open in the downtown area. Many other store owners had fled to more desirable suburban locations. Errol's Bookstore and Café was a proud survivor.

On the walls hung political posters of the era, large photos of such radical heroes as Eldridge Cleaver of the Black Panthers and Abbie Hoffman. One of the most startling posters featured Huey Newton, founder of the Black Panthers. He sat in a wicker chair with his eyes poised and a gun in his lap. It was a powerful symbol of left-wing resistance.

Several senior citizens loitered in the rear of the store, reading the books or sipping cups of coffee. They wore shirts with fiery political slogans splashed on the front of them. Errol's bookstore was a burial ground for many a worn copy of a trashy bestseller. At the heart of the bookstore was the treasure trove of rare and exotic political books and tracts.

Danny browsed the shelves of used books. It was like a journey back in time. Several of the more recent titles that grabbed his attention were *Wretched of the Earth* by Frantz Fanon and *Rules for Radicals* by Saul Alinsky.

The shop was full of musty, old, worn-out books that had found a new home at Errol's. It was an intellectual's haven. The books were crammed into the wooden shelves. Several portions of the aisle were piled waist-high with paperbacks of all types. Some had barely legible labels.

"Just got a new consignment of books," called a stentorian voice from the rear of the store. Errol Anderson, Black, with a bushy Afro hairstyle and jovial disposition, emerged from the back of the room carrying some books. He wore a faded army jacket with a patch indicating that he was a veteran of the First Air Cavalry Division.

Danny smiled at Errol. "I'm looking for a book called *History of the Cold War* by Feinberg. My school bookstore is sold out and Professor Curtis said that you might have a used copy."

Errol set down his handful of books. Almost by memory, Errol knew exactly where to find the books that his patrons were looking for. He walked over to the shelves and plucked out a well-worn, faded copy of the book that Danny needed.

Danny examined it, thumbing through the pages with a look of hopefulness. He glanced again at Errol's army insignia on the sleeve of his faded olive drab army jacket.

"My brother's serving with the Air Cav in Quang-Tri province."

Errol sighed. "How long has he been in-country?" he asked.

"Few months—should be home soon," Danny said. 'In-country' was Army slang for serving in Vietnam.

"I'll keep my fingers crossed for his safety. It's a tough slog. I'm against it."

Danny seemed stunned that an army veteran would be against the war. "I grew up in a small town," Danny said. "We said the Pledge of Allegiance every morning at school. America, right or wrong, that is what we learned. It sounds corny now, but we believed it," he said. It was more than a slogan: it was ingrained into America's very soul. "My brother is serving in Vietnam, and I'm troubled by what I've heard. I just wanted to hear the other side."

Errol opened his shirt and displayed a faint scar on his chest. It was a war wound that was a mark of distinction. "I served in Vietnam back in '67. I volunteered to serve my country. But after being in-country for several months, I began to see things. I heard the rumors and the stories from some of my fellow soldiers. I saw what both sides did. We marched into a village that was supposed to be a VC stronghold. We searched for weapons for an hour. Finally, the Commander told us to torch the village. The villagers were upset about losing their homes. The look of hatred and mistrust was intense. A villager grabbed a weapon and charged at us and one of the guys shot him." Errol shut his eyes to block out the terrible memories.

"I should have listened to Abbie," he concluded. "Abbie Hoffman and I grew up in the same hometown. We were sort of friends. He advised me against going to Vietnam. I didn't listen," continued Errol in a wistful manner.

"You really know Abbie Hoffman?" Danny repeated, flabbergasted.

"We went to high school together. He was a scrapper. Always getting into fights. One time, one of his teachers objected to his paper proclaiming that God was dead. The teacher called him a Communist. The two of them got into a fight. Abbie was suspended for three days."

Danny absorbed the story, but Errol ended it on a sober note. "I got this wound as a painful reminder. There are a bunch of us veterans like me that oppose the war."

Danny could see that Errol was missing two fingers on his hand. "I'm not sure how my brother feels about the war. The last letter that I got from him seemed pretty gung-ho," said Danny. "It was a while ago."

"It wasn't easy for me to have a change of heart, but I applaud your efforts to see the other side."

Danny smiled. Errol was soothing to talk to.

"Anytime you want to talk about politics or just hang out, Errol's got you covered," he said with an engaging smile. Danny thanked him, sure that he would return. "I offer free coffee at my cafe in the back." Errol handed him a copy of another book, entitled, *The Hidden History of the Vietnam War.* "Read this and let me know what you think."

Danny smiled and gave Errol the thumbs-up gesture as he exited the shop. Just as he was leaving, Errol called out. "Hey man, if you ever run into Abbie, say hello for me. Ask him, are you serious or delirious? He'll recognize it."

Danny chuckled and nodded 'sure' but shook his head, certain that such a meeting was unlikely. He had entered the store seeking easy answers. He left shaken in his beliefs, feeling deeply about his encounter with the older veteran. He was already looking forward to another visit after he'd had a chance to read Errol's book, and trepidation at what it might contain. He was feeling uneasy about whether the book would challenge his viewpoint and force him to confront some of his deeply held beliefs.

17

Pamela's Fateful Journey

As soon as Danny returned from the bookstore, he circled back to visit Pamela Winters and sat in his reclining chair, listening to Pamela s complain about her latest problem. Danny had gotten used to listening to freshmen regale him with their issues. However, he seemed to have formed a real empathy for Pamela. She had been stuck with a roommate that did not like her very much.

Pamela was an accommodating type of person and fidgeted as she sat on the chair. She was not the type to easily reveal her feelings. However, at this moment she was close to tears. Danny leaned forward in the chair and listened sympathetically. "She hates me," Pamela said flatly.

"I know, I can hear the two of you arguing from down the hall, but it's probably an adjustment to this new living arrangement."

Pamela wiped away her tears.

Danny shook his head and whispered softly. "Why can't the two of you make peace?" he said, questioningly.

"We just—don't gel. Every weekend I come back from a mixer, and I find the same big note on the door!" Pamela cried and pulled a wrinkled piece of notepaper from her pants pocket. The sign read 'Do Not Disturb.' It was in big, bold, unmistakable letters. "She always has some guy inside," recalled Pamela.

Danny attempted to conceal a smile. "Maybe you should have some guy over some time." He laughed, but she remained stone-faced.

"After all," he smirked, "turn-about is fair play. I read that in some ninth-grade play by Shakespeare."

Pamela bristled, but in an odd sort of way that caught Danny off-guard. He felt that there was something else going on, but he did not want to probe too deeply. Danny sighed. "You're just roommates. You do not have to like each other that much, but if it is that much of a problem, let me talk to her."

Pamela was visibly relieved. "I knew that I could count on you. Thanks, Danny."

Danny peered at his watch. "It's dinner time. You want to join us?"

"No thanks, my friend and I are going to a seminar for pre-meds this evening in town."

"I heard about your missing a class because of the protest," said Danny.

"My professor understood. He said that I could take a make-up."

Danny nodded. He admired her determination.

Pamela leaned over and stared at the *Targum* with a headline about the protests. She began to scowl. "You know why I don't like the protests?" she said.

Danny's curiosity was aroused. He raised his eyebrows.

"My cousin, Sergei," she continued, "he dropped out of medical school to go to Chicago and join the protesters at the Chicago Convention. He got arrested."

Danny was listening closely.

"Well, the medical school found out and kicked him out. He was unable to get back in. He pleaded with them, but they refused," she lamented. "What a stupid waste of talent."

Danny listened sympathetically. "And my family disowned him. I wouldn't make that mistake." Pamela concluded, leaning forward, "I hope you don't get kicked out of school because of them."

Danny shook his head. "Thanks for the warning, but don't worry. I have no intention of getting involved in the protests," he uttered. He did not want to argue with her. She felt so strongly about it. Danny changed the subject. "So, I guess that's a no. Okay, the invitation is always open," said Danny.

Pamela smiled and rose to leave. "Thank you," she said. Danny felt that he had done his best to comfort the young woman. He had earned his pay for the week.

Pamela did feel relieved. She was happy that she had gotten some of her feelings out in the open. Danny's talk had been a big help. She felt better for the rest of the day and accepted an invitation from her friend Vicky to attend a lecture later that night.

Later that night, after the Pre-Med lecture, Pamela and her friend Vicky walked down the dark streets of New Brunswick. Vicky was an earnest young woman, who was always the sidekick but never the star of any dating situation. The two women were *simpatico*. Neither was extraordinarily successful with men. Both were good at sharing inner secrets. However, Vicky sensed that there was an unseen layer to Pamela that she would not reveal.

"That was a great discussion. I'd love to go back tomorrow night for the follow-up," said Vicky.

"The bus stop is that way, I think," said Pamela with a singular lack of confidence. She scanned the unfamiliar street. They searched for the bus stop that would deliver them back to the main Rutgers campus. For a few minutes, they wandered around the quiet streets. Several mom-and-pop stores were lit up and others appeared to be empty or simply abandoned. The two girls were searching for a familiar landmark but saw nothing familiar.

"We're lost," said Vicky sadly, with regret in her voice.

Pamela delicately stated, "I know where we are, I think," but her eyes darted around the street, and she saw nothing that rang a bell.

Vicky was clearly annoyed. She fidgeted and tapped her feet.

Pamela pointed to the end of the street. "I think that's the corner where we get the bus," she said, struggling to remember.

"This is the last time I let you get directions," Vicky said in a huff.

The two women walked further. Vicky spotted a building down the street. The word 'Bar' popped off the sign. Vicky tugged at Pamela. They passed the seedy, poorly illuminated bar in the middle of the block. Enticing bold letters proclaimed, *The Rendezvous*.

"Are you thirsty?" Vicky said, wetting her whistle, simulating thirst.

Pamela shrugged. "Can we wait?"

Vicky was thirsty and this bar seemed to be the only oasis in the desert of closed businesses. "Maybe there are some hot guys inside." She laughed in a hopeful, sort of desperate manner. She visualized cuddling up to some handsome young man who would sweep her off her feet. It was not a strong possibility, but she did not give up hope.

Pamela halted by the door. She eyed the place. She sensed something unusual, maybe something off about the place. It was not well-lit like most bars and the windows had the shades drawn down.

"Maybe we shouldn't," said Pamela.

"C'mon, it could be fun."

Vicky grabbed her by the hand and dragged her inside the dimly lit establishment. "Don't be a spoiler. You'll have a good time."

Pamela and Vicky entered the bar. It was a dark teakwood bar, illuminated only by the bright lights of the bartender's station. It took a few seconds for both women to adjust their eyes to the harsh light. The garish decor was filled wall-to-wall with women. Some were short and muscular, others wore cut-off shirts, vests, and bold tattoos. A few of the women had short, buzz-cut hairstyles and wore overalls. Even the plump bartender was a woman. Vicky looked around, unhappy with what she saw. It was not what she expected. The noise from the jukebox blared a monumental, soulful hit song by Helen Reddy entitled, *I am Woman, Hear me Roar*. It would become a feminist anthem in its day. Vicky leaned over and whispered, her voice full of acid disdain, "Dykes, fucking dykes."

Pamela was distracted. "Oh, come on, they can't all be." Pamela was not an innocent, but she realized that her friend's analysis was correct.

"Really, look around you, what do you see? This is no mixer," said Vicky with distaste in her voice.

Pamela looked around the room, unsure of her own feelings. "Shhh, not so loud."

"Pam, I don't think this is our type of place. Let's go," Vicky said in a pleading voice.

"How can you tell?"

Vicky was incredulous. "Isn't it obvious?"

Pamela was intrigued. She stared at an overweight woman who strolled over to her, inspected Vicky, then focused her gaze on Pamela. "Buy you a drink, sweet pea?"

Vicky had had enough. She tugged at Pamela's hand. But Pamela stood her ground. She was determined to make up her own mind.

"Pam, let's go," she said softly and almost in a maternal way.

Pamela gawked at the woman, hesitated.

Vicky tugged on her arm. "Let's get out of here." The pleading voice had turned harsh and demanding.

Vicky hauled Pamela towards the door. The gay woman winked at Pamela and blew a hot kiss her way. Pamela hesitated for a moment more, then sighed, exiting. Vicky dashed out of the bar as if she were on fire. Pamela strode out slowly in a deliberate manner as Vicky hurried away. "Are you coming?"

Pamela stared back at the bar. She was conflicted and her eyes lingered for a few seconds.

"Why are you just standing there? You're not getting weird on me?" Vicky exclaimed.

Pamela said nothing. She began walking. They turned the next corner and spotted the illuminated, glass-enclosed bus stop. Vicky was out of breath and plunked herself down on the cold wooden bench. Pamela walked slowly, preoccupied. Vicky pulled her aside and said in a determined, even threatening, voice, "Don't you dare mention this to anyone! We'll never hear the end of this!"

The two women stood by the bus shelter in silence. Within a few minutes, a campus bus pulled up to the bus stop. The women entered the bus. Pamela smiled as she recognized the bus driver: it was the same driver who had tried to take her up to the class during the protests.

"Did you ever get to your class?" he said with a smile. He recognized the determined young woman.

She smiled and shook her head. "But my professor canceled the class after he found out about the protest, so I was okay."

The bus driver shook his head and closed the doors. He floored the gas pedal and the bus jerked forward, out toward the street. The two women ambled to the back of the bus. As the bus rounded the corner, Pamela stole a furtive last glance at the garishly illuminated bar proclaimed the *Rendezvous*.

Later, the two women returned to their respective dorms. Danny watched Pamela arrive at her dorm. He greeted her and asked how the seminar went. "Did you learn anything interesting?" No response.

Pamela turned around and motioned for Danny to move closer. "Can I speak to you, in private?"

Danny motioned for her to follow him back to his room. Within a minute, both were sitting in chairs. Pamela noticed Errol's book on the Vietnam war was bookmarked and sitting on his desk.

Pamela restlessly tried to say something. "Have you ever felt different?" she whispered. "I mean, like you arrived at the college thinking one way and then you discover that you are a different person?"

Danny pondered the question. "Yes, I came here thinking about the protests one way, and now I'm beginning to see things differently." Pamela nodded, looked down.

"Something that you saw tonight?" he said softly

Pamela grew flushed. She began to stammer. "I'm embarrassed to mention it."

Danny patted her on the shoulder. "Everyone has to deal with their lives in different ways. This college will bring changes. Sometimes despite what you believed before you started college. It certainly has changed me."

"But what if it makes you feel different from other people?" she questioned.

"Do you want to tell me what happened?" he said.

Pamela struggled with her thoughts. She blushed and grew embarrassed.

"I can't tell you. You'll think I'm weird."

Danny reassured her. "I run into a lot of people on this campus. People with ideas and behaviors that a few years ago I would have laughed at."

"And now?" responded Pamela.

"I'm learning that there is a whole new world out there. I don't understand it all, but don't beat yourself up for being different."

Pamela sighed and relaxed her shoulders, forcing herself to smile. "You're a good man, Danny. Thank you. I think I need to go to sleep now."

Danny ushered her out of the room. She turned and smiled at him. "You've really helped me," she said. "I knew that I could count on your help."

He sighed to himself. He seemed satisfied that he had helped her, despite her not sharing the source of her conflict. He took satisfaction that he was able to help the young woman with her problems. He only wished that he could navigate his own problems as easily. Danny would need a sympathetic ear to help him through the complicated events that would inflict themselves on him in the coming days. For many in the Rutgers community, the lyrics of the Bob Dylan song, *The times, they are a-changing*, were coming true, faster than they could have ever imagined.

18

Dining Hall

Days later, Danny headed out into the lobby of the dorm to gather the troops for dinner. He enjoyed dining with his freshmen because it gave him a chance to relax and meet the students in a more relaxed atmosphere. Barry, Fred, Pamela, and Alex were seated in the lobby waiting for Danny. Alex carried her sketchpad as was her custom. She enjoyed creating impromptu caricatures of the students she observed in the cafeteria. The group walked out of the dorm and across campus to the school cafeteria. Inside the school cafeteria, the group walked down the thinly carpeted stairs on the ramp towards the food line.

"Is Ryan going to join us?" questioned Alex.

Danny smiled and motioned toward the cafeteria. "He has a test, he said he might make it later."

The hall was a cavernous space capable of holding several hundred hungry students. The din of the many voices joined together into an almost insect-like buzz. Huge linen banners with the scarlet R for Rutgers dangled from the ceiling. It was almost like a tribal custom for the students to come together. Friends and dorm mates alike met for the evening meal. It was an informal, unspoken ritual that was understood by all. It was a chance to blow off steam from the pressure of their studies or just exchange good-natured banter with friends.

The smell of a wide variety of food wafted into the air. The quality varied from night to night. Cafeteria workers collected the trays full of leftover food and dumped them into the huge plastic garbage bins, as several gray-haired ladies wearing hairnets and plastic gloves dished out the food onto the plates of the famished students as they passed by their stations. They were all business, as they waited on each student. Steam wafted up from the serving trays as they ladled the current day's gourmet delight onto the plates of the oncoming famished students. It was important to keep the line moving and they developed indignant facial signals to hurry students on who could be indecisive as to whether they liked the meatloaf or the baked cod. Outside the line, workers deposited fresh cutlery onto the serving areas. The students carrying trays of food dodged the cafeteria workers as they wound their way over to the long, brown wooden tables.

Danny had hoped for a quiet dinner with his fellow classmates. He hoped it would be a relaxing meal free of any controversial comments. The sound of a blaring radio station became a distraction for the group's conversation, as someone in the back of the dining hall adjusted the dial and filled the room followed by the voice of the station DJ.

"Scott Muni, WNEW FM, 104.3, with the latest from the Moody Blues. This song has dominated the play charts for over five weeks," he intoned in his distinctive, gravelly voice.

Alex listened for a few minutes, then she gazed up at the voluminous black speakers hung on the wall with admiration. "Scott Muni, I love his voice. It's so rich."

Barry gestured with a thumbs-down gesture. "Give me Allison Steele any day," said Barry, with a touch of reproach.

Allison Steele was the velvet, sexy-voiced DJ who enchanted a generation of young listeners with her silky delivery. It was as if she were speaking directly to each listener. A 1970's classic rock song, *Knights in White Satin* by the Moody Blues, reverberated throughout the dining hall. It drowned out the conversation at the tables. The band's innovative use of electronic sound and lush orchestral music made the Moody Blues a fan favorite for over a decade.

Alex pulled out her sketchpad and a pencil. Alex smiled and began to sketch Danny. It was a caricature depicting him as a sort of wise, Sigmund Freud figure looking after the freshmen. He fidgeted and struggled to sit still for more than a few minutes.

"Hold still." Alex continued to sketch and build up the portrait of Danny. "How do you get along with Morris?" she inquired.

Danny shook his head indicating his dislike for the man.

"He's strange, but I don't let him bother me," Alex replied.

"He always gives me crap assignments," said Danny.

Alex appeared sympathetic. She appreciated his vulnerability and honesty.

Danny admired the finished drawing. "Sort of like a father figure. Genuinely nice, can I keep this?"

Alex smiled at Danny. The mention of father figure triggered a memory in Alex. She palmed the locket on her chest. "My father gave this to me on my fifteenth birthday. He was proud of my artistic ability. He took me to the local museums."

She grew uncomfortable and leaned back in her chair and recalled her childhood to the group of friends at the table. She recalled hiding in her room as her mother and father clashed over marital issues. Her father was a handsome, gregarious man, who enjoyed spending time at the local bars and held down jobs that were beneath his ability. Alex had cringed as her mom and dad would yell at each other for long periods of time. As with many marriages, the arguments revolved around money or the lack of it.

"She tried to explain it all to me. I never fully understood what had happened between them." Alex grew somber and drew on her memories. "She took me to Paris after the divorce."

In her mind, she recalled images of the two women riding around the city and enjoying the sights of Paris and being enchanted by the magnificent scenery. She recounted how excited she was to go to the top of the Eiffel Tower and see the city lit up at night. However, her greatest moments were the time she spent in art museums like the Louvre. She would spend hours wandering around the gallery. She would stare intently at the pictures and admire the brush strokes of the master painters.

"Very cool, some nice memories," everyone agreed.

Barry seemed anxious to bring the subject back to his first love, that of politics. He interrupted her reverie. He was never one to shy away from making strong comments. In fact, he thrived on it. He could always be counted on to bring his controversial opinions to any discussion. Barry unfolded a copy of the New York Times. The headline screamed, 'Deadliest Day in the War.'

Danny's eyes narrowed. He craved a calm and peaceful conversation at dinner. Barry was determined to set it on fire. Danny respected Barry's intellect and opinion but it sometimes got on his nerves. "Can we talk about something besides the war? You and the Revolution. You're like a broken record."

Everyone at the table chuckled and nodded their heads at the well-deserved rebuke.

"Thirteen Marines killed at a place called Khe-Sahn. I'm telling you—this war has to end!" Barry pounded his fist on the table for emphasis, then gazed around the table and, realizing that he was indeed like a broken record, he stopped in mid-thought.

Fred looked up from his plate. "My cousin served, came home wounded. He was never the same," Fred uttered.

Danny swallowed a mouthful of potatoes. He leaned over to address Fred. "My brother said he served with several negro soldiers. They fought well."

The table became quiet for a few moments, as everyone concentrated on their food.

"Ahh, the Sounds of Silence," purred Pamela, breaking the silence.

"The song by Simon and Garfunkel?" inquired Fred.

"No, the sound of Barry not talking about the war for a change," interjected Pamela.

Everyone roared with laughter. Barry's face reddened with embarrassment.

"If I get picked by the draft, I'm going to Canada," declared Barry, introducing yet another controversial topic with a flourish. Everyone groaned.

Danny shook his head. He had heard this before. He tried to decide if Barry was serious in his intentions or just trying to be provocative. "Really?" challenged Danny. Danny stared at Barry. Barry did not change his mind very often. Once an idea had fixed itself in his brain, it was hard wired to the inner reaches of his mind.

"I'm dead serious. I'm gone, man." His fingers drummed the table. He had a determined look in his eyes.

Pamela picked up a forkful of meat. She began to speak as she ate. "I'll probably go if I'm called," she said as she shook her head.

Barry waved his hands in the air. He was dismissive. He had his doubts about that assertion.

"Women don't get drafted. Besides, you'll probably get assigned to a nice cushy job as a doctor stateside."

"My brother volunteered. He's there now," added Danny. "He's in the Central Highlands with the 101st Airborne Division."

"Hey, maybe if you got to interview a famous person, you could do it for the newspaper," offered Fred.

Everyone paused to reflect. Alex shook her head and stared off into the distance.

"I thought it was my patriotic duty to join, but after listening to you guys, I'm not sure," Danny stated with emotion. Everyone stared at Danny with a shocked expression. No one had expected that reaction to come out of his mouth.

"You're sure, Danny?" asked Pamela with a puzzled look on her face.

"Been giving it a lot of thought lately," said Danny.

"Bold statement, my man," smirked Barry. Barry offered him the thumbs-up gesture.

The group grew silent and thoughtful. One by one, the freshmen gathered their books and exited the cafeteria.

For a few moments, Danny reflected on the evening's dinner. He checked his watch. Ryan had left him a note that he would be late for dinner and wanted Danny to wait for him. Barry had offered to wait with Danny, but Danny had waived him off, preferring quiet and time to think. Shortly thereafter, Ryan descended the long staircase. Danny spotted his friend and motioned for him to join him. For a few moments, they sat quietly at the table.

Ryan seemed a bit down. "Thanks for waiting for me."

Danny nodded. "No problem. Are you okay?"

Ryan nodded and listened to the music. The music resonated in his mind. Danny rested his palms on his chin. He was in a meditative mood and consoled his friend.

"My dad wants me to major in economics in order to take over his business someday," Ryan shared, "but I failed a micro-economics test. I might not pass the course."

At that moment, a drop-dead gorgeous blond wearing red hot pants, knee-high boots, and sporting a healthy bosom wrapped in a blue halter-top popped up from a table in the back. She sauntered past the men. She smiled with a coy expression, gliding past them in slow motion so that they could fully savor the view. She enjoyed the attention and made no pretense of being modest about her curves. Ryan and Danny spun around in their seats. Their eyeballs fixated at the vision of loveliness that had entered their lives for a few precious moments. She was the sort of woman every young man fantasized about having as a girlfriend or lover.

She spotted Ryan and stared at him with a dreamy expression. "Hi, Ryan," she cooed and batted her eyelashes in a seductive fashion.

"Who was that?" Danny asked, barely able to remove his eyes from her.

Ryan just shrugged and turned away. He was almost blasé about the whole thing. It was as if the girl were merely passable, instead of a major ten on the knockout scale. "Some chick from my class." He smiled nonchalantly. He was toying with Danny but enjoyed it.

Danny was awestruck. "Bullshit, not just a girl but a goddess."

Ryan remained almost non-committal in his response. The girl realized that Ryan was not going to pay attention to her. She appeared disappointed and headed over to another table.

"What's your secret? I haven't had a date since Tracy, and you have to fight 'em off."

"Danny, my bro, it's a talent," said Ryan, with a knowing smirk.

Danny pouted. "Are you born with it, or can you buy it at Woolworth's five-and-dime? Life's not fair."

Ryan smiled. He had the mojo that all men craved. Finally, bursting with pride, Ryan revealed his secret formula. "It's the technique." He leaned over to Danny and stared into Danny's eyes. "Just gaze into their eyes, then show them you will take care of them and say things like, 'I'll pick you up at seven.'"

Danny scoffed at the remark. "It can't be that easy." Danny shook his head. He admired his friend's cockiness. It was a quality that he tried to cultivate within himself. Like most people, Danny was plagued with self-doubt. Ryan might have been better at camouflaging it, but still was skillful in showing his more confident self.

"Whatever you got, you ought to bottle it and sell it," said Danny, shaking his head.

"How's it going with Morris?" said Ryan, changing the subject.

Danny made a face and tried to change the subject. "Still on his shit-list. He had Kevin rewrite the thing. But a thought occurred to me over dinner that if I managed to get a great interview, Morris couldn't hold me back."

Ryan could see that Danny needed a pick-me-up. As the two men finished their dinner, Ryan leaned over to Danny. "How about a game of pinball back in the dorm?" He'd thrown down the gauntlet—would Danny pick up the challenge? "Loser buys cheesesteak from the Greasy Truck."

"Be prepared to be humiliated," Danny smirked.

The idea of an evening game of pinball cheered up both men as they raced toward Danny's dorm. It was a matter of honor to win the nightly pinball match. And on this night, both men needed something to be proud of, especially Danny, whose uncertainty about everything weighed heavily on him.

19

Pinball Challenge

D anny and Ryan raced back to the dorm to have their nightly death match over the dorm's pinball machine. Inside the dorm lobby, a large Zenith brand, black-and-white television was mounted on the wall. The television proudly broadcast all 13 magnificent television stations. In the 1970's, television would end its day around midnight and then resort to a display of cringe-worthy static, or display a huge American flag as patriotic music played in the background.

Tonight, a group of students were huddled around the television to watch the nightly news program. Danny, Ryan, and a few of the students watched as a reporter finished interviewing a student protester from Rutgers before turning to the camera. "A massive protest today at Rutgers. It's reported that over two thousand people gathered around the Henry Rutgers statue."

Hearing the name of Rutgers, a cheer rose from the students in the lounge. The cheering drowned out the rest of the report and within a minute the broadcast had switched to another subject. The students switched channel to watch a baseball game. Danny and Ryan hurried to start their nightly pinball competition.

Meanwhile, across the campus in the Student Center, Morris conferred with one of his editors. He had just gotten off the phone with a member of the administration. Morris stared up at his wall chart. "The Regents want us to cut staff. Who should I cut?" Morris pondered his options: he shook his head, having not determined if any staff cuts could be made. "I'm going to fight this. I don't want to cut short anyone's career." Kevin, the chubby-faced rival of Danny, sat nearby and eavesdropped on the conversation. He piped up. "That is easy, the douchebag from Jersey Shore. All he does is botch stories about the cafeteria."

There was no love lost between Danny and Kevin. Morris scolded Kevin and warned him that this was a private conversation and not to repeat this to anyone. Kevin huffed and offered his apologies. He packed his belongings and swiftly exited the office.

A few minutes later, a gleeful Kevin trotted into the lobby of the Tinsley dorm. He spotted Danny and walked up to him. He was in a mood to try and stick it to Danny. "Hey, hayseed," bellowed Kevin.

An aggravated Danny looked up from the game. "What do you want?"

"I heard about your article on the cafeteria." Kevin gloated over Danny's status with the paper. "Morris is looking to cut staff and you're number one on the hit parade," he gloated.

Danny was not going to take the bait. He turned away, ignoring Kevin.

Kevin would not let it rest. "That's the best you're ever going to get. Stories about food. If you don't get cut."

Danny grew angry. "What do you mean?" he yelled at his plump rival.

"You'll find out!" Kevin sneered.

The two faced each other. Danny was furious about Kevin invading his space and then ruining his evening. "Get out of my dorm!" Danny shouted as a bunch of students watched. They had never seen even-handed Danny so angry and red-faced. Ryan moved closer to add ammunition to Danny's defense. Danny waved him off. He would handle this interloper.

"I'm going to get the best stories on the paper. Just you wait," said Danny. "This is my dorm, get the fuck out of here."

Kevin did not move.

"Are you deaf? You heard Danny," yelled Ryan.

The other students glared at the chubby reporter. Kevin realized that he might have gotten in over his head. He furnished Danny the middle finger and smirked as he walked out the door to the street. Danny sat down and forced himself to relax.

"Forget it, the guy is just trying to be an asshole," Ryan comforted Danny.

Danny took in a few deep breaths and began to calm down. His composure returned to normal. Ryan pointed to the pinball machine and Danny nodded, ready to continue the match. "Can you believe the balls on that guy?" said Danny.

The pinball machine was a large metallic object with flippers and bumpers and would light up and make loud sounds as the ball careened wildly up and down inside the machine. The longer you kept the ball from flying down the middle or the 'gutter' of the machine, the more points you would score. Players would grab the machine and shake it to keep the ball in play. Care had to be taken to avoid shaking the machine too hard. At that point it would proclaim TILT and the game would be over.

Loud groans and gnashing of teeth would emanate from the players when the balls bounced into the gutter. Danny went first; he kept the ball in play and knocked the ball into the bumpers. Clang, clang, as the ball rocketed to the top of the machine. It rounded the curve and then rushed down toward the bumpers. Other dorm students strolled over to watch the death match.

Danny's quick hand movements shook the machine in order to flip the ball back toward the point-scoring devices. The pinball rolled down the gutter. Danny threw up his hands and cursed his defeat as Ryan prepared for his turn. Watching from a distance, Danny noticed Fred watching and motioned for Fred to join them. Fred had boasted of his prowess with the pinball machine.

Danny leaned over and whispered to Fred. "I saw that kid you roomed with at the beginning of school," said Danny.

Fred grimaced; it raised unpleasant issues.

"How are you getting along with Barry?" Danny inquired.

"He's okay for a white boy," Fred said with a grin.

"He can be single-minded, but I think he means well."

Barry and Fred had become roommates in the middle of the semester. Fred's original roommate had made clear his displeasure at rooming with a black kid. After stopping a fight between Fred and the kid, Danny had agreed to transfer the student to another dorm. Barry was happy to make the switch. It improved his radical credibility.

"One big favor though, tell Barry to stop snoring. He keeps me up at night."

Danny laughed then gestured to Ryan, hard at play. "I hear a rumor that you're the best pinball player in the dorm," said Danny.

"It isn't a rumor. Put up some serious coin," said Fred, digging some quarters from his pocket and laying them on the cold steel of the pinball machine. He grabbed hold of the machine. He was indeed the master. The bells clanged and lit up with each swipe of the bumpers.

"Gooch that little bastard! Keep the ball moving," said an excited Danny.

As the death march concluded, it was clear that Fred was the winner. Ryan made a face; he had bragging rights and was certain that he would win the night's match. Danny and Ryan reluctantly pulled some dollar bills from their pocket and handed them to the winner.

"I have a few cold Budweisers in a cooler up in my room. I will bring them down," said Fred.

Despite the fun evening, Danny was troubled by his encounter with Kevin. He had hoped that his position at the newspaper had been secured after the fiasco of the cafeteria. Tonight, Kevin's taunting had raised doubts in Danny's mind. He would have to double his efforts to secure his spot. Like Benjamin in the recent hit movie, *The Graduate*, Danny was a little concerned about his future.

20

Bennett's Celebration

The next afternoon, Danny poked his head into Fred and Barry's room for a friendly chat. Fred was not around, but Barry sat hunched over in the corner smoking a rolled-up joint. He grew red-faced at seeing Danny, but Danny motioned to Barry for the joint. Danny took a toke and inhaled some smoke. "Good shit, man."

Barry grinned, relieved. "Did you read that article I gave you?" Barry inquired.

Danny did not want to tell him that he had read it but that the radical newspaper had turned him off. Danny shook his head. "Sorry, been swamped with my schoolwork. However, I was impressed with the protest. Very organized and peaceful."

"C'mon, be honest," Barry insisted.

"Okay, I found it a bit over the top and one-sided."

"Well, at least you read it, that's a start," Barry said, confidently. Barry's eyes lit up. He thought for a minute and blurted out, "Are you hungry?"

Danny eyed Barry with suspicion. He appeared mystified with the connection. "What's the catch?" said Danny. It seemed to be less about food than something else.

"Bennett's having a celebration. Plenty of good food, maybe some hot chicks," Barry noted enthusiastically, with a grin.

Danny was not sure that he was interested in listening to the protesters, but the idea of sexy girls and free food appealed to him. "Can I offer my opinions without getting my ass yelled at?" said Danny.

Barry laughed. "No worries, it'll be great."

A few minutes later, the two men walked down the hallway. They encountered Ryan sitting in the lobby. He indicated that he was planning on inviting Danny back to his friend's fraternity for another round of beer and protestor-bashing politics. "You want to join me at the frat for another night of drinking?" said Ryan.

Danny smiled. "No, I have other plans. I have been invited to go to Bennett's for some food and drink. You want to join us?"

Ryan made a face at Barry. He knew it was Barry's idea. Ryan's face dropped. It was as if he were invited to swallow something unpleasant. "When pigs fly," he voiced, in a dismissive tone.

"Don't let them brainwash you, my brother," Ryan retorted, then walked away.

"Party of the year, bro," Barry chuckled, calling out to Ryan.

"Bite me, I'd rather die," said Ryan without turning.

"Don't mind him, he has no manners," joked Danny.

Ryan turned and offered Barry his middle finger. Barry bristled, but Danny took Barry by the arm and the two men walked out of the building. The two walked a few blocks away from the campus.

"I knew Ryan would rather die than attend that party," joked Barry. "You still think that we are defending America from Communism?" asked Barry.

"Can we have this discussion another time?" asked Danny.

"You're right, just can't help myself at times," chuckled Barry.

Barry patted Danny on the back. The two men continued their trek.

A short time later, Barry and Danny walked up the stairs to Bennett's apartment. The apartment was in a fancy section of the city. They entered the apartment. The party had been underway for a while. Bennett's apartment was a posh high-rise in a middle-class section of the city. It was not the type of area that poor students rented. It featured manicured, well-kept lawns and even a doorman to welcome and screen guests. It was the opposite of most penniless student apartments of the time. Most students decorated their apartments with Salvation Army hand-me-down furniture.

It was a cheerful apartment. Billowing white curtains hung from the ceiling to the floor, shag carpeting, velvety cushions on the couch, and a giant Zenith, 24-inch color television sat in the middle of the living room. A large, table-sized fan blew cool air into the apartment. The aroma of food wafted into the air. A red tablecloth covered the table, loaded with food. A mixture of cold cuts and spicy Italian foods dominated the senses. Tiny sandwiches, cans of cold beers and an Italian dish populated the table.

The members of Bennett's militant organization were clumped in small groups around the room. They were eating, talking, and celebrating the success of the prior day's protest.

Bennett emerged from the kitchen, carrying an over-sized tray of sandwiches. He placed it on the table. The men's eyes popped at the delicious assortment of goodies piled before them. Everyone was in a celebratory mood. The food on the table began to dwindle as the members of the group devoured the makeshift sandwiches and snacks.

"Let me know if you want more. I have the girls slaving away in the kitchen," said the ebullient Bennett. The members sitting in the living room were all men. Many of the women of the Movement were slaving away inside the kitchen preparing the food. Despite the beginnings of the Feminist movement, many of the male members of the group still displayed large amounts of male chauvinism about the role of womenfolk in the Revolution.

Bennett entered the kitchen and stared at the women busy running around the kitchen preparing the meals. Betsy, blond with curly hair and freckles, one of the young girls in the group, looked up from the table. She wiped the perspiration from her brow onto her apron. "Let us know when we can join you."

"This meeting is for the men. You can serve the Revolution by preparing food," he huffed. Betsy looked aggravated. "We're part of this group too," she exclaimed, nearly spitting on one of the piles of newly minted sandwiches. "What about the women? Women's Liberation. You might have heard of it?" She threw up her hands and exclaimed in an irritated voice. She appeared eager to wipe the arrogance off his bearded face.

Bennett leaned toward her and smirked. "You want liberation?"

Betsy leaned up from the kitchen counter. Her face indicated that she was not amused. She knew that she was about to be verbally abused by the arrogant Bennett.

Bennett chuckled. "I'll liberate you in the bedroom tonight." He laughed and grabbed her by the waist. He planted a sensual kiss on her lips.

"Male chauvinist pig," Betsy roared defiantly. Betsy pulled away. Furious, she grabbed a half -finished sandwich and tossed it at him.

Bennett thought that it was amusing. "More roast beef sandwiches. The men are getting hungry." He ducked out of the room. The other women in the room were unhappy at the treatment that they received. Bennett re-emerged from the kitchen. One of the members saw the remains of the sandwich plastered on Bennett's shirt. He quickly wiped it off with a laugh.

"They're still looking for liberation," joked one of the members of the group as he devoured the remains of his sandwich.

Bennett sneered, "I'll liberate them. Right here." He pointed to his bulging crotch. The rest of the group roared at the crude joke. "Make them scream and beg for more." They laughed in response. The group settled back down to the business at hand.

"To a memorable rally," said one of the members. Everyone raised their glasses in unison to toast Bennett, the hero of the hour.

"My friends, this is a time to celebrate. Let us try to put politics aside for the evening."

Barry Lipkin and Danny had settled on a couch near the back of the room and were quietly sipping drinks as Bennett walked over and introduced Danny. Bennett focused in on Danny.

"Barry's told me a lot about you, Danny, welcome," said Bennett. Danny nodded and then offered, "I thought the protest was remarkably interesting. I told Barry that I would listen. Keep an open mind." Bennett grinned. "Feel free to join in, but I told people to go light on the politics tonight."

The men kept eating and listening to the music. Everyone was enjoying small talk about college and girlfriends. Most avoided talk of politics as demanded by Bennett. Some of the members kibitzed with Danny about his role as student advisor.

"I have a great group of freshmen. I think they're going places." He grinned and pointed in Barry's direction. Barry beamed with delight.

Barry and Danny returned to the back of the room with their plates loaded with food. Danny was astonished to see Errol in the middle of a crowd of men.

He looked up and waved as Danny approached. "Well, stranger, fancy meeting you here," chuckled Errol. Danny returned the greeting. "Barry told me that you play a mean guitar and sing at the local coffee houses."

Danny blushed. "Yeah, I am no Elton John, but I can carry a tune."

"Well, bring your guitar down to the store sometime, we'll do a jam session," said Errol.

"Sounds good to me," said Danny. Danny felt that what had started as a simple book purchase was beginning to blossom into a friendship.

The revelry was disturbed by Tom Klonsky sitting in the back of the room. Klonsky had been drinking and was growing more hostile with every drink. He sat with several of his friends, arguing about politics. He could not resist talking politics even for the evening. Klonsky's voice grew louder and more passionate with every word. "We are bombing North Vietnam. Just the other day, we blew up a village and killed over two hundred villagers. I think that we should hold some of the administration as war criminals."

Danny grew uncomfortable listening to the volatile rhetoric. He shifted uneasily in his chair. He tried to ignore it and admire the furnishings, but Klonsky's bombast grated on Danny's nerves. Danny could not control his opinion any longer. "My brother is serving in the

Central Highlands. He's out there defending your freedom to mouth off," Danny said defiantly.

Klonsky was taken by surprise for a few seconds at the outburst of the stranger. "Your brother is a war criminal," Klonsky roared.

Danny was ready to explode. "What the fuck are you talking about?"

With every passing moment, Klonsky grew more red-faced and more strident. He was just short of blowing a fuse with his passion. Finally, Errol got up from the couch and confronted the hostile Klonsky and motioned for him to calm down. "Chill out, he's our guest," hissed Errol.

Klonsky disregarded the friendly warning. "Screw him and the horse he rode in on."

"Leave the kid alone, this is a party. Save your energy for the protests," said Errol, attempting to inject a bit of humor into the proceedings. He placed his hand on Klonsky's shoulder, but Klonsky brushed it off in a hostile manner. Errol was about to get physical but decided not to start up with him.

"I'm not going to calm down," Klonsky hissed. "This kid is defending a baby-killer."

"Don't be a dick," said Errol.

Danny was in no mood to be civil; he doubled down on his comments. "You're a fucking Communist asshole."

"Cool it, Danny," warned Errol.

Danny recognized that he was standing on the edge of the precipice. However, he was not going to back down. Some of the members were hesitant. They stared at each other. A stunned moment of silence permeated the room. Everyone recoiled from Danny's comments; they did not want to be part of the fireworks. Danny was left isolated in the rear of the room.

Klonsky sized up his opponent and the members of the group. He decided to push the issue. "What did you say?" roared Klonsky, with a haughty look of hostility.

"I said that I think that US involvement is a good thing. The people voted in a new government, and we bring in modern medicine." Barry eyed Danny, but the damage was done.

Klonsky glared at him for a moment. "Anyone else want to defend him?" he continued. A hush fell over the room. The members ducked their heads, not wanting to be involved in any discussion. He said it with a level of evil relish. He was flexing his verbal muscles and had successfully intimidated the group. There was a level of fear in the room. No one disagreed with Klonsky, at least not openly. He looked around and saw that glint of hostility and fear on the member's faces. He pounded the table for a second. His face grew profoundly serious. The volunteers murmured to themselves. The afternoon had just moved up a notch from being a mundane celebration to an unexpectedly ominous one.

Bennett had been inside the kitchen speaking to Betsy when Errol stormed into the kitchen and informed Bennett that Klonsky had become unhinged. Bennett bounded out of the kitchen in time to witness the conversation.

He strode to the back of the room to confront Klonsky. He stepped in front of him, eyes blazing. "This is supposed to be a party, not a shout fest," Bennett warned.

"Did you hear what this warmonger is saying?" roared Klonsky, in full belligerence mode. Klonsky was in the mood to be aggressive and maybe even hoped for a fist fight.

"I came here to listen, not be intimidated and insulted," shouted Danny.

Bennett looked around the room. He saw that Klonsky's outburst had spoiled the mood of the party. He decided to become the peace-maker. He lifted a sandwich from the platter and handed it to Danny.

"This man is our guest. I don't want him leaving thinking that we are a bunch of intolerant assholes." He stared directly at Klonsky. Klonsky took the hint and sat down and attempted to cool off.

Danny was surprised that Bennett had come to his defense. Barry sighed and appeared relieved. He figured that Danny would never talk to him again after this party.

"We appreciate him joining us and listening. He's very brave," said Bennett.

"I just wanted to be fair to Barry and listen to the other side."

111

Bennett appeared pleased by the remark. "I applaud him," said Bennett.

Everyone in the room grew more relaxed. The fireworks had died down. They raised their glass and saluted Danny. Danny offered them a half-smile. He sat back down and took another bite from his food. Danny had gotten more than he bargained for, but he realized that perhaps they had something of value for him to learn.

As he walked toward the door, Errol gave him the high sign. He thanked Errol for defusing a dangerous situation. "Thanks for your help. I really didn't want to get into a fight."

Errol smiled. He offered him the thumbs-up gesture. "Klonsky can be an asshole. Everyone knows it."

The two men shook hands.

"Thanks for giving me the book. I looked at it briefly. I'd like to discuss it further with you. I'll try and keep an open mind when I read it."

"Any time, you are welcome to stop in the store and bring your guitar," said Errol.

"Count on it," Danny said.

Barry and Danny packed up a few sandwiches and left the party. They walked back to the dorm in silence.

"I was afraid you'd never talk to me again," said Barry.

"I was afraid that the asshole would beat the shit out of me."

"We may not agree on everything, but we had your back," said Barry. When they returned to the dorm, Danny knocked on Ryan's door. Ryan was in a grouchy mood. He looked up as Danny approached. "I need the notes to the Curtis class."

Danny nodded. "Give me a few minutes."

"Well, did you at least yell at them?" he growled.

Danny smirked. "As a matter of fact, it was relatively pleasant. Bennett thanked me for coming and for being willing to listen." Danny omitted talking about the near confrontation with Klonsky.

Ryan was stunned at Danny's amiable description of the celebration. "Danny, you're a pussy. I would not have gone, but if I did, I would have yelled or cursed them out," Ryan snorted.

Danny grew red-faced and angry. "Don't call me that."

"You've earned it," replied Ryan.

The two men's hostility boiled over. It grew red-hot in intensity.

"Well, fuck you very much. I had a nice time," remarked Danny.

Danny and Ryan scowled at each other. They would not compromise their positions. They moved nose-to-nose. It was beginning to get loud and ugly.

"You can play the stupid Mine Street Cafe gig by yourself," Ryan fumed.

The discussion grew louder. "I'm the better singer," said Danny.

"Bullshit," replied Ryan. "They come to see me, and you know it."

Danny was surprised how quickly things had turned nasty. Just like the party, the political divide was far more dangerous than Danny realized. Even his best friend was now turning on him for daring to have nice things to say about the protestors. Danny realized that certain lines should not be crossed, but he realized that his sympathies for the protesters were beginning to change. He had gone to the party feeling neutral about the protesters. However, he was impressed by Bennett and was beginning to see a different side to the protesters. Perhaps the protesters had been right about the war. It was a difficult thing for Danny to admit. He had been brought up with a rigid set of views on the world and now he was being exposed to viewpoints that he would have dismissed out of hand a few months ago. He was growing less certain about how strongly he supported the Vietnam War.

21

Bennett Writes an Op-Ed

D anny sat in the office of the college newspaper and stared blankly at the wall. His mind was not on his work. He was still angry about the previous evening's argument with Ryan.

Morris handed him a revised copy of his cafeteria story. It was loaded with red marks and comments. "Rework it and give it to me when you're done," said Morris.

Danny forced himself to rework the story. He absorbed the comments and then began his rewrite. He was nervous that Morris might not approve the revision. He walked it to the back of the room. Morris read it over and gave it his stamp of approval. Danny was relieved. "It works this time. Take it to typesetting," said Morris.

Danny was happy to oblige. He got to talk to the lovely Alex. Alex sat in the cubicle in the back of the room in front of the typesetting machine. Danny admired the pretty redhead but had decided that attempting a relationship with her was out of bounds if he was her Student Advisor.

She was an amazingly fast and meticulous typist. Danny handed her the typed story. "Morris said it was ready for typesetting." Alex grabbed the paper and began to typeset the story. He was amused to see several caricatures of different staff members posted over the cubicle. One of the drawings showed Morris as the King, sitting on a toilet, staring down at the reporters who were his loyal subjects.

"You get any flak from the King?" questioned Danny.

Alex smiled. "He almost smiled when he saw it."

"He has a sense of humor, who would have guessed?"

Alex's face lit up with a beautiful smile. Danny could see why men could be smitten with a woman like that.

"I'd like to see you and Ryan play at the coffee house on Saturday. I heard you two are really excellent together," she said with a touch of admiration.

"It's going to be a solo act," he declared. His shoulders hunched, indicating that the statement left him feeling dejected. Alex raised her eyebrows. She was surprised by the news.

"Yeah, Ryan and I had a bit of a blowout. No, we had a fucking shouting match and nearly got into a fight." Her curiosity was piqued to a new level. "He and I had a fight over politics. I told him to shove it."

Alex sighed. "I'm sorry to hear that. The two of you seemed to be good friends."

"Past tense; all good things must come to an end," he said morosely.

Alex was genuinely sad. She liked Danny and felt that he made a serious effort to help his freshmen. In addition, he was respectful about her ambitions.

Danny watched as Morris approached. Danny waved goodbye.

"Catch you on the flip side," he said.

Danny passed Morris who did not say a word. Morris walked over to Alex and patted her on the shoulder. He appreciated her beauty but tried to remain detached. "I have the front page ready to go for typesetting," said Morris.

Alex pulled the front-page proof copy from the machine. It was fully typeset. He analyzed it as if he were a jewelry inspector analyzing a precious stone. He was satisfied and patted her on the shoulder. He began to smile and then immediately caught himself. Morris resumed his gruff managerial style.

Morris held out his empty coffee cup. "Sweetie, fetch me a cup of coffee. Not too much sugar."

Alex bristled at the request but agreed to give the coffee cup a refill. She got up from her seat and poured a cup of coffee for the King.

After leaving the newspaper, Danny walked into the office of the Mine Street Coffee House. He told the manager that he would be doing the show as a solo act. The manager questioned Danny about his erstwhile partner. Danny was adamant that it was him alone or nothing. The manager shrugged. He did not want to be in the middle of some personal dispute. He just adjusted information on his playlist chart and waved Danny out of the office. Danny stood outside for a few minutes to clear his head. He had finally raised the courage to set his own course. He and Ryan had been good friends, but it seemed that they were on the outs for the foreseeable future.

Danny walked into the Student Center and up to Bennett's office. Bennett smiled as Danny approached him.

"I just want to thank you for the other night."

Bennett smiled and shook hands with Danny. "I have to watch Klonsky. He's a good man but can be an asshole and a hothead."

"Well, I think he's an asshole, but it did give me time to think. I am beginning to change my opinion on things."

"You are more than welcome to join us. Sit in on a few meetings."

"How about an interview?" Danny asked cautiously.

Bennett took a deep breath. "I promised to give an interview with someone that Morris picked. Sorry Danny, maybe another time."

"No problem, just keep me in mind, if the opportunity opens up."

Bennett patted Danny on the shoulder. "I understand that you're a good musician."

"Great, not merely good. You should attend one of my concerts sometime," said Danny. He smiled. "Maybe you need to write something for the paper. Explain your position on issues in ways that others can find non-inflammatory."

Bennett's eyes grew wide. It was an interesting idea.

Danny checked his watch. "I got to go, but I just wanted to stop by and say thanks."

After Danny left the office, Bennett sat in his little office in the Student Center. He stared at some of the political documents like the Declaration of Independence that he had framed and mounted on his wall. He had not given it much thought; he was more comfortable speaking instead of writing his own thoughts. However, the more he thought about it, the more sense it made. This would be his contribution to the writings of such great minds as Thomas Jefferson. He chuckled at his own lack of humility. He put his other chores on hold to write his own contribution.

He pulled a yellow writing pad from his desk and sat with it perched in front of him on his desk. He sipped his cup of tea as he prepared to write his political manifesto. He jotted critical ideas on the paper pad.

Bennett Andrews was the son of a labor lawyer who worked for the American Federation of Labor (AFL-CIO). He had been indoctrinated into politics at an early age. His family had been politicians serving in the New York City area for decades. He had spent his summers at sleepaway camps in the mountains of Pennsylvania. His great-grandfather had served in the Teddy Roosevelt administration in NYC. His family had been active in the Eugene Debs Socialist Movement in the early years prior to World War One.

Betsy entered the office and noticed Bennett sitting at his desk, absorbed in his thoughts. "Hard at work?" she asked. Bennett smiled and resumed his writing. She began to file papers from Bennett's desk in-basket.

"Just immortalizing my words and thoughts," Bennett said with a smirk.

"How's this for a thought: don't forget to go food shopping for dinner tonight."

She had met Bennett at the beginning of the year. Her family had also been involved in the Civil Rights Movement. She admired Bennett's ability to speak and command people. They had dated for a few months before Bennett invited her to move in with him. She had some feminist passions but accepted the fact that, despite his leftist leanings, he was still a big bad male chauvinist when it came to women. He let her do all the cooking and cleaning.

She watched him scratch out numerous ideas on the pad while she filed some papers in a nearby cabinet. She observed him feverishly cobbling together his wordy masterpiece. He was a bit of a perfection-ist, as he would scratch down a thought or a sentence, ponder it for a moment and then cross out the sentence. He repeated the process several times. Finally, after crumpling up numerous sheets of paper and tossing them on the side of the desk, he admired his work.

"It's not the Gettysburg Address," she muttered, clearing up his trash.

Bennett looked up. "Just maybe it's my fucking Magna Carta," Bennett snorted with self-importance. "The entire student population is going to read it, so it better blow their socks off." Betsy dismissed his delusions of grandeur and shook her head and returned to her business.

"It's my Declaration of Independence." His eyes lit up and he spoke in a pompous tone of voice. She sniffed in amusement. Bennett doubled down. "I want it to rock the Board of Regents and establish our posi-tion for University policy." He continued writing for another half an hour, then with a flourish, handed her the corrected final copy. "Please type this for me, honey."

Betsy dutifully sat down and banged out the copy on the typewriter. She paused for a few seconds and verified what Bennett had written. She was a fast typist and within a few minutes had pulled a fresh copy from the typewriter.

Bennett inspected it and gave it his stamp of approval. He leaned over to give her a peck on the cheek. "Be a dear and run this up to the *Targum* office," he said. She hesitated. Bennett sighed and stared at the pile of papers needing to be filed. He waved her away from the cabinet. "I'll take care of that. Don't worry." She placed the manifesto inside an envelope, sealed it and clutched it in her hands. He patted her on the ass as a thank-you gesture. She protested, but not too hard. "Give it directly to Jim Morris," he said.

Within a few minutes, Betsy had walked into the *Targum* office. It was quiet, as the day's edition had already been published. Jim Morris sat at the editor's desk chewing on his Number Two pencil, reclining with his feet propped up on the desk. He was skimming a stack of new articles from the wire-rimmed basket marked 'Future Articles' when Betsy entered and handed him Bennett's masterpiece. "Bennett wanted you to have this. It's his Declaration of Independence." She smirked.

"Thanks. Tell him it will be in tomorrow's edition," Morris uttered without even looking at it. She smiled and headed out the door. Morris scanned the typed copy and began to smile. The ideas popped off the page.

Morris began to read the paper out loud. "'We demand immediate and continued opposition from all Americans to stop the war.'" He beamed as he scanned the rest of the op-ed. "'We demand that the Dean stop classes for one day to have a Teach-In on the war. Students will be invited to discuss the war with the faculty,'" he intoned. "I knew I could count on him for an interesting op-ed." Morris chuckled. "'This demand is not negotiable and any attempt to refuse this is considered unacceptable to the student body.'" Morris continued to read aloud excerpts from the op-ed. "'We demand an end to classes for that day to protest the greater problems of inequality in our society.' Not just interesting, incendiary. He sure knows how to light a fire," said Morris.

Across the campus meanwhile, Dean Mansbach sat talking on the phone, arguing with a member of the Board of Regents. The Regents were the ultra-conservative governing body that ruled the University, like a Board of Directors for a major corporation. Mansbach reassured them that he would handle any demands that the radical protesters would hand to him. He was adamant in his judgment. He closed his eyes; he had gone through this dance with board members many times in the past.

"Yes, I saw the Cronkite piece on the protest." Mansbach listened for a few more minutes. "Of course, I understand how it makes the University look." He was determined to make his point. He drummed his fingers on the wooden table. "I understand the position of the board." The voice at the other end grew louder and more strident. "Yes, the meeting is tomorrow." Mansbach was a methodical and patient man and was growing tired of the conversation. He jotted down some notes as he listened to the member of the Board. "Rest assured, we will not give in to their demands," he said.

He buzzed his secretary and directed her to set up a meeting between Bennett and himself for the following day. He clicked the phone back onto its cradle. He looked forward to the upcoming confrontation with Bennett and his followers. He was confident that he would dominate any meeting with Bennett. He was certain that Bennett would crawl out of his office begging for rhetorical mercy. Not a man known for his sense of humor, Mansbach envisioned himself as the lion in the Coliseum devouring the quivering Bennett as a tasty lunch.

22

Bennett Meets Mansbach

The next morning, the cafeteria buzzed with excitement as the students read Bennett's inflammatory op-ed. Danny sat in the cafeteria, having a leisurely breakfast with Barry. Everyone was enthusiastic about the article. Danny was impressed with how easily Bennett had translated his often-soaring rhetoric into easy-to-understand ideas. He was growing more impressed with Bennett's style and compassion as a leader of the protest. His sympathies for the radical's positions were beginning to grow stronger. Much to his astonishment, he found much to like in the column. He was still on the fence in many ways, but he found that he often agreed with some of Bennett's ideas.

Barry was hunched over his breakfast and scanned the newspaper with Bennet's manifesto. Finally, he looked up with some admiration in his eyes. "Man knows how to turn a phrase. He'll be all over the Dean," said Barry.

"Well, I'm starting to like Bennett very much, but my money is on Dean Mansbach. From what I have read about him, he is no pushover. He'll eat Bennett's lunch," countered Danny.

"Either way, I think that this is a game-changer for Bennett and the movement. It forced Mansbach to take the protest seriously," boasted Barry.

Danny was more cautious. "I think that the Dean will be ready for Bennett."

After breakfast, outside the cafeteria, Barry and Danny passed by a table with several protesters. The protesters had set up a table with fliers and newspaper clippings of the editorial. Danny glanced at the articles and turned away. Barry scooped up several copies and shoved them into a book bag just as several fraternity members passed by the table. They were from a different fraternity and Danny did not recognize any of them. The two groups glared at each other. The fraternity brothers stared back at the long-haired protesters manning the table. Tensions simmered on both sides. One of the frat brothers yelled, "Get a fucking haircut. You guys look like a bunch of freaks!" Another shouted, "You look like a bunch of sissies." The protestors ignored the jibes. However, cooler heads on both sides intervened and forced both sides to 'cool it.' The bad feelings subsided for the moment, but both sides knew it would not last.

Later that morning, an ebullient Bennett, Klonsky, and several rowdy radical students marched over to Sproul Hall and crowded into the Dean's office as if they were headed for a 'Love-in.' They appeared to be a giant party and not a serious meeting between two of the most powerful campus figures. They gathered in the Dean's office. Bennett had invited them to join him in a show of solidarity. It was quite a show. Several of them carried their wooden placards. Many of them were sloppily dressed in sweatshirts and love beads dangling from their necks.

The secretaries frowned and made it clear that they were displeased by the lack of decorum shown by the group. However, they maintained their control and pretended to ignore them. Several members of the group practiced meditation and others strummed a musical instrument.

They were animated and eager for some sort of confrontation. The radical students were a motley collection of shabbily dressed boys with long, stringy, unkempt hair, dirty army fatigues, sandals, and headbands. Some radicals lounged on the black leather couch, while others sat cross-legged on the floor. The contrast between them and the plush environment of the Dean's office was stark.

Mrs. Fitzpatrick, the Dean's secretary, was a middle-aged woman, elegantly coiffed, with shiny jewelry dangling from her wrists and fingers. She wore a print dress and black high heels. She was offended by the body odor and lack of decorum of many of the protesters. However, she maintained her distance and was determined to not raise an issue over it, though she could not help frowning. After a few moments the phone rang, and she answered it.

"Mr. Andrews, the Dean will see you in a few minutes," she said firmly and pointed toward Bennett. The radicals grabbed their protest signs and eagerly bolted toward the Dean's office. Mrs. Fitzpatrick intercepted the crowd and barred the doorway. She raised her hands to object. "You can't bring them in with you," she snapped at Bennett. "It's a private meeting, just you and the Dean." Bennett frowned and Fitzpatrick loudly tossed in an emphatic command. "It's the Dean's orders!"

Bennett was visibly annoyed but seemed determined to handle things on his own.

She addressed the rowdy students with a hint of condescension. "The Dean wanted to meet with Mr. Andrews by himself."

Bennett motioned to his followers and ordered them to sit down and be patient. "Stay chilly. Let me handle the old man," he snapped. They groaned in unison but obeyed Bennett's directives.

At that moment across the campus, Danny pulled an official-looking letter from his mailbox. It was a letter filled with a request for information about his scholarship. It was unclear what information they were requesting. He decided to take a trip to the Dean's office to get further information. He stopped off to grab an ice cream from a nearby vendor and then proceeded on his way.

In the Dean's office, Fitzpatrick led Bennett down the carpeted corridor to a small conference room. The walls were decorated with wallpaper showcasing the history of the college. Paintings and fine furnishings adorned the room. Inside the room, the Dean sat calmly collecting his thoughts and jotting down notes. The Dean was dressed in his usual tailored suit and tie. It was supposed to be a pleasant discussion or meeting of the minds between the leader of the protests and the Dean of the college. They would meet and discuss the group's demands. Both sides could be flexible, but both sides arrived with fixed expectations for what they wanted to accomplish with the meeting. Bennett sat on the opposite side of the Dean at a beautiful oak table. Bennett fidgeted in his chair. He appeared to be uncomfortable in the plush surroundings. He was dressed for a no-holds-barred political discussion group rather than a meeting with the formidable, stone-faced Dean Mansbach. Bennett gazed around at the fine linen and furnishings. However, he was determined not to let the surroundings distract him from his mission. Mansbach made the first move. He picked up a cherished silver tea set and offered Bennett a cup of steaming chamomile tea. "Do you take milk or sugar?"

Bennett was taken aback by Mansbach's genteel manner.

"This teapot has been in my family for three generations." He beamed, as if he were some proud collector of antiquities. "Perhaps we could have a cup of tea like civilized men before we begin the discussion." He spoke in a civilized, modulated voice.

Bennett nodded agreeably and sipped his steaming cup of tea, feeling as if there was no reason to appear belligerent. He would listen to what the Dean had to say and be civilized in discussing his agenda.

"You're a particularly good speaker. Very persuasive," Mansbach offered, amicably.

Bennett soaked up the compliment. He knew it was the opening volley, but he was happy to accept it. An odder couple than the two men at the table could not be found. Bennett had envisioned sweeping into the room and offering the Dean his set of non-negotiable demands. The Dean would be forced to accept the demands without fighting back. Bennett was surprised by the Dean's attempt to disarm him with small talk. He decided to play along momentarily.

"I find that brand of tea is very calming," said Mansbach, in his refined, soothing manner as he watched Bennett enjoying the drink. "I was familiar with some of your relatives. Your Uncle Samuel and I worked together in Selma," Mansbach continued. "We are two strong-willed men with strong and divergent opinions," the Dean stated. "And I am in charge of this institution."

Bennett wanted to be the rabble-rouser and Mansbach continued to act as if it were a meeting of a literary society with polite conversation. He stared at the Dean with a strong penetrating glare. Mansbach was immune and leaned back in his chair to take a measure of the man. "You live up to your reputation, Dean."

The Dean offered him a small smile in return. "I'll take that as a compliment."

"Let us get right to the issues," Bennett demanded.

The Dean sipped his tea. He was not in a rush. He continued to stare at Bennett like a boxer analyzing his opponent's weaknesses. It was the Mohammed Ali boxing strategy of Rope-A-Dope: wear out your opponent, take his punches, and then hit back.

Bennett grew tired of the civility. He stood and pointed his finger at the Dean accusingly. "As you know, we are not just an anti-war protest group!" The Dean responded with a sigh. "We are also strong advocates of the civil rights movement," said Bennett.

"We are in complete agreement," said the Dean.

Bennett looked at his opponent with surprise. He was taken aback by the remark.

"I was a strong supporter of civil rights when you were still in grade school," the Dean chided Bennett. "I was a volunteer during Freedom Summer, the voters' registration drive in 1964."

This took the burst of wind out of Bennett's sails. Bennett was not to be outdone. He doubled down on his demands. "We demand a greater number of negro students be admitted to the University."

The Dean nodded in agreement and jotted down facts and figures on a sheet of paper. "However, we need to establish certain guidelines, such as grade point average, and conditions as to grants and scholarships," the Dean stated.

"We also want more black professors and a department of Ethnic Studies created."

The Dean firmly held Bennett's gaze. "The Board of Regents has no desire to create such a department. We believe that the existing Political Science and History departments handle the course material that you desire. Nothing is done without the approval of our Board of Regents."

Bennett pounded the oak table to show his disapproval. It vibrated slightly. If Bennett thought he could rattle the Dean, he was wrong. "There can be no preconditions," Bennett hissed. "In addition, we demand that the University cut ties to the military recruiters on campus and programs such as ROTC. There can be no negotiating this point!"

"That is where I must draw the line," the Dean replied. His eyes narrowed and his expression became harsh and unyielding. "I was an officer during the Korean War. I served with distinction. This university has strong ties to the military going back to the days of our founding. I will not allow you to make such a demand," he rumbled.

Bennett attempted to switch back to his charm mode. "Dean Mansbach, you must recognize the power of the student protest movement. We had over two thousand students chanting to end the war the other day. The student movement is growing in power. We want an equal voice in the direction of the university."

Mansbach was an excellent chess player, and he was two moves ahead of Bennett. "Very impressive, but students on a field chanting doesn't move me. Strident demands for unearned power are not acceptable," said the Dean.

Bennett began to lose his temper. He rose from the table and began to shout, his face contorted in anger. "We'll come back with greater numbers. We are not going away," warned the impatient Bennett, shaking his fist.

"Lower your voice, Mr. Andrews," said the Dean, utterly unmoved. "I am not receptive to threats of any sort. Good day, Mr. Andrews."

He thrust open the door and motioned for Bennett to leave the room. Then he turned his back on Bennett and returned to sipping his tea. A dejected Bennett walked out of the conference room and trudged out to the main office. He waved to the impatient mob and motioned for them to leave the building. He did not utter a word. The down-trodden expression on his face made it clear how he was feeling.

Just as the group was leaving the office, Danny waved to Bennett, but Bennett did not respond. The protesters continued to leave the office. Danny had entered the office clutching his scholarship letter. He went over to the desk of one of the secretaries and showed her his letter. "I'm not clear on what paperwork you are looking for?" he said to the administrator. Danny continued to press the administrator for information about the scholarship. After a brief discussion, the administrator handed Danny some of the forms he needed. Satisfied, Danny exited the office.

Outside the building, Kevin, his arch nemesis, approached Bennett. He had been assigned to get the story on the Bennett-Mansbach meeting. He began to pepper Bennett with questions. "Any comment for the paper?"

Bennett waved his hands and offered a terse statement. "Where is Danny Watkins? I'll talk to him."

"Hayseed Watkins? The editor doesn't trust him with a big story."

Bennett made a face at Kevin's use of the term 'hayseed.' "We gave the Dean a simple list of demands that will keep the spirit of the protest alive until our demands are met."

Danny exited the building and watched Kevin attempt to interview Bennett.

"Will there be more protests? Are you going to raise the pressure on the University?" injected Kevin.

"The Dean has not heard the last of us," warned Bennett. His response seemed half-hearted compared to the firebrand rhetoric of the previous day. Bennett led his dejected group out of the building. Bennett had been rope-a-doped by the old fox, Dean Mansbach. Bennett turned around and shook his fist in a defiant manner. This was a temporary setback; he was not about to go away without a fight.

A short time later, an ebullient Dean sat in his office; Williamson, a member of the Board of Directors, sat in front of him.

"Congratulations are in order," said Williamson.

127

Mansbach's face was flushed. He took a few seconds to recover. "Are you okay?" asked the Regent.

Mansbach acknowledged a moment of stress but recovered within a few minutes. "Did you expect anything less?" he said firmly.

Williamson beamed. Mansbach pulled out a typed letter. He would send it to the *Targum* for publication. It would demoralize the radicals.

"Do you think that it will drive Bennett to any acts of violence?" asked Williamson.

"I will not tolerate any threats of violence," he countered. "I will outline the University's position. Mr. Morris has agreed to publish my article in the next edition of the *Targum*." Mansbach was not a man to rest on his laurels. He had no illusion that this was merely another step in the protest.

Later that morning, Danny wanted to find a nice sci-fi book to get his mind off the day's events. His bookshelf was empty, and he decided to walk down to Errol's store to find a good science fiction book to help him relax. He entered and spotted Errol putting books on the shelves. "Just wanted to thank you for your help at Bennett's party."

"Klonsky was being an asshole," Errol recounted. "Bennett had a serious talking to him later after the party was all over."

The discussion turned to the day's confrontation between the Dean and Bennett. Errol offered him a cup of coffee. He showed Danny his guitar and blues harmonica. "Let's hear a few bars," Errol said.

Danny sat on a chair and began to strum the guitar while Errol played the blues harmonica. They made a great combo and both men began to pour their heart and soul into the music. The bookstore rocked with the music of the two men. They were beginning to bond.

"Good music." Errol offered Danny a grin.

"Maybe we can do a gig sometime," said Danny.

Errol smiled; his respect for Danny was growing. A few minutes later, Barry stormed into the store. He was visibly angry.

"What's up, Barry?" Danny asked, as he and Errol paused the music.

"I'm pissed that the protesters have been forced to cool their heels by the Dean!" Barry ranted. Errol handed Barry a cup of tea to calm him down. "Fucking Dean," he muttered again. "Bennett is not the type to accept the situation," Barry shouted.

Danny and Errol nodded. "As they say, sometimes payback can be a bitch," joked Errol.

Danny and Barry nodded in agreement. Danny began to feel a kinship with Barry and Errol that he had not felt before. "I agree with you guys," said Danny.

Barry and Errol were surprised by Danny's change of heart. He was surprised how quickly his viewpoint was changing toward the protesters.

"I read some of those chapters in the book you gave me," said Danny.

"Eye-opening, isn't it?" said Errol.

Barry was astonished that Danny was beginning to change his opinion on politics. "Are you feeling okay, Danny?" suggested Barry.

Danny smiled and offered him the thumbs-up gesture. "We'll talk about it later," said Danny. "Bennett's not the type to accept defeat at the hands of the sly fox, Mansbach."

Everyone knew that a day of reckoning was not far in the future.

23

March to Dean Mansbach's House

That evening, Morris sat in his office reading the Dean's op-ed response to the Bennett-Mansbach meeting. The Dean had it typed up and sent it to the newspaper for publication. Mansbach outlined his feelings about the meeting. He expressed disappointment that the protesters assumed that they could march into his office and provide non-negotiable demands. He made it clear that he was not a man to be trifled with. Morris was as eager to print the column as he had been with Bennett's Manifesto. It made good copy for the paper. He ordered it to be printed in the next edition. He hoped that it might get captured in a wire services story. It would be a feather in his cap and show the world what a brilliant editor he was.

That night, Danny sat across from Morris's desk. He had hoped to advance in the world of reporting. Morris had approved his last story and he hoped that he would get better assignments. Finally, after a few minutes, Morris handed Danny a new assignment. Danny eagerly read the assignment sheet. He was not pleased with it.

"I'd like you to do a story on new parking spaces. The sergeant of the Campus Patrol is waiting for one of my reporters. I would like you to cover it. Just straight reporting this time. Do we understand each other?"

Danny nodded his head. "Of course," he muttered. It was not the most exciting story, but at least for the moment, he was temporarily off Morris's shit-list.

"Just remember not every story is going to win you a Pulitzer Prize," warned Morris.

Danny sighed, grabbed the assignment sheet and walked out the door.

Meanwhile, that afternoon, Bennett and his followers, including Barry Lipkin, had retreated to Bennett's apartment for a strategy session. The mood was somber. Bennett felt the need to recoup from his disastrous meeting with the Dean. He had suffered a tactical defeat and wanted to send a message. He was determined to regain the initiative. Bennett sat in his living room with Klonsky and several members of the leadership to discuss strategy.

"We have to send a message that he cannot ignore," uttered one of the protesters.

Another member interjected. "The Dean is determined to turn down our demands," suggested another member of the group. Everyone nodded their heads in agreement.

"Maybe we could have a sit-in at the cafeteria," suggested yet another member of the group.

"Maybe we can offer the kids to rally around something besides bad food," joked another.

"A sit-in would involve the campus police, not a good idea," stated Bennett with authority. He demanded that someone come up with something more creative.

Barry raised his hand, leaning forward, his mind working faster than his mouth formulating an idea. "If the Dean won't listen to us, we need to bring the protest to him," suggested Barry.

Bennett looked up from taking notes. "What are you suggesting?" he added.

"Bring it home to the Dean, I mean literally. March outside his house and hold a candlelight vigil." Bennett was paying attention.

"The Dean will think twice about ignoring us," quipped another member. Everyone laughed and nodded their heads in approval. It was a very promising idea and Bennett seized upon it to make it official. They would mobilize and march on the Dean's home. The group conferred with the plans to organize the march for the following evening.

"How about renting a small sound truck," suggested Barry. "We could organize the students better with it as a command post."

Bennett smiled and gave Barry the high sign of approval for the idea. Bennett warmed to the idea and suggested that they investigate a way to rent the small truck. Bennett made a note to call the truck rental agency and rent a truck for the following evening. The next morning, he was on the phone arranging for the group to rent the sound truck.

The following night, the protesters gathered on the field near the statue. The group gathered around and admired the small sound truck with its giant speakers attached to the sides of the vehicle. It would be a great rallying point for the protesters.

Across the campus, Danny sat in the headquarters of the Campus Patrol, doing a story on the increased parking areas planned by Campus Patrol for the spring semester. It was another boring story, but Danny was determined to do straight reporting. He did not want to ruffle Morris' feathers. He was questioning the shift captain about parking issues. He sat and diligently took notes. "We are renovating a grassy area and paving it over. It should bring parking closer to the Student Center for about a hundred drivers," said the officer. Danny dutifully took notes.

Suddenly, the phone rang and one of the officers cupped his hand over the phone. "You're not going to believe this," he gasped as he handed the phone to his superior officer. The officer's expression grew intense as he listened to the news.

Upon hearing the news of the impromptu march, Danny asked if he could ride along. The officers were enthusiastic and offered him a lift. However, they warned him to stay on the side lines and just report any story that occurred. "Don't get involved, stay on the sidelines for your safety," said the officer.

"Remember, you're a student journalist, not a patrolman," growled another officer.

Danny was excited. A mundane story had suddenly grown more interesting.

It was dark as Bennett led the growing band of protesting students marching down the street. He drove ahead of the group in a small, rented truck with bulky speakers perched on the side of the vehicle. He spoke into the microphone that was connected to the speakers. He barked out commands for the group. He had decided that the sound of his voice emanating from the speakers would help organize the long line of marchers.

"Single file, stay in line," Bennett commanded.

Klonsky, the enforcer, walked alongside the crowd to keep them organized. Barry was amid the crowd with his small group of friends.

"Take your positions in the field across from the Dean's residence!" Bennett barked.

The protesters proceeded to march in single file down the street. The crowd snaked down the empty street. Other students, huddled at the campus bus stop, watched the proceedings with a hint of curiosity mixed with alarm. They wondered if this would remain a peaceful protest or would tempers flare and someone incite them to violence.

At the same time, inside the library, Pamela and Alex sat in cubicles on the second floor. Pamela was hard at work deciphering an arcane formula for her Chemistry class. Alex thumbed through her hefty art history book. She paused periodically to make notes in her notebook.

Hearing a tremendous amount of noise emanating from the open window, they observed the mass of protesters marching past the library. Alex was fascinated by the moving mass of protestors. "Want to join me?" she asked. Pamela declined. She had a quiz on some of the formulas the next day. Alex stared at the protesters. "Could be fun. See you later." Alex gathered her books and placed them in her knapsack. She raced down the stairs to exit the building.

That night, Ryan sat in the ROTC office handling some late-night paperwork. He was also being drawn out of his work by the sound of the crowd as it began to filter into the quiet office. He peeked out of the window and observed the students marching past the building. He could only shake his head in disgust and resume his work.

After a few blocks, the mass of protesters stopped in the small field directly opposite the Dean's house. It was a stately brick home with white columns, befitting the head of the College. It sat on a small plot of well-manicured land. A proud flag flapped above the house from a tall pole.

Bennett drove to the front of the group and dismounted from the truck. He motioned for the group to form up in the field opposite the Dean's residence which was well lit inside.

Dean Mansbach and his wife had just finished dinner. They had their usual dinner-time conversation, he tells her about the difficult decisions that day. Rumors had been flying about some sort of protest. The Dean had dismissed the rumors. He felt that he had soundly defeated the protesters. He had left the office confident that they would not be active so soon.

But now, the phone rang. The Campus Patrol was calling to alert him to the movements of the students. He took the news calmly and suggested that they stand by in the event of any serious disturbance. He reassured the commander that he was okay and would be an observer of the student march. He asked the Campus Patrol to break up any attempts at violence.

Mansbach moved into the living room to his favorite rocking chair. He enjoyed rocking as part of his unwinding process. Then he rose and pulled his rocking chair to where he stood and peeked outside the window of his living room. He watched the growing crowd with fascination. He stroked his chin and seemed positively relaxed. His wife drew in a breath, alarmed at the sight of the outsized crowd violating the quiet of their evening.

"Did you know they were going to be here tonight? asked his wife. She had begun to quake but was reassured by his steadfast manner.

"I heard rumors about some action, but nothing concrete or brazen.

However, if this is an attempt to intimidate me, it has failed. I faced down a Chinese human wave attack in Korea."

"Shouldn't we do something?" inquired his wife. She began to panic as she peeked out of the billowing white curtains, growing increasingly frightened.

"They are putting on a show for us. Let them have their moment," he said firmly. He turned and stroked his wife's shoulders, as if to reassure her that all was well. He told her that the Campus Patrol would be standing by in the event of an emergency.

The students formed lines in the vigil in front of the Dean's house. The crowd pulled unlit candles out of their pockets and passed around sets of matches to the growing mob. They lit the candles and hoisted them high into the air. Some of the crowd, including Barry, took the opportunity to lit up a marijuana joint and pass it around to some of his friends.

"Don't Bogart that joint my friend, just pass it around and light up another one," sang Barry in a jovial, off-key voice. However, some of the other protesters believed that the lit joints were deflecting from the mood of the crowd and urged them to extinguish the joints. They motioned to Barry that the joints were a distraction.

The field appeared to be a giant moonlit parade. There was no need for electricity. The field lit up like a hundred overhead lights. It was indeed an electric moment. The students held hands and swayed to the lyrics of a John Lennon song. Their voices grew louder and more passionate. The ground seemed to sway along in perfect harmony with the crowd. The feeling of the crowd was complete tranquility and togetherness. Barry stood with some of the members of the group. Alex had joined the crowd and waved at Barry and some of the other dorm residents. Barry moved through the crowd and waved her to join his group. "You ready to join the movement?"

"No, just looked like fun. I was a bit bored studying." She laughed.

Barry lit up another joint and offered it to Alex. "Take a hit." Alex inhaled the smoke and coughed before handing it back to Barry. The group joined hands and began to sway back and forth and burst into song.

"All we are saying is give peace a chance!" the group sang in perfect harmony." They repeated the lyrics several times before Bennett stepped up to the makeshift microphone.

"Dean Mansbach, I know you're listening. I demand that you end the military program and end support for the war." The crowd cheered. Inside the house, the Dean and his wife continued to watch the proceedings as if it were a live reality show, a show staged for their benefit and entertainment.

On the sidelines, the Campus Patrol officers unloaded from their vehicles. They stood vigilant at the front of the park. They wore their vests and riot gear. The officers hoped the protest remained peaceful, but they were prepared for the worst. Danny sat in the Campus Patrol car parked on the street, scribbling notes. When the officer's attention was captured by the growing masses of protesters, Danny slipped out of the car and raced toward the waiting patrolmen. An officer attempted to intercept him, but Danny was faster. He approached several of the officers and requested some comments. The officers were happy to unofficially voice their disapproval. One of the offices bounced his wooden baton off the palm of his hand in a show of strength. "These kids better not do anything stupid."

"These kids should be in the bar drinking instead of bothering the Dean," joked another officer. "Aren't they missing a new episode of *All in the Family?*" said another.

Kevin showed up at the police lines. He flashed his *Targum* credentials. "I'm here to cover this protest." The officer smiled at him and pointed to Danny, who was busy taking notes and talking to the different Campus Patrol officers. "It's okay, we have a reporter here now. We don't need you." Kevin sputtered in anger, but it was a futile gesture. Another officer escorted a furious Kevin off the field. Danny watched with amusement as his rival was escorted away. He began jotting down the quotes and recording the actions. For once, he was at the forefront of a good news story. Tonight, at least, he got revenge on the smug Kevin. Danny obeyed the Commander, remaining on the fringes of the crowd. He was satisfied interviewing the officers and jotting notes about the spectacle on the field.

"It's all a show," one of the officers had said before and then crossed his fingers and placed them behind his back.

All the students seemed unified in their purpose. After a few more bars of the song, Bennett again leaned into the mike. He did not disappoint.

"We asked for action, but the administration would not listen. We tried to speak in a civilized manner, but they refused to listen." They booed in unison. Bennett stopped in mid-thought and stared out at the crowd. He smiled at the strength and integrity of the crowd.

"I hope this sends a message to the administration. Dean Mansbach, I know you're still listening," he bellowed. "We will keep coming back every night until our demands are met."

The crowd roared its approval. "It's time for action!" he yelled. Some of the crowd cat-called, while others remained silent.

"Are you going to just stand there?" Jerry, a boisterous, pudgy radical, with a loud tie-dye shirt, ponytail, and hostile manner, tried to rile up the crowd. He waved his hands and raised his voice until he grew hoarse. He picked up a rock and chucked it in the direction of the Dean's house. Bennett frowned as he watched the impulsive Jerry attempting to stir up the crowd. Klonsky approached Jerry and grabbed his hand. His frowning expression told the story. He informed him in no uncertain terms to stop trying to incite the crowd. The leaders were determined not to let this moment get out of hand. They were determined to keep the evening peaceful to maximize the impact. The crowd returned to passive mode. They lit a second candle and resumed their 'Kodak Moment for Peace' among men and women.

At the same time, a group of conservative students mixed in with some of the fraternity brothers mobilized to engage in a counter-protest. However, the Campus Patrol, seeing them, cut them off at the pass. They blockaded the path and prevented the counter-protestors from gaining access to the field. After several speakers gave their speeches, the crowd grew restless and began to filter off the field. They felt that the point had been made and it was time to return to their dorms.

The Dean and his wife watched with relief as the crowd slowly dissipated. Mansbach phoned the Commander of the Campus Patrol.

He was ordered to stand down. Everyone was ordered to return to normal duties. Mansbach reassured his wife that events like the evening were all part of the game of confrontation that the students played. He assured her that he was prepared to take countermeasures.

Soon, the night was as tranquil and calm as it had been prior to the beginning of the march. The students were buzzing with stories about the protest. Bennett and Klonsky went back to the office to evaluate how effective the night's protest had been. They congratulated themselves and discussed potential future protests if the Dean was not going to cooperate with their demands.

Leaving the Campus Patrol office, Danny ran back to the office of the *Daily Targum*, where he found the office filled with staffers who had been called in at the last minute. He clutched his notebook as though it were gold. He passed by the sulking Kevin and slipped him his middle finger. Kevin turned away, having been humiliated at losing his assignment to his arch-rival.

Errol had closed his bookstore and driven over to the Student Center. A few minutes later, Errol entered the newspaper. He handed Morris an article on his courses. He explained that he was trying to drum up interest in some upcoming African American history classes that he would be teaching at his bookstore. He explained to Morris that he had not been able to attend the evening's protest because of a backlog of work at the store. He noticed Danny sitting at his desk, churning out the story. He walked up to him. Danny looked up and smiled. They chatted for a few minutes. Danny told him about his upcoming story for the paper.

Errol yelled over to Morris. "Treat this kid right, he's an upcoming star."

Danny smiled at the compliment.

Errol patted him on the back. "Stop by the store anytime, you ever want to talk politics or just jam on the guitar."

Morris frowned, but was not going to make an issue of it to Errol. Danny was feeling positive. He had discovered a good friend in Errol. Danny spent the next half hour typing up his story, then presented it to Morris.

138

"I love the quotes from the officers, nice touch," Morris concluded, in an unaccustomed jovial mood after reading it over and making a few corrections. "Shows you've got reporter's instincts." This was almost high praise from Morris. He even moved Danny's name up the wall chart for preferred stories. Danny beamed! Perhaps he would find a path to his future dream job after all.

Danny left the newspaper feeling on top of the world. He walked back toward the dorm. He spotted Ryan as he passed the Student Center. Ryan seemed fixated on ignoring Danny. He glared at Danny before walking away without saying a word. For a moment, Danny lingered. He wondered if this were the final word, then Ryan turned to Danny.

"Were you at the rally?" demanded Ryan.

"Yes, I did the story for the paper."

Before Danny could finish the sentence and explain himself, Ryan turned his back on his former friend. From a distance, Ryan yelled, "Sell-out!" Danny was in too good a mood to yell back. Ryan thrust his arm out and gave Danny the middle-finger salute before disappearing into a nearby building. *The Lord giveth and the Lord taketh away* was a favorite hymn around Danny's home. Danny had left the office feeling encouraged at the success of the story, but his altercation with Ryan left him with a feeling that he could not shake—that his pride and his elation could be so short-lived. It would be replaced with something much darker in the near future.

24

Alex the Peacemaker

Despite the restlessness Danny felt at leaving Ryan, he felt relaxed enough to join the regulars in their late-night game of poker, seeing that Barry was nowhere to be found. Several of the players asked Danny why he was in such a chipper mood, and he recounted his experience writing the article for the newspaper. They offered their hearty congratulations and then returned to the serious business of taking each other's money at cards. Danny did not last long; suddenly exhausted after losing a few dollars, he excused himself and went to bed.

Alex had spent an hour after dinner at the library and then recalled that she had an assignment at the newspaper. She spent the rest of the evening sketching some new layouts for the paper. Danny had enjoyed watching her engrossed in her impromptu late-night sketches of students in the dorm. She had enjoyed some late-night discussions with Danny and felt that Danny understood her struggles to maintain her independence.

Both felt that they needed to explore their college experiences. She was sorry to learn about the split between Danny and Ryan. Danny had lent her a sympathetic ear about her artistic ambitions and even about some of her dating disappointments. Danny was always a good friend to listen to you when you wanted to complain about life's ups and downs.

Alex felt sympathetic to Danny because she had once lost a person that she considered a good friend. She recalled Sarah, a long-time friend from high school, who had broken up with her over a minor misunderstanding. Unlike Ryan, Alex was not a fair-weather friend. The two girls had vied for a position as head of a school organization. The organization picked Alex and Sarah blamed Alex for somehow influencing them to choose her for the position. Sarah held a grudge despite Alex's pleadings until the two women parted ways when they attended different schools. Alex tried to communicate with her former friend, but Sarah refused to respond to Alex's letters.

The next afternoon, Alex had completed her work at the *Targum*. She had finished typesetting the paper and waved to Morris as she exited the office. Morris was absorbed in editorial matters and barely noticed her departure. She had decided on an early dinner, so that she could get a head start on her studies. While sitting in the dining hall, Alex noticed Ryan eating by himself at a table. Alex had felt an enormous sense of attraction to Ryan. Despite his bravado, he seemed like someone that Alex could like. This would be the first time they would be alone together, and she displayed a hint of shyness as she walked over to him.

"Mind if I sit down?" She spoke with a hint of shyness in her voice.

Ryan was flattered and was not about to turn down the lovely Alex. "To what do I owe the honor?"

She was cautious as she uttered, "It's about Danny."

Ryan frowned and his body posture grew rigid and unyielding. "Not interested in talking about that Judas."

Alex was about to give up when she decided to try one more gambit. She placed her hand on his arm. The smell of her perfume enticed him to change his mind. "Look, Danny is visibly miserable about the fight. He regrets it. Could you cut him some slack?"

"Have the two of you been gossiping about me?" he demanded.

Alex seemed hurt that her efforts had been rebuffed. "No, I hate to see you and Danny end your friendship over this," Alex countered.

"Is he going to apologize?" Ryan asked frostily.

Alex shrugged. She had no idea.

"No, then I have nothing to say," he said curtly. Ryan stood up to leave.

She was very disappointed: she had made the effort, but it had been rebuffed. She checked her watch and picked up her books. She had to meet some of her classmates.

Alex and several co-eds carried book bags slung over their shoulders as they walked toward the lecture hall. Across the street, Alex observed Professor Jacobsen. He was mid-thirties, bearded, and sported a delicious English accent. He was the epitome of what a college professor should look like. He was Professor Henry Higgins with a beard. He walked down the street and was talking animatedly to an attractive female student. She wore a brown miniskirt that was cut off at the knees and wore shiny black knee-high boots.

"I hear he's a tough grader," said Alex to one of her friends, who also observed the professor and the young student.

The co-ed chuckled at her naivety. She thought that Alex was occasionally naïve about how the world works. "I also hear he likes to get friendly with his students," she said with a smirk.

"He likes girls with big boobs," chimed in a third co-ed.

"I think he encourages the girls with promises of good grades."

The women broke up into a hysterical laugh. The other co-eds joined in on the joke. Alex stared longingly at Jacobsen. She observed him gently stroking the sexy young woman's shoulder. The female student giggled and responded to Jacobsen's attentions by moving ever closer to him. She seemed to be enjoying the undivided attention of the professor. Was she aware that others might be staring at her? Did she even care, or was she so enraptured by his wit and charm? Nothing else seemed to matter. She turned to face him and kissed him passionately on the lips. The professor seemed to be savoring the moment, oblivious to any critical outside observers. Alex decided that she had better things to do than be a voyeur and decided to walk down the street.

A few minutes later, Sandy walked up to the group and headed toward Alex to confront her. There was an air of disbelief in her voice and on her face. The two stood face-to-face. Alex and Sandy had exchanged hostile words from the first days of school. Alex had effortlessly stolen a boy's attention away from the chubby Sandy. Alex chalked it up to mere jealousy and tried to avoid the young co-ed.

"I noticed you signed up for the museum position," said Sandy with a hostile expression on her face. "You can't be serious," said Sandy, mockingly.

"Really, that's what I want to be," said a defensive Alex, "A curator."

"How boring!" Her voice was a soundtrack of disapproval.

Alex reddened and grew defensive. "It's not boring. I went to Paris as a kid with my mom. I fell in love with the Louvre. That's why I want to be an art historian. Study the great works of Rembrandt."

"Oh please, spare me the bullshit. We all know you are here for your MRS degree, just like the rest of us, but you parade around like you are all about brains and beauty not being hard to get!" she snarled.

"MRS degree?" Alex responded with a puzzled expression on her face.

The co-ed smirked. She tossed the long, curly locks of her hair as if it were a weapon against Alex. "Don't play stupid on me, honey, MRS, as in married with husband and family."

Alex was having a hard time accepting the discussion. She lashed out at her opponent. "Any of you hear about Betty Friedan or Gloria Steinem?"

The other girls shrugged. The names did not ring any bells for them. "Wake up!"

"Do they have columns in *Cosmopolitan*?" asked one of the co-eds.

Cosmopolitan was the primary women's magazine of the day, with Helen Gurley Brown as the editor. Alex's chest heaved as she struggled for breath, visibly upset. The other girl motioned to her watch. "It's time for class."

Alex could not escape fast enough. She entered the huge building surrounded by a massive crowd of students. The hallway was filled with students walking to various classrooms and lecture halls inside the mammoth building. Modern ornate silver sculptures and wood paneling decorated the building's walls. Scott Hall was the biggest lecture hall in that sector of the campus. Professors would enter the building and lecture to the crowd of students. The crowd of earnest students would sit in their chairs while the professors would pontificate in front of the lectern and drone on about some dull subject related to the coursework. This was a lecture hall for Jacobsen's Art History class. The class consisted mainly of women.

They buzzed as Jacobsen entered the lecture hall. He mounted the stage in front and turned on his projector. The lecture hall was almost filled. Alex sat in her usual front row seat, immediately absorbed in the lecture as the professor began to speak, her head bobbing up and down, and jotted down notes at a furious pace. Jacobsen stood by the wooden lectern and switched frames on the slide projector. He clicked the machine, and it would advance to the next slide in progression. "This is an example of 15th-century artwork by the master. Notice the fine lines and the broad brushstrokes. Giacomo was considered a patron of the arts. He supported several of the painters as they struggled to produce paintings for him."

Later, Jacobsen snapped off the projector and leaned up against his lectern. "He was imprisoned for insulting the king and died in jail." The audience was enraptured by his style and skill with luring his class into the world of art appreciation.

Jacobsen grabbed a piece of paper on the side of the table. He displayed it for the class. "I just want to bring your attention to one of the essays that I read last night." He held up a paper for everyone to see. "We have an outstanding student. I am overly impressed with her essay. Alexandra Doherty. Please stand up!"

Alex blushed and appeared shocked and embarrassed by the sudden recognition. She hesitated and remained seated. Another co-ed nudged her, and she reluctantly stood up from her seat.

Jacobsen gestured for her to come up on stage. "Fine work, it should be rewarded." He continued to offer praise to the blushing student: "A very fine paper. It's time someone understood the nuances of 19th-century Impressionists," intoned Jacobsen.

Alex blushed as she turned to see a sea of familiar faces staring at her. After the lecture, the class filed out. Alex carried a flier and approached Jacobsen. "I'm really interested in the museum tour this summer," she said shyly, almost embarrassed to ask.

Jacobsen's eyes evaluated her from head to toe. It was no coincidence. She was indeed a fine, looking young woman. He had seen her in class and might have boosted her grades to bring about the meeting. "You're one of my best students," he said, admiring her like a fine piece of sculpture.

Alex was hopeful that the professor was merely interested in her artistic ability. She continued to gush about her enthusiasm for the tour. "My cousin worked for a museum. She showed me all the paintings. I could sit for hours analyzing the artist styles." She spoke in a rapid-fire manner, attempting to convince the professor of her genuine interest.

Jacobsen did not need to be sold on her talent or beauty. "Can't let such enthusiasm go to waste. I think you have a good future," purred the professor. Jacobsen eyed her.

It was now apparent that it was more than the admiring look of a proud teacher to his prize student. Alex blushed and grew embarrassed at the lavish praise.

"If you need someone to be sort of a mentor, let me know." His eyes dwelled on her breasts.

She noticed his roving eyes and grew uncomfortable. "Thanks for thinking of me," she muttered quietly. Alex blushed but grew apprehensive at his continuous leer.

He closed the gap and wrapped his arm around her. His voice grew even more seductive. She pulled free. "You know my office hours." He smiled and jotted his private phone number on a piece of paper and handed it her.

She thanked him and escaped quickly. Alex had always accepted her natural beauty without a second thought. After her encounter with the professor, she began to wonder if maybe she was cursed instead of blessed with her natural beauty. She wanted to be taken seriously as a person and an artist. She decided to take a closer look at her attitude and try and blend in with the other women in the school. She found a bench nearby the lecture hall and sat down and cried.

25

Letter from the Brother

L ater that morning, Danny sat in the cafeteria by himself. He wondered if the rift between him and Ryan would ever be resolved. He was disappointed but decided not to dwell on the issue. After finishing his meal, he decided to visit the campus post office. His weekly ritual was to empty his post office box of any mail or packages from home. Danny reached into his post office box and pulled out a letter. It was strange because the postmark indicated that it was from overseas. In addition, the postmark indicated that it had been mailed a few months earlier. It took him only a few seconds to realize that the letter was from his brother, who was serving a tour in Vietnam. Danny was thrilled at the prospect of hearing from his brother. He was also nervous at the prospect of some bad news. After all, the letter had been mailed a few months ago and was just now arriving in his mailbox. He peeled open the letter and began to read.

I've been in-country for several months now. I hate to say it, but I'm beginning to wonder if I did the right thing.

Danny let out a deep breath as he devoured the rest of the letter. It went on outlining his brother's growing disillusionment with the war. He grew sober as his brother outlined some of his feelings. The letter ended with a somber, cautionary note: *Please don't mention this letter to Dad. He would not understand. I'll explain it to him when I get back, if I get back.* Danny gulped as he read the final section.

Normally, Danny would talk it over with his friend Ryan. Ryan would lend a sympathetic ear to Danny's feelings. Suddenly, Danny felt alone and vulnerable. He had no one to share his innermost feelings with about the letter.

He took a deep breath and decided to take the letter and visit his newfound friend, Errol. He had begun his discussion over the war with Errol. He was certain that he might want to talk with him further. Then he recalled that Errol was indeed a veteran. He felt that if anyone could comprehend his feelings it was Errol. Errol might lend a sympathetic ear and offer his opinion.

Danny soon arrived at the bookstore and found Errol deep in conversation with another patron. They were arguing the fine points over some political discussion. Danny waved the letter in front of Errol. The discussion was over, and Errol smiled and waved Danny over.

"It's from my brother... the one in Vietnam." Danny handed it to Errol.

Errol immersed himself in the letter and nodded his head in agreement. "Sorry you have to deal with this shit."

Danny nodded. "My brother was totally gung-ho when he volunteered."

Errol was sympathetic and patted Danny on the shoulder. "I'll keep my fingers crossed that he makes it back okay." said Errol.

"Thanks for listening, I needed that."

Errol was about to make a further comment when a voice boomed from the back of the store. It was a familiar one: it was Bennett. "Do you have any more copies of that book that I ordered?" he called.

Errol yelled back, "It's on back order."

To Danny's surprise, Bennett Andrews exited the section of the store hidden by a partition and strode up to Errol. "You'll let me know when it comes in." He turned and was surprised to spot Danny. He smiled in a solicitous manner. "Thanks for the advice about writing the op-ed. Hey, I liked your article about the protest, nice writing, very fair," added Bennett.

Errol interrupted the conversation. He told Bennett about Danny's letter. Danny was reluctant to discuss the letter with a stranger, but Errol revealed the contents to Bennett.

Bennett shook his head in dismay. "No hard feelings. We are not taking it out on guys like your brother. It is the anger that we feel about President Johnson lying to the public about the reasons for being in the war. For all the needless bloodshed on both sides."

Bennett grew passionate and then realized that he did not have to make a speech. He grew calmer, more reflective. "Whatever we personally feel about the war, I hope he makes it home," he intoned. Bennett reflected on his summers spent in rural Pennsylvania. Bennett questioned Danny about some of the country fairs that were held near Danny's hometown. Bennett had played baseball in some of the local competitions. He and Danny might have even been on opposite sides of the game. A sort of kinship had grown between two men on different sides of the political aisle. The two men shook hands.

Danny was pleased to hear this from Bennett: "Look, you're welcome to join our little group anytime."

Danny thanked him and added, "Just don't tell Barry. I don't want him to know that I'm coming around to his point of view." Bennett chuckled and agreed to keep their meeting a secret. Danny folded the letter and placed it in his pocket. Bennett might have been a fierce opponent with the Dean, but he had his gracious side. Danny might have told Ryan that Bennett had a warm and fuzzy side to him, but Ryan would not listen even if the two men patched up their differences. It was no longer just the fight against some existential threat of Communism. Danny's perspective on the war grew more intense as he realized the human cost to the soldiers who had gone off to fight the war with the best of intentions. Many of these young men would return with mental and physical wounds that would haunt them for the rest of their lives. Many of these young men would be haunted by their memories of an unpopular war. They would witness destruction and sometimes the death of a close friend. It was no longer a John Wayne movie to Danny or the thousands who served. Danny's mind had not been firmly made up, but he was beginning to reevaluate his long-held beliefs about the war.

26

Danny and Ryan Make-Up

Later that afternoon, Ryan returned to his dorm from his classes. He found a note from Tomlinson pinned to the door, inviting him to meet some of the fraternity brothers at the local bar. He plopped his books on a pre-determined spot on his desk. The room was meticulously neat, everything in its place. The word 'clutter' was not part of his vocabulary. Ryan smiled and slipped the note into his pocket. As he passed the Mine Street Coffee House on his way, he decided to check on the status of the upcoming music event at the coffee house. He was informed by the church director that Danny had requested to do a solo act.

"Just like that?" demanded Ryan.

"He insisted that you were not going to be available," responded the director. The director was firm that he would not get in the middle of any dispute between the students. "You two should work it out. It is not my role to handle your petty squabbles. I have more important matters to deal with. Good day, Mr. Marshott." The director grabbed his schedule and exited the room.

Ryan was livid and dashed out of the church basement.

Danny had also been walking back to the main campus, consumed with the feelings from the conversation between him and Errol and Bennett. As Danny passed the Mine Street Coffee House, he spotted Ryan walking down the steps. The two men glared at each other.

"In case you're wondering, I told them that I'm playing a solo gig on Saturday," said Danny.

"Yeah, he just told me. Probably best, since I'm the better singer." Ryan offered a sarcastic remark.

There was dead silence for a moment. Ryan did not wait for a response. He turned his back on Danny and walked away.

That morning, Danny had invited Barry and Fred to join him at the same bar as Ryan. He had no idea that they would be at the same bar. So that evening, both Danny and Ryan showed up to hang out, but at separate tables. Danny carried a pitcher of ice-cold Budweiser to the table and poured a round for the people at the table.

Barry crowed, "I heard about you and Bennett bonding at the bookstore."

Danny was annoyed that the news had gotten out. "Yeah, good news travels fast. He's a cool guy, what can I say."

Alex breezed into the bar and apologized for her lateness and thanked everyone for inviting her. She had just finished one of her classes. A few of the guys in the bar stared at Alex and gave an appropriate wolf-whistle of appreciation. She never felt comfortable with the response of the young men, but tonight she simply smiled at the young men, and then continued walking over to Danny's table.

Danny tried to ignore Ryan sitting in the back of the room, but he could see Ryan observing Alex. He tried to ignore his ex-friend's presence and concentrate on having a fun evening with his classmates sitting around the table. In the rear of the bar, Ryan sat with Tomlinson and some of his friends from the jock fraternity. Ryan noticed Danny but refused to make eye contact.

Tomlinson smiled at Ryan. "We got a big party coming up. We're depending on you to bring some of your best-looking girls for the brothers."

"Make sure they're not acting like drunken assholes," snorted Ryan. The two made loud farting sounds with their mouths and laughed. It was all in good fun.

He turned and shook his head at Danny and offered him a frosty expression. It was as cold as the beer they were drinking. Danny made no effort to come over and talk to him. Both men kept their distance. Neither one was willing to take the first step.

Alex had grown comfortable hanging with Danny and some of the guys in the dorm. In some ways, they treated her as one of the guys rather than just the sexy girl. Alex appeared distant and a bit downhearted. She explained that she'd had a confrontation with one of the co-eds in the dorm. Alex had not been invited to go with the other girls to a frat party. The other girl made it clear that the girls did not want competition from Alex for the attention of the available boys.

Danny attempted to cheer her up. "You're a good person. Do not take it personally. She is probably just jealous. Hey, I found something at the church that might cheer you up." Danny pulled out some posters from his knapsack. They were the posters that Danny had found pinned to the church bulletin board. They announced the opening of a contest for aspiring artists. He handed them to Alex, who responded with delight. She offered him a peck on the cheek. She brightened up and turned her attention to the guests around the table. Alex turned to Danny as if to change the conversation. "I tried talking to Ryan about making up, but he wasn't interested."

As she uttered those words, she observed Ryan out of the corner of her eye in the back of the bar. She explained her attempts at being the peacemaker.

"Yes, I see him, thanks for trying," muttered Danny. Danny turned to Fred. "This guy bothering you?" he said, referring to Barry.

Fred repeated, with a smile, "He's okay for a white boy."

"How about the other kids in the dorm?" Danny finished.

Fred smiled and reassured Danny that everything was okay. "Yeah, one of the kids from the floor is in my math class. He helps me with my math assignments. We're cool."

Danny motioned for the two to play a game of pinball on a vacant machine at the end of the bar. Within minutes, they were engrossed in a lively pinball competition.

A few minutes later, Kevin, the chubby-faced reporter from the *Targum*, walked through the bar with several friends. He spotted Danny and walked up to him. He was drunk and in a combative mood, wanting to stick it to Danny. "Morris said that you don't have much of a future at the paper." He smirked.

Danny grew red-faced and angry. "You're lying. Morris told me I had great instincts."

"Don't bet on it, loser. You were just lucky. He said that the article would have been better if I had written it."

Danny grew red-faced and got close to Kevin. "What did you say?" Danny demanded.

"Hayseed, you're a fucking loser. Everyone at the paper knows it," said Kevin.

Ryan had observed the confrontation from across the room. He rushed over to Danny's side and added a stern warning. "Take your shit and get outside, or you'll have a real problem with me to deal with."

"Hey, butthead, stay out of this. It's between me and the loser over here," crowed Kevin.

Ryan fumed. He contemplated punching the chubby Kevin, but he did not want to start a fight.

Danny took the initiative and grabbed the pitcher of cold beer from the table and poured it over Kevin's head. The bar erupted in laughter and cheers. A soggy, red-faced Kevin beat a hasty retreat. He gave Danny the middle finger and stumbled out the door to the street. Everyone gathered around Danny and Ryan.

"That guy had it coming," said Alex.

"Forget it, guy is just trying to be an asshole," said Ryan.

Danny sucked in a few deep breaths and began to calm down. "Now he's a soggy asshole," intoned Danny.

Both men looked awkwardly at the other. Ryan was about to turn around and head back to his friends in the back of the bar, but Alex and Barry stood up.

"You work better together," she said.

Barry nodded in agreement. "Dig it man, you guys can't stay mad."

Ryan pondered the comments and offered a bit of a smirk. "You're right, he needs me to save his ass from embarrassment at the coffee house next Saturday night." Danny just chuckled and disregarded the comment. Ryan shook his head. "Look, I don't want a little disagreement over politics to come between us."

Danny nodded in agreement. "Yeah, I agree, we can agree to disagree."

Ryan noted, "I can't stay mad at you, even if your politics piss me off."

"Same here, "said Danny nodding his head, struggling to conceal a smirk.

The two smiled and shook hands. They gave each other a big hug.

"You can't play for shit without me," said Danny.

"You suck without me," replied Ryan.

The two men bumped fists. "You're still a pussy," said Ryan.

"Least I get some," Danny hooted.

Alex, overhearing the remark, blushed at the off-color remark. Barry simply sat back in his chair and smiled.

Ryan stared at Alex with a wistful expression and added, "Yeah, you're a stud."

The two shook hands. They all adjourned to the table to share a beer.

"Let's keep this party going. I think this calls for another round of drinks," Ryan uttered. He ordered another pitcher from the bar and the burly bartender poured a fresh pitcher for the group. "On the house," said the bartender, nodding with pleasure at the good atmosphere.

Ryan carried the pitcher back to the table and then took a seat next to Alex, smiling sweetly. She seemed receptive to Ryan sitting next to her.

Danny sat back and smiled. The evening had become a success, but he realized that a greater test was just around the corner.

27

Danny the Folksinger

S everal days had passed and it was late Saturday night. Danny and Ryan checked in with the director of the Mine Street Coffee House. He stared up from his scheduling book and motioned to Danny. "I thought you were going to be a single tonight," said the director.

"I changed my mind. I'm going to be generous and let my associate play," Danny quipped. "He needs the experience."

The church official shrugged and scribbled Ryan's name onto the cast list. He motioned them toward the dressing room in the rear of the church, where they sat waiting for the beginning of the show. They caroused with the local talent in the impromptu dressing room. Each folksinger would do a short set of three songs. They tuned up their guitars and sipped a small can of beer to steady their nerves. They were about to go out in front of a large crowd and entertain them.

The students sat on wooden chairs in a small semi-circle or circle-in-the-round style. In the middle of the stage was the performer's space.

The level of talent ranged from the total novice to acts that could, with a lot of luck, blossom into major performers. The performers would sit on a wooden stool or stand in front of a mic and perform for the audience. Along the side of the room were several wooden tables containing cups of coffee, stacks of cakes and creamy chocolate donuts. The strong smell of freshly brewing coffee percolated the air as the students mingled and exchanged small talk.

It was a very informal environment. Boys could approach girls without feeling too self-conscious. It was more relaxed than the traditional college mixers. These were large dance halls filled with large speakers blaring music and strobe lights that gave a psychedelic feel to the evening. It was life-threatening for a young man to cross the dance floor to ask a girl to dance. The dangers to the male ego upon rejection were strong enough to deter even the most stouthearted of men. The loud music and lights were distracting and made the moves intimidating. In a coffee house setting, many men found girls and promising relationships consummated over a friendly cup of coffee.

Having waited through several acts, the spotlight focused on Danny and Ryan, as they performed astride tall wooden chairs. They strummed guitars and sang a folk song called *You've got a friend*, written by rock and folk icon James Taylor.

"*Isn't it good to know, you've got a friend? Oh, baby, you 've got a friend.*" Danny's voice was strong and melodious. He strummed the guitar as he wrapped up the tune. The audience broke into polite applause. The two singers took a bow. They leaped off the makeshift stage and plunged back into the audience. Another folk singer waited in the wings for his turn on stage.

The sound of a loud argument in the back of the room caught Danny's attention. He spotted Tracy, his ex-girlfriend, curled up in a chair in the corner. Tracy was crying as Storzillo, the large, blond-haired jock, loomed over her. It was the same guy he had seen with her only days before. He was berating her for some minor offense.

"I said let's go back to my room." His voice was strident and unyielding. He yanked her by the hand. She resisted with every fiber of her being. She sat cowed and shivering, no longer interested in the guy.

"You embarrassed me in front of my friends," the jock thundered.

"I'm sorry," Tracy said, softly sobbing and dabbing her eyes with a tissue.

"Tired of your bullshit," he said arrogantly.

She sat in her chair with her hands covering her face, sobbing.

"Why couldn't you be like the other girls?" he demanded, without an ounce of remorse. The blond-haired boy did not seem bothered that he was creating an unpleasant scene in the church. He was oblivious to the fact that Danny and Ryan were staring at him from across the room. "Then you drag me to this stupid coffee house." He was unrelenting in his criticism of the young girl.

At first, Danny was ambivalent. He had been hurt by the girl's cruel rejection. He felt that it was no longer his business what happened to her. However, the longer he watched as the blond jock make her cry, the more his blood began to boil. And then, adding insult to injury, Storzillo slapped Tracy across the face.

"Isn't that Tracy?" asked Ryan.

"Yeah," said Danny, "but she was pretty nasty to me the last time."

"Dude, the girl needs help! You can't ignore this."

Danny nodded in agreement. Whatever anger he had felt towards Tracy, it melted as he watched the young girl being berated. Danny gathered his courage, as he crossed over to the jock and confronted him.

"What do you want?" demanded the angry Storzillo. He recognized Danny and grew indignant. He jabbed at him with his finger and made it clear that he was not interested in anyone stopping him from reprimanding his date. Ryan watched with fascination as Danny, full of fire, bore down on the blond-haired boy.

"Leave her the fuck alone," Danny stated.

"You and what fuckin' army are going to stop me?" bellowed the belligerent jock. The blond-haired boy flexed his muscle as though he were going to strike Danny.

Danny grabbed his hand. He stared hard at the blond-haired boy. "I'm her dorm adviser, I said leave her alone." Danny took a deep breath. "I don't think the Dean or Campus Patrol would take kindly to what you're doing." He was bluffing, but he put enough authority behind him to make it sound feasible.

The blond-haired boy seemed angry but decided that maybe Danny was not bluffing. He had had enough for one evening. "Here, she's your problem." He unhanded the tearful young woman and stormed out the door of the tiny church.

Danny grabbed a handkerchief from his pocket and dabbed her eyes. The knight errant, Danny Quixote, had a new friend. Tracy stopped sobbing and looked up at Danny. She appeared grateful and stared up at Danny with newfound gratitude. She grabbed him and gave him a deep passionate kiss. Ryan was impressed at the scene from a rom-com.

"I was wrong. I apologize," she said, in between fighting off tears.

Danny responded by blushing and then returning the favor. They exchanged soft smiles and eye contact.

"I'm sorry, Danny, I really am," she sobbed.

He grabbed her hand and led her over to the coffee table. Ryan watched the proceedings at a distance.

"Have a cup of tea. Make you feel better." He handed her a cup of steaming tea. It made them both feel better.

"Call me, I'd like to go out with you again," she cooed. Tracy finished her cup of tea and walked out the door. At the last moment, she turned and blew Danny a goodnight kiss.

Ryan walked up to Danny and stared at his friend with a new level of respect. He was surprised at Danny's bravery. "Way to go, Danny boy. I didn't think you would do it."

The two men walked out of the church. They were silent for a few seconds. Ryan nodded his approval and gave him the thumbs-up sign.

"Nothing to it," said Danny with conviction.

"Buy you a cheesesteak? Lots of grease?" The two headed to the Greasy Truck. Danny was feeling ten feet tall and expansive over the evening's events.

When Danny and Ryan entered the dorm, Danny spotted a note pinned to his front door. It was a simple note that said that his mother had called. The note mentioned that his parents were coming for a visit on Sunday. Danny sputtered that he had no time to protest the upcoming visit. He grew pale and the blood drained from his face.

"Are you okay?" questioned Ryan.

He handed Ryan the note. Danny's mood had shifted dramatically. He had been in such good spirits. Now he faced the harsh possibility of a visit from his disapproving father. He slunk back into his room and slammed the door shut.

Ryan stood outside for a few minutes. "Danny, answer me, are you okay?" Ryan repeated his call.

There was no answer. Silence was the only sound that could be heard. Standing outside the door, Ryan could hear Danny inside, cursing to himself and knocking books and items off the furniture.

Ryan pounded his fist on the door. "Danny, are you okay?" This was met with silence and then the pounding began again. Ryan called out another time, but again was met with silence. He sighed and understood that he had to give Danny some time to deal with the situation. He was worried about his friend.

28

The Gym

The next morning, Ryan cautiously knocked on the door to Danny's room. He was not sure in what sort of mood he would find his troubled friend. He clutched a leather gym bag with the Rutgers logo emblazoned on the sides.

Danny opened the door and stared directly at Ryan. He looked frazzled and pale. "We're closed," he bellowed.

He attempted to shut the door in Ryan's face. Ryan grabbed the door and propped it open. "Don't be a grump. Let us talk," said Ryan in a hopeful manner.

Danny grimaced and said nothing. He just stared into space. Finally, he spoke. "I'm doomed. My parents are coming. There's nothing I can do to stop it."

"Call them, tell them you have a social disease," Ryan added, trying to make Danny laugh.

Danny frowned. "That's pretty lame, even for you."

"Why not level with them? Tell them that you are leaving the family." Ryan shrugged. He spat out any lame excuse that came to mind.

Danny wanted to shut the door on his friend. The discussion proved to be unhelpful. However, he realized that Ryan was a good friend and wished him well.

"Well, if you can't do anything about the visit, maybe you just want to knock off some of that anxiety and the beer gut," chuckled Ryan.

He pointed to Danny's small, but protruding gut. Danny shook his head. Unfortunately, this time he had to agree with Ryan. Danny loved his beer. Someday, he might transform into Norm, the beer-drinking patron from the future TV show, *Cheers*.

"Get dressed. We can sweat off some of the stress," said Ryan. Ryan hefted his gym bag over his shoulders.

"What do you have in mind?" Danny asked his friend.

"I got the boxing gym reserved for us." He waved a small gold key in front of him. "For the side door, we can get in and out faster."

Danny waded into his cluttered room and grabbed a gym bag stashed in the corner of his room. Boxing was not what he had in mind but was willing to work out some of his frustrations. "Okay, but I get the first punch," said Danny.

"Dream on, pal." Ryan laughed at the idea.

Danny walked quickly down the street. He stared down at the ground and seemed preoccupied with his thoughts. His face revealed his inner turmoil, as he wrestled with demons. He walked ahead of Ryan.

Ryan quickened his pace to keep up. His eyes were downward cast as he moved along. "Just be straightforward," Ryan said, walking in lockstep after catching up.

Danny snorted in derision. "I'll bet that works with your father?"

Ryan shrugged. He had to admit that it was no more effective. Ryan's father could be as demanding with his son as Danny's father. "My father was a colonel in the Army," Ryan sighed. "He wants me to join the Army and become an officer." Ryan was ambivalent about being an officer. It was a matter of pride for him, but sometimes he wished that it had been his idea rather than a commandment from his unyielding father. Danny nodded, understanding his friend's plight.

The two men entered the tiny boxing gym inside the large, imposing Alexander Gymnasium. They hefted their gym bags and trotted down a set of rickety wooden steps to a tiny room located in the bowels of the large basement. Ryan plucked out his key and opened the door. Danny appeared in better spirits than the previous night. However, he still looked like a young man carrying a heavy weight of the world on his shoulders. Danny was the type who could keep his problems wrapped up inside himself. He did not like exposing them for fear of having to confront his fears. Sometimes the fear turned out to be the monster of the week, other times it was a mere phantom that trampled inside the fertile fields in the back of his mind.

The boxing gym was a tiny room located in the basement of the large gym. It featured a canvas boxing ring. The canvas reeked of sweat. Some say it also reeked of desperation, as the would-be pugilists pounded the equipment in hopes of training to become famous athletes.

Danny and Ryan changed into their gym clothing. They examined the work-out equipment. They wore shorts and tee-shirts with the Rutgers logo emblazoned on the front of the shirt. They did a fast warm-up, skipping with the jump rope, then stood in a makeshift boxing ring composed of canvas bags and rope for the ring. Danny took out his rage and frustration on the defenseless canvas bag. He pounded the bag with a series of blows to no effect. The bag was resilient and kept bouncing back for more. It seemed to be mocking his attempts to conquer it.

"Never good enough," he muttered loudly. "Never fuckin' good enough."

Ryan mused, "I think you should definitely confront your father."

Danny grew annoyed. "You don't think I thought of that?" It was more of a blanket statement than an accusation.

Ryan understood. He had felt pressure from his own father for different things. He was sympathetic to Danny's dilemma. Ryan's dad had similar high expectations for his son. Ryan felt that he would not have to work hard to achieve success. He was the son of a successful businessman and gifted in many ways. His father felt that Ryan took advantage of his good fortunes and never fully exerted himself. "Why can't he leave you the fuck alone?"

"He knows how to push my buttons." This was Danny's low reply.

"Is he still talking about you going to school closer to home?" said Ryan.

"He told me that he's getting older, makes me feel guilty." Danny bowed his head. He breathed hard. It was a painful situation.

"You got to tell him off," Ryan insisted.

Danny rolled his eyes. Not so easy, he thought to himself. His father had always intimidated him. Danny always felt under pressure to follow his father's wishes. Danny had resisted him as much as possible. He wanted to scream at his father, but something inside of him held him back. He wiped the sweat off his brow with his shirt. Danny stared at the heavy bag. A weary expression told the story.

Ryan had hit on a temporary solution. Ryan motioned for Danny to step in the ring. The two danced around each other. Danny held the gloves tight against his body. He warded off a few punches as Ryan lunged at him. Then Danny walked over to the heavy bag. It was a gray leather bag dangling from a silver chain on the ceiling. He grunted and slugged the bag with little effect. He danced around the heavy bag; it bounced and swayed as he punched it, but not with much impact.

Ryan motioned for Danny to stop. He would demonstrate the fine art of hitting the heavy bag. He launched himself at the heavy bag and began to smack the heavy bag with his gloved hand. that bounced around with every punch. "You got to smack the bag dead center," muttered Coach Ryan.

Danny copied the technique. He danced around the bag, throwing punches, and accepting his rage. Danny picked up a towel and wiped off the swath of sweat from his midsection. The towel was soaked. "You think I can't," said Danny. "Just watch."

The veins in his neck started to pulse. He pounded the gloves with both hands and advanced on Ryan. He jabbed in Ryan's direction. Ryan easily dodged the punch and danced around. He seemed to be taunting Danny with the ease with which he dodged Danny's efforts. Ryan's eyes narrowed, and he hurled another punch.

This one caught Danny by surprise in the solar plexus. For a moment, the breath shot out of Danny's lungs. He sat down on a stool in the corner of the ring to regain his breath. Ryan was alarmed and approached Danny. Danny waved him off. "I'm okay. Just give me a second," he huffed.

After a few seconds of rest, the color returned to his face. Danny was not intimidated. He had taken the punch in stride and was determined to dish out some punishment. He was nimble on his feet and lunged at Ryan. They exchanged a series of blows and Danny landed a shot. It caught Ryan by surprise.

"Lucky shot," taunted Ryan. Ryan mouthed the words. The words were having an effect. He saw that Danny was growing angry. Danny digested the words. They made him mad. His best friend giving him negative suggestions. He leaped forward and torpedoed a shot into Ryan's gut.

Ryan took it and rebounded. He smiled. "You got it in you?" said Ryan. "That's what I want you to feel when you talk to your dad."

Danny understood what Ryan was doing. He wanted Danny to channel his anger. Ryan mounted a fierce counterattack and lunged at Danny. The two of them exchanged blows with their gloves, dancing around each other until the bell clanged and the round was over. They retreated into their respective corners. Both men were exhausted and covered with sweat.

"Feeling any better?" Ryan grinned.

Danny slumped into a corner. They both reeked of perspiration. They gathered their equipment and headed for the door marked 'shower.' Danny was worn out yet exhilarated. For a moment, he felt like he could take on the world. Danny wondered if the exhilarating feeling would last into his upcoming confrontation with his father.

29

The Parents' Visit

The next afternoon, Danny sat alone at his desk in the dorm. It was deathly quiet. He preferred it that way when he desired to study. Several textbooks were spread out on the desk in front of him. His eyes focused on his bulky, formidable math textbook. He tried to solve several complex equations from the text. Several scraps of paper on the floor around the desk were bleak testaments to Danny's inability to grapple with the problem.

Frustrated, he turned on the television to distract himself. The show was called *Gunsmoke*. The TV image depicted the local saloon, Marshall Matt Dillon sharing a drink with Miss Kitty, the lovely saloon keeper, as they exchanged concerns for the safety of Dodge City.

"Can't let the cattle rustlers force you out of town, Marshall," said Miss Kitty.

Marshall Matt Dillon put down his glass of whiskey and strapped on his holster to battle with the bad guys. "Time to hold my ground," declared the Marshall.

Danny was glued to the television. It helped take his mind off the vexing math problems and impending visit from his parents.

A call pierced the evening air. Danny froze as he heard the chilling words, "Danny, you've got a phone call. It's long distance."

He had anticipated another phone call from his father and dreaded it. Perhaps if he focused on his work, the call would fade away and he could focus on more important matters. Danny trekked down the hall to the floor's telephone booth. He picked up the phone. "Hello?" he said.

"We're coming for a visit," replied his father.

Panic again enveloped Danny. His heart pounded as the reality of the impending doomsday visit sank into his thoughts. "Yes, I got your message, but it's not a good time, Dad."

"We haven't seen you in a few months and we need to discuss things," said Matthew in a firm take-it-or-leave-it tone of voice.

"I'll be home for Christmas. We can talk then," said Danny, in a defensive tone. He hoped that would placate his dad. He knew that would not happen, but sometimes hope springs eternal.

"Danny, I got word from my doctor. My health is not good. I may need you to come home," said his father. "For good. I mean, to hold down the fort here."

Danny's heart sank. His breathing became more rapid. His heart palpitated, and he felt dizzy in the same way that he felt after working on the farm for extended periods of time.

"We'll be over for dinner on Sunday. Find a nice restaurant for your mother and me," said Matthew. Then there was a loud click, followed by a blissful silence.

Danny sat still, staring at the smooth, light brown walls of the phone booth. As he sat there contemplating the visit by his mother and father, he began to panic even more. Was this visit necessary? he thought to himself. He realized that there was nothing that he could do to postpone it. He stared at the wall of the booth at a loss for how to make it okay.

That Sunday, Danny's parents' vehicle drove down the paved driveway toward the dorm. Their car was an old, sky-blue vintage Cadillac. In its day, it was considered a luxury car and had a large set of pointy fins protruding from the rear of the car. Many families envisioned it as a sign of wealth or success to drive such a fancy car. Matthew and Sarah emerged from the car. They were tired after the long trip. Sarah, Danny's mother, was a pleasant, matronly looking woman. She had a creamy-complexioned oval face and auburn hair with streaks of grey. Her pink floral dress was very conservative, and she wore little in the way of makeup. The general sadness in her eyes had been elevated by the problems of raising a family and the tension created by her marriage to a very domineering husband. It had robbed her of her youthful beauty. She had become attractive in a matronly sort of way. Her clothing camouflaged the weight that she had gained. The skin on her face, once taut and smooth, had begun to show wrinkles and signs of aging. She walked behind Matthew and appeared to be deferential. This was the common tradition back in the 1970's. She had been a secretary but became a full-time stay-at-home mom. Like most women of the era, she learned to remain content raising the children.

Matthew was a large, burly man. He had muscles on his arms, but his stomach protruded from his pants. He looked haggard, as the years had worn on him. His ruddy complexion and rough-hewn hands indicated a man who spent much of his waking hours working in the fields of the family farm. He looked uncomfortable and out of place wearing a pair of slacks, a loud Hawaiian shirt and penny-loafer shoes. He was more at home dressed in casual blue jeans.

Matthew and Sarah emerged from the car. They looked around at the buildings. Even though they had dropped Danny off at the beginning of the year, it was an unfamiliar sight. The campus and city might as well have been on Mars for all the similarity to their small town in Pennsylvania.

Danny peered out of the window. He raced out of the dorm to intercept them before they introduced themselves to too many people. Danny was not sure why, just that he did not want to be embarrassed by their sudden appearance. Sarah walked over to kiss her son. She leaned over to hug him. Instinctively, Danny pulled away from his mother. It was embarrassing to be seen with his parents, as it potentially reduced his status in the eyes of his peers. At least, that was the thought running through his mind at that moment.

"Can't a mother kiss her son?" she questioned. Danny nudged his way out of the embrace and finally relented. She gave him a peck on the cheek. "There, that wasn't so bad," she said with a hint of a laugh.

Danny offered her a half-smile. Yes, it was, but he had to accept it, he thought to himself. At least no one had seen his personal degradation. He turned to stare at Matthew. There was no warmth in his father's eyes. No sign that he welcomed the chance to spend time with his youngest son. He offered his hand to shake Danny's hand. It was not a welcoming grip, more like a crushing grip. The purpose of the handshake was to intimidate the young man.

"So, where are we going for dinner?" he demanded.

A few minutes later, Danny hopped into the back of the car and lounged in the back seat of the Cadillac. He rolled down the window and stuck his head out and enjoyed the cool autumn breezes as the car sped down the college street. The sounds of country-western superstar Johnny Cash echoed inside the vehicle, as the singer blasted the latest soulful ditty from the car radio. Sarah suggested that he lower the radio's volume, but Matthew refused the request and glared at her. He made it clear that he would determine what was played. After all, the car was his domain. He got pleasure listening to the latest from his favorite country-and-western stars. He even hummed or mouthed the lyrics to the song.

Danny attempted to make innocuous conversation, but it was strained. "How was your trip?"

Matthew sat in the driver's seat, concentrating on his driving. He wanted to make sure that the ride was smooth and uneventful. He was also not a big conversationalist. "We made good time on the Pennsylvania freeway out of Lancaster," he said dryly. He was a man of few words on most occasions. He could talk for a long time about farming or his favorite baseball team. However, ordinary chit-chat was not something he enjoyed. He felt it was a waste of time and energy.

The Cadillac rolled through some pothole-ridden streets in the run-down section of the inner city. New Brunswick, like many cities of the day, had some sections that were inhabited by middle-class families, and others containing large, run-down housing projects and multi-family homes.

Matthew rolled down his window to inspect the run-down neighborhood. His eyes fixed on the dilapidated buildings. His expression indicated his dissatisfaction for what he saw from his spot in the car. He noticed many boarded-up apartments in need of repair. He observed people lounging outside the apartments, sunning themselves, or watching shabbily dressed children playing in the cluttered backyards.

"When do we get out of this section of town?" he asked. He was clearly uncomfortable and wanted to get out of the ghetto as soon as possible. "These people should be ashamed of themselves," he added, in a voice of authority and revulsion.

"Oh hush," said Sarah.

"Another couple of blocks," Danny said, leaning over the driver's seat to address his father. "We will be on Richmond Street. Make a left and that takes you over the bridge into Highland Park."

"You would think those people would have fixed their houses up," he said firmly. He turned to Sarah who only smiled, with a look of satisfaction that part of her family was together, at least for a few hours.

The streets whizzed past. There was an uncomfortable silence between the family members. After a while, Danny sat and stared out the window. He stared up the road and spotted the restaurant ahead. He pointed to the restaurant. Matthew made a sharp turn and steered the car into the crowded parking lot. Once out of the car, the family headed toward the fancy home-cooking restaurant called The Hearth.

"Someone recommended this place. They said it was really nice."

Once inside, the maître d' led Danny's family into the main dining room. They sat at a table with a fancy, pearly-white linen tablecloth spread on top. A beautiful vase holding a flower sat in the middle of the table. It was the type of restaurant that people reserved for special occasions. Everyone stared at the menu as intently as someone reading one for the first time. The family peered around the room, admiring the fine décor. Several oil paintings hung on the wall, along with pictures of celebrities.

A flaxen-haired waitress stood at a table in the back of the room. She fiddled with her red polished nails and appeared bored. She was young enough to be a graduate student. It might have been her first job upon graduation, or simply a job that helped pay her expenses while attending school. When she noticed that the family had been seated, she ambled over to take their order.

"I'll be your server, my name is Darlene," she had an engaging smile. She tried to make every visitor welcome. She felt that it would garner larger tips for her. She was quite charming and earned substantial amounts of tips. People responded to her warm smile and courteous service.

"What are your specials?" Matthew asked. He could see the list attached to the menu, but he wanted to test her memory. Darlene rattled off the various menu choices and offered helpful suggestions regarding ingredients and alternatives. Matthew was happy and Sarah seemed pleased at the multitude of choices. Danny eyed the pretty young waitress. She avoided his gaze. She was someone that Danny might have enjoyed meeting under different circumstances. Darlene was aware of Danny's welcoming glances but remained aloof and stayed in her professional capacity. She took the order and walked back into the kitchen.

"How is school going?" asked Matthew.

It was an opening to a barrage of questions that Danny had prepared himself for in advance. "Pretty good. I have an A average in my Political Science and Economics classes," responded Danny.

Matthew nodded with satisfaction as he stared at the fancy décor. "We could use a nice restaurant like this in our town," he said.

"Have you met any nice girls?" Sarah asked. Her face and expression were full of curiosity.

Danny never felt comfortable revealing his personal feelings. He grew uncomfortable with the question because his social life was anything but a roaring success. "I've dated a few girls, but nothing long-lasting," he said, growing red. His mind shot back to an image of his short-lived romance with Tracy.

"Plenty of nice girls on this campus," said his father, dryly. It had all the passion and curiosity of someone taking inventory of farm equipment. Danny's mother stared at her son for a reaction.

Danny felt guilty and backtracked. "I'm sure I'll find someone nice, but I want to concentrate on my studies."

Sarah accepted Danny's practiced answer and returned to admiring the décor of the restaurant.

A few minutes later, Darlene emerged, carrying several platters of hot food. She placed them in front of each of the family members. "Some of the plates are hot," she warned. "Be careful."

Danny grabbed one of the plates. His hand bounced off the plate. It was indeed hot. His fingers tingled with the burning sensation that lasted for a few minutes. "How do you handle them?" he inquired.

Darlene smiled and was ready with a response. She seemed happy to offer some small talk. It was a question that she had gotten many times. "I've gotten used to it and learned how to avoid grabbing the hottest parts." She smiled. "Anything you need, I'll be back in a few minutes to check up," she added, before retiring to the back table. Periodically, she glanced at the contents of a textbook spread out on the table. She would glance up to see if any of her customers needed her assistance. Danny realized that she was indeed a student.

Matthew bowed his head and led the family in saying Grace before the meal. "Heavenly Father, thank you for this meal that we are about to eat."

"Amen," repeated Danny and Sarah.

"We ask the Lord's blessing for this meal," said his father.

Danny and his mother bowed their heads and said together, "Amen."

Danny looked at his father. It was unusual to hear the sight or sound of prayer at a meal in school. He had grown used to just digging into his food. After Matthew was finished, everyone devoured their chosen meal.

"Danny, it's getting harder and harder for me to run the farm," his father finally started.

Sarah chimed in. "He took a terrible fall the other day."

"You okay, Dad?"

Matthew glared at Sarah. He did not want to over-dramatize the issue or divert the discussion. "We may need you to come home," said his father.

Danny cringed inwardly. He could see that the responsibilities weighed on his father, but he was not going to be deterred. Danny stood his ground and tried to answer the question as calmly as possible. "I plan to finish school here," he said without looking up from the plate.

"If we aren't able to pay tuition, you may have no choice but to come back home," Matthew continued.

Danny's manner changed. He simmered and finally had had enough. He was tired of playing defense. His voice grew stronger, more determined. "It's important for me to get my degree. I want to be a journalist. Work for Walter Cronkite or the New York Times."

Matthew bristled at the mention of Walter Cronkite's name. "He's losing the war for the American People," Matthew stated. Danny glared at his father. Matthew pulled out a folded copy of the local hometown newspaper. He pointed to several stories about the student revolts on campus. "I've been reading about the riots on campus," Matthew continued.

"They are protests, not riots," Danny shot back.

"Bunch of violent radicals, if you ask me," said his father.

"I've had a chance to talk to some of them. They may have a point," Danny now volunteered, provocatively.

His father glared at him. He put down his utensils, disgusted. "Bunch of communist agitators," he said flatly, as if daring Danny to dispute him.

"Some of them are quite serious about social change for minorities," said Danny, unwilling to be intimidated.

An air of tension grew at the table. Matthew was not taking this. "If they were in my unit, I'd send them to the brig."

Danny snickered at the image. He barely concealed his amusement at his father's remark. "Dad, this is 1970. People don't do that anymore," said Danny firmly. Danny had hurled down the gauntlet. He was not going to be pushed around. "Maybe you should listen to some of these people. I had an incredibly good discussion with Errol Anderson.

He is a veteran who came back from the war," Danny repeated.

Matthew glared. "You weren't raised to believe that stuff!"

"I've changed. I am wondering if we should even be in Vietnam. I read that we are bombing innocent villages. We bombed this little village thinking that it was a headquarters for a Viet Cong base camp. It resulted in two hundred innocent deaths."

"Lies, damn lies. America would never do such things. We have a history of fighting against that stuff. Just ask the Nazis." Matthew pounded the table with his fists. He was not going to listen to such talk. Danny noticed that some of the diners were staring at them.

Matthew hissed, "Your brother is over there fighting for his country, or have you forgotten?"

Danny was caught off-guard, but quickly recovered. "Of course not, Dad. How could I forget?" he said defiantly. "You would never let me forget."

Sarah shifted nervously, carefully taking a bite.

"I would love to hear from him. See how he feels now that he has been over there for a while. I will bet he would have interesting things to say," Danny retorted, raising his voice a degree.

"You are not my son, not the son that I raised to love America, my country, right or wrong," Matthew barked.

"Maybe we are not as innocent as you thought," hissed Danny.

Sarah sighed. "Time to eat, not argue," she stated. She looked back and forth to both husband and son for a reaction. The two men gazed at their food. Neither was very hungry, but they were tired of fighting and wanted the meal to end as quickly as possible. They sat in silence and finished the food on their plate.

At the end of the meal, Danny eyed his dad and one more time, he reiterated, "Dad, I intend to stay in school and get my degree."

"We'll see when it comes time to pay the check for next semester," warned Matthew.

"I'll get a scholarship or get a part-time job if I have to," Danny confirmed, shocking both parents.

"Is that how you speak to your parents?" Matthew glared daggers at his son.

"Let him speak," said Sarah. Her voice was firm and decisive. It surprised even her.

Danny had said all he needed. He smacked the napkin down on the table to emphasize his point and locked eyes with Matthew, catching his father off-guard. Sarah secretly smiled, happy to see the boy stand up for himself. The rest of the dinner was wrapped in silence.

Danny sat in silence. His mind was buzzing with thoughts about how proud he was that he had finally stood up to his father. He had dreaded the visit by his parents for that very reason, but he'd stood his ground and might even have made an impression. Perhaps his father would finally accept that Danny could make up his own mind about things. Danny felt that he was growing up. He could express himself freely without being intimidated by his father.

After paying the check, they walked back to the car and piled in the car. The ride home was filled with a deafening silence. Neither father nor son spoke during the entire ride back to the campus.

When they returned to the parking lot, Sarah leaned over and kissed her son goodbye. She seemed proud of him for standing up for himself. Danny offered his father a farewell handshake, but the gesture was not returned. Danny opened the rear car door and sprinted out of the vehicle and headed back to the dorm. He'd had enough of warm-fuzzy family visits for a lifetime. He disappeared into the dorm. He mounted the stairs to his floor and sat on the couch in the lobby. He pondered his position. Several people passed him in the lobby and called out to him. Danny was lost in his thoughts and did not hear them or just was too tired to deal with anyone now. He breathed a sigh of relief as he slammed the door behind him.

He flicked on the television screen to catch up on the latest sports program and take his mind off the day's events.

New worlds had been explored in Danny's universe tonight. He felt emboldened and a new sense of his own power. Moreover, he felt a sense of relief that the ordeal with his parents was over for the moment. He had made the break into adulthood on his own power, and to his surprise was not feeling a bit overwhelmed.

30

Ryan Invites Alex Out on a Date

Later that evening, Danny was still in his room, reflecting on his parents' visit. He felt that he had been right about his shifting viewpoint. He would try to attend a meeting of Bennett's group to see if his feelings for perspectives were genuine, or just an attempt to piss off the old man!

A few minutes later, Barry popped into the room to borrow an album. Danny unloaded the details of the family discussion. Barry sat transfixed. "I'm proud of you, man. Standing your ground. You're the man, bro."

"It wasn't easy," said Danny.

"Are you going to share this story with Sergeant Rock over at the ROTC?"

"I'll tell Ryan later. I'm sure he will want to know all the gory details."

Barry offered him the thumbs-up sign. Then he reached into his pocket and pulled out a joint and offered it to Danny. Danny broke into a huge smile.

The next day, Danny ventured up to Bennett's office in the Student Center. The only occupant was Betsy, Bennett's girlfriend. She was filing papers in the cabinet when Danny entered the room. He was disappointed that Bennett was not in the office. "I just wanted to tell him that I'd like to attend one of the meetings." Betsy thanked him. She handed him a flier that broadcast a meeting schedule for the group. Danny shoved it into his pants pocket.

"I'll make sure he knows that you stopped by," she said sweetly. "And your name again was...?"

Danny smiled. "Just tell him that Danny Watkins stopped by to see him." Betsy nodded and offered him a soft drink for the road. He gulped the drink down right there in the office, then left.

As Danny descended the stairs, he spotted a stranger wearing a military uniform milling about the Student Center. Captain De Vincenzo was a ramrod straight man wearing a military uniform. He walked around the floor as if he were inspecting it. It occurred to Danny that the man seemed out of place. The officer seemed to be looking for something. Danny decided that he was a bit lost and volunteered to help him. "The ROTC office is a block away," Danny offered.

"Yes, I know where it is," offered De Vincenzo. He seemed noticeably confident of his mission and shrugged off Danny's help. Apparently, the officer did not need his help and appeared to be making mental notes about the arrangement of the floor. It was odd, but Danny decided that it was not his business, and besides, he was late for lunch with Ryan.

A few minutes later, Ryan and Danny sat down in the school cafeteria for lunch. The table was nearly deserted. Danny started to relate his encounter with the military officer, but it was clear that Ryan was not interested. It was Ryan's turn to appear glum and rant. "I bombed that quiz," Ryan noted. "I have to pass it, if I want to pass the course."

Danny consoled his friend. Ryan was normally the cheerful one helping get his friend out of the dumps. Now it was Ryan's turn to be down in the dumps. He tried to cheer up his friend, but to no avail.

He spotted a pretty girl walking past them toward the exit. He motioned over toward Ryan. Ryan spotted the girl, but quickly turned away from her.

"Didn't you date her?" Danny asked. Ryan gazed up from the table and looked at the pretty girl again as she walked in the opposite direction, then shrugged. "Jesus, who haven't you dated?" said Danny, half serious, half in jest.

"Can we change the subject?" Ryan whispered; his tone more brittle than Danny had ever heard him sound.

"Love sucks," he blurted out. Danny squinted at that remark. Had he heard correctly? Was this the same Ryan or some alien life-form? Ryan spoke softly, barely above a whisper. "I rarely date a girl more than once." Danny looked stunned. Ryan liked to brag about his love life, but the truth had never surfaced as it was doing right now. He remained quiet and let Ryan continue with his painful discussion. It was indeed a painful admission for Ryan. His expression was crestfallen. "I wanted you guys to think that I was some sort of stud, but I'm a fake."

"You didn't have to prove anything to me or anyone else," replied Danny.

Ryan repeated his story about how his mother had cheated on his father. He appreciated having people view him as this god-like creature. In truth, he had dated in high school, but they were superficial events. He felt that his mother had let him down. She formed a pattern that he saw all women fall into—flirty, but superficial.

"Girls at this college... All they are looking for is some guy to get married. I need someone serious. Have some sense of purpose. Do something with their lives," he exclaimed.

Danny was surprised. He let Ryan rant and emote his feelings without disturbing him. "Must be someone out there that will change your mind?" Danny said, sensing that he already had the answer.

"'Love 'em and leave 'em.' That's my motto." At that moment, Ryan's eyes wandered over to Alex. She sat at a nearby table immersed in her textbooks and seemed oblivious to everyone.

Danny observed Ryan's fixation on Alex. He called her over. Alex stopped by, but it was apparent that she was not interested in a lengthy conversation. She seemed lost in thought.

"Want to join us?" said Danny.

Alex stood by and did not utter a word. It was unusual for her to be so solitary.

"You're usually more conversational," said Danny.

"Got a lot on my mind," she said.

"Okay, some other time perhaps," suggested Danny. Danny shrugged and changed the subject. He searched for a way to make Alex more social. He saw in Ryan's expression how much Ryan wanted to meet her.

"Alex is the girl who did that caricature of me," said Danny, with a knowing smile. "I told you her story."

Ryan perked up. "Loved the picture. Looks like him in a weird sort of way."

Danny could sense the vibes between the two. He was determined to see if he could play match maker. "Maybe you could draw one of Ryan. He is in the ROTC. Draw a picture of him as General Patton." Danny chuckled.

Ryan laughed. He was intrigued.

"She wants to run an art gallery when she gets out of this place," Danny offered.

"My father is a patron of the arts. He supports our local theater group at home," said Ryan, impressed. A woman with ambition. That was refreshing.

Alex checked her watch. She was running late. Ryan eyed her as she walked up the stairs out of the building. "You can give her that stare-into-her-eyes routine."

Danny thought for a second. "Nah, she doesn't go for that sort of thing."

Ryan smiled. He enjoyed the idea. "I love a challenge." Ryan dashed out of the cafeteria and followed her at a distance. She entered the gleaming metal structure containing the Rutgers Art Gallery at the end of the street. It was her refuge from the pain of the world. She entered the building and headed for the painting's gallery at the rear of the building. For a few minutes, Alex stood alone in the gallery. She spotted a tranquil landscape portrait and imagined that she could escape into the lush greenery of the painting. The scenery and colors were tranquilizing and peaceful and it imparted a sense of peace in Alex's troubled psyche.

Ryan entered the room, relieved to find Alex standing alone, silently admiring the artwork. Alex heard shoes scuffing the marbled floor and whirled around.

"Sorry, didn't mean to startle you," he said almost apologetically as he approached her.

She bristled at the sight of Ryan. She was not looking for company. "What are you doing here? I thought you were hanging with Danny."

"I—just—well, I was hoping we could talk," he stuttered.

Alex saw Ryan was no longer playing all-conquering stud. She softened.

He studied her and could see that she was upset. "Are you okay?" he asked.

"Maybe some other time. I come here when I need to think," she said with a distant stare. "I'm having a hard time with one of the girls on my floor," she explained.

"I'm a good listener, try me."

"Some other time."

Ryan was not going to let this opportunity slip away. He decided on another tactic to keep the conversation going. He stared at the painting from every conceivable angle. He attempted to understand the appeal of the painting. His facial expression indicated that he was clueless.

"Very deep. I dig his brush strokes," he said with self-deprecation. He knew nothing about art.

Alex giggled at him. She could not believe that someone had used that hackneyed line. "Brush strokes?" she teased. She motioned to a nearby bench for the two to sit down.

Ryan sat across from Alex and smiled. "Actually, I'm going to a frat party on Saturday night. Pick you up at seven?"

Alex stared at Ryan. She had heard rumors of Ryan's boldness, but never felt that she would ever be put to the test. "That stuff work on other girls?" Alex smirked, genuinely amazed.

"I know a good thing when I see it," he said. "You are driven and ambitious. I like that."

No slick spin, just blunt purity from the heart. Alex took pause. His sincerity had hit its mark. She admired his honesty.

"What are you afraid of? Having a good time?" he pressed gently. She remained quiet. "Danny told me your story," Ryan said softly. "About your mom and dad and Paris. You think that makes you so unique and vulnerable that you do not need to keep an open heart?" He turned to leave.

Alex was floored by his honesty. Ryan was almost out of the door. "Okay," she said, slowly surrendering, "but don't bother picking me up. I'll meet you there."

Ryan smiled. "DKE Fraternity, Saturday at 7:30," he said with a mischievous grin.

Shortly, while Ryan was returning to the dorm, Danny read a note pinned to the door. It was from Bennett, inviting him to attend a meeting of the student protest committee. Ryan approached, bubbling over with excitement at the possibility of a date with Alex. He invited Danny to join him at the DKE party on Saturday night. Danny beamed since the gods seemed to be smiling on him for a change.

Danny was intrigued by the invitation to the party. He had promised himself that he was going to improve his social life. He pondered who to invite. His cupboard seemed a bit bare. "Maybe I can go stag, by myself. Maybe I'll meet some nice girl at the party."

"What about Tracy?" suggested Ryan.

Danny pondered the thought. Was she grateful and interested in Danny? He hesitated. "You think she might say yes, or was it just gratitude for rescuing her?"

Ryan had an easy answer. "Bro, that girl was practically off the charts with you. She was all over you the other night." Ryan patted his friend on the back by way of encouragement.

The more Danny thought about it, the better Danny liked the idea. Danny smiled. What did he have to lose? he thought to himself. 'Everything' was the response in the back of his mind.

A few minutes later, he ventured over to Tracy's dorm. He took a deep breath as he entered the girls' dorm section. He stopped by the room and knocked. He seemed a bit nervous. Maybe he had overestimated his feelings.

Tracy was wearing her thick black glasses and sporting her 'I'm studying' face. However, when she opened the door, she offered him a genuine welcoming smile. "I was hoping that you would stop by," she cooed.

Danny seemed relieved that his decision to invite her seemed to be returned. "My friend and I are attending a party on Saturday night. Would you like to join me?"

"You're asking me out on a date?" she said, teasingly.

Danny hesitated. A second later, Tracy broke into an infectious smile. She was only teasing. Her eyes lit up in delight and a big smile came to her lips. She leaned over and kissed Danny. "I'd be delighted," she purred in response. "Just tell me when."

She offered him a deep soulful kiss that indicated that her feelings for Danny were genuine. She beamed with excitement at the invitation and said that he should pick her up at seven. Danny raced out of the dorm. A huge smile lit up his face. His life was taking a turn for the better. Danny was excited. His love life was getting interesting.

31

Whales' Tales

It was a moonless Saturday night, which meant that it was the perfect party night for the student population. The campus was filled with mixers, socials and other entertainment venues for the boys and girls of Rutgers to meet each other. The college fraternities were clustered along Union Street, or 'Fraternity Row' in the heart of the campus. Every fraternity along the street housed a different fraternity. There were several different varieties of fraternities on the campus. There were the jock fraternities for the athletes, Jewish fraternities for the—well, Jewish kids, and then there were others that pledged a wider, hodge-podge variety of types.

The girls from Douglass College across town carpooled or took the bus to the Rutgers campus. Non-college girls from the local areas labeled 'Townies' swarmed onto the narrow streets of Fraternity Row. Many of the Townies were under-age high school girls looking for an 'older man' to date. They were dressed in fashionable jeans and makeup. They gathered in the parking lots across from Fraternity Row. They would make their last-minute makeup checks on themselves before plunging into the hard-fought battle of romancing a 'fraternity guy.' Tonight, any thought of studies had been banished from their minds. Some of the girls had decided to offer themselves as a prize for any good-looking young college boy. It was a hard-fought battle, as the prettier girls tended to outshine the plainer-looking girls.

Being a member of a fraternity was prestigious to many of the college boys. Some of the fraternity houses, such as DKE, were well-maintained models for Architectural Digest. Other fraternities such as Delta Sigma Phi were holding-pens for some of the worst Salvation Army-style furniture and behavior on the campus. The frats populated by the athletes were called jocks' houses. The jock fraternity of Delta Kappa Epsilon was a modern, brick, well-manicured house set on the main street. It featured a brick front and manicured lawns. It had a staid appearance, but inside, many of the parties were raunchy, wild events. Huge numbers of kegs full of beer would be consumed at these parties. Getting drunk or stoned was the order of the evening. The other order of the evening was bragging rights by getting laid by any willing female of either the Douglass or Townie variety.

The music from each house blared out into the street. The louder, the more enticing. Each house competed for getting the most women to show up. Some of the frat brothers maintained the quaint habit of standing on the front slab of the cement called 'The Wall.' Their job was to scoop up the most desirable young women and escort them inside to meet other members of the fraternity. The guys manning the walls would separate the pretty girls from the less attractive girls. They were ruthless in applying their standards of beauty.

Inside the DKE frat house, a live band played loud music till the wee hours of Saturday night. The rooms were dark and lit up with psychedelic lights or swirling colored lights. The swaying bodies of the boys and girls enjoying themselves would engulf much of the dance area. Some of the guys and girls would hang out and play wallflower until the liquor had kicked in. Then fearless, they would approach some attractive member of the opposite sex and ask for a dance. In the dark it was hard to tell what anyone looked like.

Danny and Tracy arrived early. She was wearing a pair of hip-hugger jeans and a shirt that accentuated her bosom. Danny wore his best pair of jeans and sweatshirt. He mentioned that they'd been invited by Ryan and were hustled down into the basement for some liquid refreshment. He was delighted to be seen with Tracy and clutched her hand as they descended the stairs to the basement.

They were led down the stairs into a furnished, wood-paneled basement. A frat member served as bartender, lining up rows of glasses of beer on the bar. Some of the frat members would stand at the bar and ogle the new female arrivals.

Danny and Tracy sipped a cold beer each, absorbing the surroundings. The space was lavishly furnished and covered with wooden tables and festive tablecloths. Everyone seemed to be having a good time. They listened to members of the fraternity bragging about their sexual encounters. After a few minutes, the talk revolved around issues of campus life. They proclaimed that the protesters were immature jerks who were ruining college life for everyone. In particular, the scorn centered on censuring Bennett Andrews. Danny wanted to concentrate on his date and not deal with any weighty issues on the pros and cons of the protestors. Danny saw that their glasses were empty. He excused himself to get Tracy and himself a refill. He talked for a few minutes to the bartender. Danny smiled to himself that the evening was going off without a hitch.

A few minutes later, from the back of the room emerged Storzillo, the blond-haired jock. Tracy and the blond-haired jock instantly recognized each other. Tracy grew nervous and began to tremble.

"Come to apologize to me?" said Storzillo.

"You're the last person I'd apologize to, you asshole."

Storzillo was incensed and was about to grab Tracy by the arm when Danny returned with glasses of beer. "Hey, I told you to leave her alone," threatened Danny. He grabbed Tracy by the arm and took her aside. "You don't have to be afraid of that jerk."

"I should have punched you out," shouted the jock.

Danny was about to continue arguing with the jock, but Tracy tugged on his sleeve. "Let's go," she pleaded.

"You're a jerk, you treated her like crap." responded Danny.

Tracy trembled but seemed reassured by Danny's determination for her safety.

Storzillo pursued the couple as they edged toward the bar.

Tomlinson had overheard the conversation and approached Storzillo. "Hey, this is a nice party. Leave the girl the fuck alone. She's with someone."

Storzillo was about to get aggressive, but several of the fraternity brothers joined with Tomlinson. They glared at Storzillo and he quickly left the floor and went upstairs.

"I apologize for him. He's a bit of an asshole at times," said Tomlinson.

Danny smiled and reassured the fraternity brothers that there was no problem. "I just want to enjoy the party and not get hassled by the cretin," said Danny.

"Don't worry, we'll have a talk with him tomorrow," said Tomlinson.

Tracy leaned over to Danny and planted a soulful wet kiss on his cheek. Danny seemed happy to see her in a better frame of mind.

She was now getting a little tipsy from the beer. She leaned over and whispered to Danny, "Let's go back to your room." Tracy smiled.

Danny smiled; he was not about to turn her down. They walked up the stairs holding each other's hand. They encountered Ryan standing in the doorway waiting for Alex.

"Leaving so soon?" questioned Ryan.

Danny motioned over to Tracy. "We have other plans," he said, barely concealing his desire to move on to the rest of the night's events.

Ryan gave the loving couple a wide smile. "Go get 'em, Tiger."

"I'll tame this wild beast," cooed Tracy.

Ryan indicated that he would remain to meet Alex.

Alex walked down the street by herself. She was consumed by her thoughts. She wondered if this night was going to turn out well. She felt bad that she had not been invited by her girlfriends to the DKE party and felt isolated from her fellow co-eds. However, she had decided that if she were not wanted by her fellow co-eds, she would take advantage of Ryan's offer. She stared at the long line of houses with their blaring music and swirling light shows.

She steeled herself for the night ahead. Several times she passed by the infamous fraternity 'Wall.' The boys ogled Alex and motioned for her to enter their frat party. Some of them whistled in appreciation for the vision of beauty or made crude gestures for what they hoped would be the end of their nightly ritual. Their goal was to find some desirable woman and convince her to partake in an evening of sexual adventure. Alex turned down the offers of the drunken frat boys. She was going to attend the party with Ryan. At least she knew Ryan and might enjoy his company.

She examined the Greek letters on the side of the houses. When she spotted DKE, she knew that this was the place that she wanted to visit. She turned into the sidewalk and jaunted past the drunken jocks. Some of them graciously offered to escort her inside. Alex turned them away and headed to the front door under her own power and unescorted.

One of the jocks stopped her at the door. "Were you invited?"

Alex smiled and said that she was a guest. Another frat member glared at the frat brother for being either blind or stupid. He elbowed the doorman. A stunning young woman had entered their domain. Of course, she was welcome.

Moments later, Ryan spotted her entering the building from his spot at the back of the room. He had almost given up hope that she would show up. It was not as if Ryan would not have found a nice girl to dance with or make out with before the night was over. However, Ryan was determined to have a date and maybe something else with Alex. Ryan sensed that beneath her defiant attitude was someone interesting and worthy of a relationship.

"I invited her. She's my guest, Tomlinson, your president invited me," Ryan said.

The other members shot an envious look at him. Alex was a prize catch, and she was about to be taken away by a non-frat brother. Ryan wrapped his arm around her shoulder and escorted her down the stairs. "Glad to see you. I was about to send a search party to look for you."

Alex chuckled at the absurdity of the remark. "I came to educate you about the brush strokes," she said, repeating her joke.

"Bullshit," he retorted, despite himself.

Alex laughed. "Okay, I figured you went out of your way to invite me. I thought it might be worth checking out."

"Glad you're not a snob tonight," sighed Ryan.

"I thought about your offer. I fit in like everyone else," she replied.

Downstairs, the co-eds from Alex's dorm stood by the bar, chugging a few beers. Several of the girls were talking to the fraternity brothers. Several of them were laughing and snuggling up to the frat brothers and offering a warm embrace. One of the girls motioned to her compatriots that it was time to adjourn upstairs to the dance floor.

The co-eds from the dorm were stunned to see Alex and Ryan descend the stairs. She might have been the last person that they expected to see that night. After the cruel rejection, the odds of her showing up were worth taking a bet. Alex offered them a delicious 'screw you' smile.

Ryan noticed as they descended into the bowels of the basement toward the bar area. "Good news travels fast," he whispered in her ear. She giggled in appreciation.

Several jocks motioned them to sit at their table. "We need two more. It's called Whales Tales, a drinking game. Requires you to think fast and let the other guy get piss-assed drunk."

The co-eds laughed. "Her?" said the first co-ed, gesturing at Alex. "No way," replied the other co-ed.

Determined, Alex headed for the table. She picked her seat, determined to be in full view of the gossiping co-eds. "I'm ready," she said, warming up. Ryan sat at the opposite end of the table, admiring Alex's spirit.

The co-eds were surprised. "Are you sure?" they said, flabbergasted.

The frat members poured beer in a series of glasses on the table. Alex sampled the beer and taking a practice swig, psyched herself up for the competition. "You're scared of a little competition?" she said, with a taunting expression.

The jocks, Ryan and Alex sat around the crowded table. Each seat was occupied by a player of the drinking game. The jocks were intrigued with the pretty, red-headed newcomer. Drinking large quantities of beer was a habit that the frat members had cultivated. Drinking games for bragging rights or money were common. They were certain that they could drink her under the table. She seemed too fragile or refined to be a big drinker. The game had attracted a large crowd of spectators and curiosity seekers.

Whales Tales was a drinking game in which the lead person at the table calls out the number of the person sitting around the table. It was a game of split-second timing. It could be a numbered position or the counterclockwise reverse of the number. One had to be sharp, quick reflexes and on their best game not to be caught unaware. The winners were the hard-core drinkers in the crowd. The lead frat member called out the instructions.

"Whales Tales, Roving Band of Eight calls on... reverse five."

Alex and Ryan analyzed their numbered position, like racecar drivers analyzing their positions in a race. Alex was in the fifth counterclockwise position. She missed the call.

"The pretty girl has to drink," said a jock sitting opposite Alex.

The jocks pounded the table. Alex hoisted her glass and consumed the beer in one gulp. Everyone around the table was impressed, especially Ryan. She gulped down the last of the beer and hammered the empty glass back down on the table. The jocks cheered.

The head caller looked around the room. Alex relaxed a little. She hoped that she would not be the target of another call. She had just gotten her first taste of the beer. She was beginning to feel its effects.

"Whales Tales calls on reverse five."

It was over in a flash and Alex's number was called. The jocks were going crazy. "Drink, Drink," they chanted.

Alex chugged her beer. Ryan stared in disbelief. She belched and dropped the empty glass on the table. The jocks laughed and patted the sexy newcomer on the shoulder. She had started off a stranger and was working her way into becoming a super-charged competitor.

The co-eds glared at her. They couldn't believe that straitlaced Alex was chugging beers with the best of them and appeared to be unaffected. They turned and left in a huff. Their vision of the world had crashed and burned. After a few more rounds, however, Alex appeared plastered. The frat brothers applauded her yeoman efforts and motioned for Ryan to take her away from the table. He did so gladly, now worried she might get sick and throw up.

Back at the dorm, Danny led Tracy back to his room, and showed her some of his personal photos and personal effects. They included a framed copy of several of his *Targum* articles. He discussed his relationship with the mercurial Morris. The conversation drifted over to his recent visit from the parents. She encouraged him in his determination to declare his independence from his father's demands. She looked at a copy of the *Targum* newspaper.

"The guy hates me, but I'm going to show him," said Danny.

"Don't let anyone stop you from getting what you want in life," Tracy said.

"Have no fear, I will do what it takes," whispered Danny.

Tracy embraced him and gave him a reassuring kiss. "You are a strong and determined man. I like you, Danny Watkins."

Danny pulled a bottle of wine from his desk and poured her another drink. Soon, both were beginning to feel the effects.

"Is there anything I can do?" she said with a dash of sympathy.

"No, just being with you helps me feel good." He smiled and went to the closet to find an album by Frank Sinatra. Danny put on Sinatra to spice up the romantic atmosphere. He had a renewed sense of purpose. They kissed and embraced. Tracy whispered to Danny that she was not ready to make love with him that night.

Danny was a bit disappointed, but he felt that if the relationship developed there would be plenty of time for that. "Don't sweat it," said Danny. "There will be more nights, have patience."

Tracy had imbibed a bit too much liquor and soon fell fast asleep. Danny sat in an adjacent chair watching the young woman fall into a deep sleep. Danny was in an ecstatic mood. He felt so good about the evening and how it had turned out. The night had turned out better than he hoped. He had shown his courage by standing up to the brash jock. He was pleased that Tracy had shown a passionate interest in being with Danny. He was beginning to feel invincible. The thought was premature, but for tonight at least, Danny felt that he could conquer the world.

32

Morris and the Letter

The next morning, Tracy awoke and realized that she had indeed spent the night in Danny's room. She blushed and appeared embarrassed. He reassured her that nothing had happened. Tracy was apologetic, but Danny explained that he was fine with the events of the evening. They shared a quiet breakfast in the cafeteria. After breakfast, Tracy informed Danny that she had a lot of classwork to finish. She left him with a deep tender kiss and the promise of more to come. Danny smiled and waved goodbye to his newfound love.

Later that afternoon, the office of *Targum* was almost empty. It was a slow news day and the job of assembling the newspaper had been completed for the day. The air seemed clearer without all the cigarette smoke hanging in the air. A few staff members lounged in the back of the room analyzing material for an upcoming edition. Morris stood in the corner of the office hovering over the teletype machine. A frustrated Morris had his hands cupped on the sides of the reluctant teletype machine. The temperamental hunk of metal and plastic was not working. Morris cursed and banged the sides the machine. He was not a happy camper.

"Why isn't this piece of junk working?" fumed Morris. It was a rhetorical question because he knew the answer: the gods were angry at him for some reason, and this was their revenge. He vainly attempted to coax it to work. It was important to him to try and send Rutgers news out to other sources. This would establish Rutgers as a credible source of news in the protest movement.

Morris flattered himself as being a future major player in the field of journalism. He had to make his mark by developing the *Targum* into a major college paper. If he did this, he felt certain that he would be guaranteed to get a great job offer upon graduation.

Across the room, Danny scanned his notes, pounding out a story on a proposed new wing for the library on his Smith Corona typewriter. He poured his heart and soul into the story. He was determined to write a story that Morris would approve on the first draft. His fingers raced across the keys. He barely had time to think, his fingers banged the keyboard with an intensity that rivaled a lightning strike. He smiled to himself as he typed his masterpiece. It would be the story for the ages, or at least pass muster with the imperious Morris. He walked over to Morris, who was still hanging over the teletype machine.

"If this machine dies on us, we're cut off from the news of the world," Morris moaned to no one in particular.

Danny looked on sympathetically but had no clue how to operate or fix the stubborn machine. On the table was an owner manual, but it was written in early technology: the diagrams and verbiage were incomprehensible. This meant that you had to be a genius to even decipher the contents. Danny suggested that maybe if he cursed the machine, it would respond. Morris winced; he was not amused.

"Come to Papa, you son of a bitch," said Morris, in a foul mood.

Perhaps Morris felt that if he cursed the machine long enough it would work to his specifications. Often Morris was wrong. He was not adept at ordering machines to act precisely, as he demanded of his intrepid reporters. This contradiction irritated the irascible young editor.

Morris grabbed Danny's masterpiece and read it on the spot. He scribbled red pencil marks all over the entire article. He shook his head in disapproval. The article resembled a young man with acne all over his face. Danny was stunned.

"The lead needs to be punched up. Not enough details."

Danny examined the red-scarred story and shook his head, dejected.

"Danny, maybe you're just not cut out to be a journalist," Morris stated.

Danny was devastated. "You liked the piece that I wrote about the vigil," said Danny, trying to control his rage.

Morris banged on the sides of the teletype machine. He took out his frustration on the poor machine. Finally, it sputtered to life. "I've seen a lot of you guys come and go over the years," he snickered. "You hit here and there but miss most of the time." Morris shook his head and walked back to his office.

Danny was speechless and picked up his belongings and headed out the door, a grave darkness overtaking his whole person.

By that night, Danny's mood had shifted as he decided to sit in on the ongoing small-stakes poker game. Several times the players had to remind him to play a card or put money into the pot. The other players could see that Danny's mind was not on the game.

The next morning, Danny followed his usual morning ritual. He went for breakfast at the cafeteria and then walked into the Post Office in Records Hall. Inside the back of the hall were row upon row of student mailboxes. Sometimes he received care packages of food, or a letter from some high school friend. Today, the only mail that he received were official notifications from the college about tuition or grades. Danny opened his mailbox. It was empty except for one lone letter. He snatched an official-looking letter from the mailbox. It looked too official, even a tad ominous. He was nervous about opening the envelope. He was not sure that he would like what he found inside. Would it make his day or doom it? He ripped open the envelope. His heart sank as he scrutinized the contents of the letter: *Dear Student: Regarding your scholarship, we need to confirm your continuing status at the college newspaper. We need to have an answer in the next week to maintain it.* Danny's heart sank. He knew that he would have to get past Morris, the Gatekeeper from Hell, if he wanted to keep the scholarship.

Danny climbed the steps in the back of the Student Center and once again entered the newsroom. Morris sat at his desk, overseeing the morning preparation of the paper. A big 24-inch Zenith television mounted on the wall broadcast the morning programs. He sat staring at the television set. He watched it, ignoring Danny's approach. On the television was a picture of Dick Cavett, the handsome, blond-haired, legendary talk show host. He was interviewing Abbie Hoffman, who sat across the table.

Hoffman was a twenty-something, frizzy-haired protest leader of the national Student Movement. He had risen in the ranks of the student protest movement and been arrested after a wild melee with police in Lincoln Park in Chicago. In 1968, the Democrats had nominated Hubert Humphrey after the assassination of Bobby Kennedy. Humphrey was an old-fashioned liberal who supported the Vietnam War. The protesters took to the streets of Chicago to protest the Vietnam war and the nomination of Hubert Humphrey as the Democratic nominee for president that year. Humphrey had his liberal credentials but was too conservative for the radicals. They had pinned their hopes on Eugene McCarthy as the nominee. McCarthy had been a popular choice by the young people on the college campus and many college-age students had gone out to campaign for him. McCarthy had not been a popular choice and was soon out of the running for the position as nominee.

After being gassed and jailed, Hoffman had been placed on trial as part of the Chicago Seven. The Chicago Seven were the leaders of the different protest groups in Chicago. Some considered it a political show trial because of the way the cranky Judge Julius Hoffman handled the case. Some considered that Abbie Hoffman and company had been arrested to demonstrate how Nixon handled law and order issues. Either way, Hoffman and his co-defendants received tons of free publicity and notoriety.

Danny stood watching the interview with Morris. "Rumor has it that you're going on a tour of college campuses," Cavett said to Hoffman,

195

who smiled back at his host. Cavett was the intellectual counterpart to Johnny Carson, the genial host of *The Tonight Show*. He was also considered the king of late-night television and the master of the one-liner. His approach was to entertain the late-night audience whereas Cavett had the reputation of booking serious intellectual or political leaders of the day for news and commentary.

"I'm the voice of my generation," Hoffman intoned, without a mild hint of humility.

"Don't be modest, tell us how you really feel," remarked Cavett in a perfectly timed response.

"I have a lot to say. I cannot be silenced. Remember that Dick," said the jaunty Hoffman. He appreciated his egotism and now reveled in the comment. The audience offered a thunderous round of applause. Abbie Hoffman got off his seat and bowed.

"You can't be silenced? Good, that means you'll stay for another segment," rejoined Cavett.

Danny stared up at the screen at Hoffman. "Maybe he would come to Rutgers and make a speech," Danny speculated.

Morris watched the interview and shook his head, a bit of envy in his expression. "Abbie Hoffman at Rutgers? Are you on drugs, Watkins? That would be a great story. Never happen."

Danny shrugged and followed Morris as he walked over to the dartboard mounted on the rear wall of the office and tossed a few darts at a picture of Dick Nixon. "Take that Tricky Dick!" Morris hit the target dead center.

Danny thought for a second. He glanced back at the image of Cavett and Hoffman. He had an inspiration, a wild implausible thought. He looked at Morris. "If I could get him here? Would it be my story?"

"If you got who?" said Morris, his eyes narrowing, his face contorted into a nasty smirk.

"Abbie Hoffman, of course," said Danny, with a hopeful expression.

Morris attempted to restrain himself. The thought of this lowly reporter getting the interview of the year was absurd. Danny had thought that Morris might laugh at the suggestion at the very worst. Instead, his amusement turned to a rant.

"Are you fuckin' kidding me? You think that you can come into my space and spin this crazy story, and that I'll smile and agree to this absurdity, this delusionary world where you exist." He threw another dart. It hit the bullseye. "When did life become a fantasy? My girlfriend tells me to stop spending so much time here. And by the way, why the fuck are you here? What do you want to gripe about now? Make it good!"

Danny drummed up his courage. He grabbed the letter from his pocket and placed the official letter in front of Morris.

"What do you need now?" said Morris.

"I know we haven't seen eye-to-eye on things, and I'll do anything to prove my worth, but I just got this from the registrar." He began to read the contents of the letter to Morris.

"*Dear Student: We need to have your status on the school news-paper confirmed by the editor for you to continue receiving your scholarship. To keep your scholarship, you must get it signed by the editor of the paper,*" said Danny.

Morris hesitated to look at it, but finally examined it.

"They want you to sign it for me." Danny was on the verge of tears. "Writing is my life. I know that I have a lot to learn, but I'm committed, and I need this scholarship," Danny pleaded.

"I thought you wanted to work here for the glory." Morris smirked.

"Glory doesn't pay my tuition. Other kids get help with a ride from their parents; mine do help, but without the scholarship I am sunk. My college career is over. Please sign it for me," Danny begged. It was unlike Danny to beg someone for help, but he had to make his case. His future was on the line.

Morris frowned, and put the letter on the nearby desk, seemingly unmoved. "I need serious news people working for me. Let me think about it."

"I am serious. I did the cafeteria story, the lack of parking spaces for the faculty story and the vigil story that you seemed to like."

Morris remained stone-faced, then motioned for Danny to follow him over to the editor's desk. He reached into the wire basket marked 'Assignments' and handed Danny an assignment sheet. "Fine, here's a serious assignment for you. I am short-staffed. I need you to cover the meeting of the faculty council. Which, by the way, starts in an hour. If it is truly well done, I'll sign your goddamn letter."

"Doesn't give me much time to prepare," moaned Danny.

"You want it or not?" said Morris.

Danny changed his attitude to one of gratitude. "You won't regret it," said an enthusiastic Danny.

Morris scowled; his face appeared to be a stone-cold warning. Danny grabbed an assignment pad and raced out of the room. Getting the assignment, he did not question his fortune. However, at the back of his mind he was plagued with doubt. Would he find a way to screw up the assignment? He was determined to do the story right, but fate had a funny way of twisting even the best of intentions.

33

Board of Directors

anny sprinted across the manicured green lawns and headed toward the administration building. It sat at the center of the complex and was impossible to miss. It was an opulent brick structure with regal columns, huge bay windows and marble statues of the college founders in the front.

Danny raced up the stairs to the office of the Board of Governors. They were the real power brokers of the University. Many of the board members were also high-powered business executives, who were the true power behind the throne. They dictated policy and had the final say in how the University was governed.

The Board of Directors met in the plush Conference Center at the top of the building. It was lavishly furnished with a glass chandelier, billowing white curtains and a solid oak wood conference table planted in the center of the room. Danny thought of the Palace of Versailles in France when he looked at this ornate conference room.

Embarrassed to enter the room as the meeting had already started, Danny murmured his humble apologies and grabbed a seat in the visitors' gallery section. He wore his ID prominently pinned to his lapel. This indicated he was the representative of the college paper. He slid into an empty seat.

The Board Members gazed up at the insolent newcomer for daring to intrude on their sacred deliberations. Mansbach sat at the head of the table. He glanced up at Danny. "And you are?" questioned the imperious Mansbach.

Danny stood there for a second. He found his voice. "*Daily Targum.*" He gulped and nearly swallowed his tongue to get the words out of his mouth.

"Nice of *Targum* to show up," recounted Dean Mansbach frostily. "You're late," he barked with no remorse. "Very well, let us proceed."

Senior faculty members sat around the table, full of a palpable sense of importance. Each one wanted to be recognized for their contributions in running the college.

The Board resumed their deliberation. Danny attempted to follow every word. Mr. Flynn began an intricate speech about maintaining costs. Mansbach and the other directors took notes or just attempted to follow the discussion. Finally, after finishing his presentation, he turned to face the members of the committee. "I'm sure that the Dean would agree?" Flynn concluded.

"We are agreed that we will back the motion for more spending on the new complex with some of the Endowment funds," agreed Mansbach.

Mr. Zalenskie, the next director to speak, stood in front of a complex flip chart. The chart was filled with arcane numbers and colorful graphs. He flipped over to the next page depicting a detailed sketch of a new building. "So, it is agreed that we support Bill 340-A for the new construction." The directors argued for a few minutes about the cost of the projects. Each of the members of the panel took turns offering their learned opinions about the value of the project.

Danny scribbled notes on his notepad as fast as his fingers could move. However, he struggled to follow the details of what they were discussing.

Williams, another governor, stood up and moved to the lectern. He popped open a leatherbound folder. "We oppose using the money as long as the faculty needs money for other projects. The new students will not use the building," said Williams in a determined tone.

Danny's gaze shifted between the complex, colorful charts and the impressive men. They were impressive in terms of their demeanor and eloquence. He scribbled the notes, but was soon mesmerized by the proceedings to the point of boredom. He found the material complicated and dry. He yawned.

Mansbach glared at him with a cold, merciless expression. "Are we keeping *Targum* up?" said the Dean with little amusement.

Danny mumbled an apology and put his head down as he continued scribbling notes. For the rest of the meeting, he felt the eyes of the directors burrowing into him. When the meeting was over, Danny scooped up his notepad and exited the room. He regarded his notepad. The notes were a jumble. He decided that he would sort them out when he got to the office. He had not enjoyed the meeting. It seemed to drag on forever.

He walked to the Student Center building and sprinted up the stairs to the newspaper. He entered the room and spotted one of the editors sitting at his desk. He eyed Danny as he entered but refused to make eye contact. He knew what was coming and did not want to be in Zeus's line of fire when he hurled his lightning and thunderbolts.

"Is that Danny? Tell him to get his ass in here!" It was the word of God, or close. Morris roared. He erupted from his office. He wagged his finger at Danny for him to enter his office. Danny suspected that the meeting would not be pleasant for some event that had transpired at the board meeting. He was expecting to be blasted with both smoking barrels. When he entered, Morris slammed the door behind him.

"I just got a phone call. It wasn't good," thundered Morris with a totally if-looks-could-kill expression on his face. Morris's mouth twisted into a demonic grimace.

He demanded Danny's notepad and scoured the notes with a look of acrid distaste. They were gibberish. "Where is the stuff about the Dean's decision on the Endowment fund?" said Morris.

Danny sputtered. He had no glib, easy answer.

Morris pounced on the reporter's vulnerabilities. "Where are your notes on the building fund?" Morris hissed. "There are no direct quotes or the names of the different Regents!" Morris raged.

Danny scratched his head, then turned pale as the words sunk in.

"What makes this worse is the fact that the faculty members said that you seemed bored. You're supposed to be representing the paper." Morris was just getting started. Danny knew that his ticket had been punched. Morris's voice grew more unpleasant by the second.

Danny grew defensive and tried to think of a logical excuse. "'I did them in a hurry," he said.

Morris continued to shake with anger. He shook his head at the pages of gibberish, ripped them into shreds and tossed them into the nearby garbage can. "Danny, I gave you an important assignment."

Danny bowed his head. He felt sick. It was getting worse.

Morris stared at him with a cold expression full of disdain. Not an ounce of remorse. It was his job to punish Danny for his misdeeds. "You represent us, the paper," thundered Morris.

"I understand," said Danny, his voice full of doubt.

"Do you? Do you really understand?" Morris paced around the floor and ranted. "You know we depend on them for our funding."

Danny felt his facade crumble. "I'll call and explain that I was completely engaged, just short of sleep, nothing more." Danny hoped to mollify Morris and deflect any errors that he committed. Danny had missed the boat.

Morris was not in a conciliatory mood. He rose out of his seat, face beet-red. "There isn't going to be a next time," he bellowed at the young defenseless reporter.

Danny was riveted to his spot. The words echoed through Danny's brain. All he could hear was 'there will be no next time.'

"We'll print an apology. Don't bother to sign out."

Horrified and embarrassed, Danny quickly exited the building. His world had just collapsed. He had visions of packing up his belongings, taking the bus back to his hometown and having to confront his parents' disappointment. Things could not get any worse.

34

Danny's Doom and Gloom

The next morning, Danny stood in front of the counter at the financial aid office. He presented his scholarship letter to the female clerk at the counter. "Is there some sort of mistake?" he asked.

The female clerk examined the letter and shook her head. "No mistake," she said.

"Could I have a supervisor give a second opinion?"

"It was signed by the manager, no mistake. It says that the scholarship will be cancelled at the beginning of the month if it is not signed," said the clerk.

"It's my lifeline. I need this. Can one of the professors or someone else sign this apart from Morris?" he said, with his voice almost declining into pity. Danny wanted to shout at her but realized that she was only doing her job, as she sympathetically shook her head. He took a deep breath and grabbed the letter. Dejected, he walked away from the counter.

Later, Danny headed back to the dorm and dialed his home. He wanted to discuss his disastrous situation with his family. However, he was reluctant to have the discussion.

Luckily for Danny, his mother Sarah picked up the phone. "Hey, Mom," Danny started.

There was a pause on the other end of the phone. Sarah paused; she was delighted to hear from her son. "What a surprise to hear from you," she said.

Silence on the other end. Danny stared at the floor, unable to speak. "Is everything all right?" said his mother.

"Can I speak to Dad?" he said slowly. Danny's voice shook.

Sarah paused, concerned. "Do you want to tell me about it?' she said, concern in her voice. "He's talking to a customer. I'll get him," she said.

Danny waited, his heart pounding. He really did not want to have this conversation.

"I'll get him, wait a minute, hold on."

Danny's heart pounded and raced as the seconds passed. He hung up the phone before his father could answer.

Later that night, a downcast Danny trudged into the crowded bar full of students. They seemed to be without a care in the world. He just wanted to crawl into some dark corner and drink himself to death. Dejected, Danny sat down alone at a table in the rear of the bar, even seeing Ryan across the room playing darts.

He spotted Danny sulking at the table and made his way over. "You look like the world just collapsed."

"I screwed up a story and Morris fired me. Other than that, everything's wonderful," moaned Danny. Danny offered the most dejected expression painted on his face. The world could have collapsed, and it would not have made a dime's worth of difference to him.

"That good, huh?" said Ryan, evaluating his friend. "Want to talk about it?" he continued. Danny stared at the wall, saying nothing. Ryan patted him on the shoulder. "Nothing like a tall frosty to get you going." He tried to sound cheerful but sensed his friend's bottomless depression.

A few minutes later, Ryan returned carrying a pitcher of cold, golden Budweiser beer. He filled Danny's glass and Danny chugged the cold brew in one shot. Fixing his eyes on the table, he spoke softly with his voice muffled. "I'm so embarrassed. Maybe Morris was right," Danny moaned.

A few seconds later, Danny chugged a second glass of beer in one shot and then downed another just as fast.

As he went for more, Ryan placed his hand over the pitcher and offered him an uncompromising stare. "Haven't you had enough?"

Danny belched, acknowledging Ryan's searing indictment. "Let me drown my sorrows," he lamented.

Ryan slid the glass away from his friend. "You're going to let him beat you down?" asked Ryan.

"Damn straight," said Danny. "It's over, I screwed up big time."

Another student passed by the table and stared at Danny.

Ryan frowned and waved him off. "Hey, motherfucker, this is a private conversation."

The other student beat a hasty retreat to his seat.

"Speak to the Dean," Ryan said in his most authoritative voice.

Danny stared at Ryan as if to say, 'easy for you to say.' He grabbed the pitcher from Ryan's grasp and poured himself another glass.

"Danny, I'm serious," Ryan stated.

"Are you serious or delirious?" said Danny defensively, then chugged his glass.

Danny was about to pour another when Ryan yanked it out of his hands. He stared at his friend for a few seconds, then dragged the drunken Danny off his chair and escorted him out of the bar. Ryan escorted his friend back to his dorm room. "You'll feel better in the morning."

Danny said nothing. He was now very drunk. When they finally reached Danny's room, Danny opened the door and flopped down onto his bed.

"Hope you feel better in the morning," Ryan concluded. He shut the door and walked down the hall.

The next morning, the two friends met for breakfast. Danny seemed to be in a better mood. He suggested that they check their mailboxes. The pair finished breakfast and walked over to Records Hall. Danny opened his mailbox and found an official-looking envelope jammed into it. He opened the letter and blanched at the contents. "It didn't take them long, those greedy fuckers!" wailed Danny.

He handed the letter over to Ryan to read. Ryan read it twice. "This must be a mistake," Ryan agreed.

"They can't just cut off a student's scholarship, like flipping a switch overnight without a warning. Can they?" Danny whined.

Danny was ashen. The two walked back to Danny's room. He lay on the bed for a few minutes, immobilized, as Ryan sat by his desk wanting to figure out how to help his friend.

"What am I going to tell my folks?" Danny moaned. "They want me home, but not this way." Danny pondered his future; it did not seem promising. He sat at the edge of the bed with his hands covering his face.

Ryan had never seen his friend so depressed. Ryan knew that it was pointless, Danny was inconsolable. He lay down again and soon fell fast asleep. The bottom had just fallen off his world. At that moment, it seemed unlikely that he would find the strength to get up again. Helpless to fix anything, Ryan let himself out, planning to check on Danny within the hour.

35

Danny and the Dean

The next morning, a hungover, miserable Danny wandered into Dean Mansbach's outer office looking like a condemned man facing death row. The cheerful, well-furnished office with its brand-new paint job and the latest editions of magazines on the coffee table only served to intimidate him and depress him even more.

Danny snatched up a copy of the latest *Sports Illustrated* magazine from the nearby coffee table, then approached the secretary's desk, glancing up at the clock. It read 11:30 a.m. De Vincenzo, the ram-rod-straight military officer he had seen days earlier at the Student Center, stood at the secretary's desk. He was collecting his mail from her before heading into his office. He eyed Danny with suspicion before heading into the office.

Danny approached the secretary. "My name is Danny Watkins and I have an appointment with the Dean," Danny said, his voice choking with anxiety.

The secretary glanced down at her appointment book, nodded, and motioned for him to sit down and wait for his appointment. He steeled himself as he prepared to enter the lion's den.

A few minutes later, De Vincenzo walked out of the Dean's office. He strode over to the secretary. He announced in his booming voice that the meeting with the Dean had gone well. He had granted him an appointment to meet with the commander of the ROTC unit. He exited, carrying some papers propped under his arm.

The secretary glanced over at Danny. "The Dean has a full schedule. Perhaps you can come back tomorrow?" she said.

Danny was totally intimidated by the surroundings. He jumped out of the chair and turned to leave. Perhaps this was not such a good idea, he thought to himself. His mind was a minefield of potential excuses. However, at the last moment, he spun around and indicated his need to stay. "I'll be fine," he croaked. The secretary smiled politely, and then sat down at her desk and returned to work. After finishing every magazine on the table, Danny looked up at the clock. Three hours had passed.

The phone buzzed and she picked it up and listened to the Dean. After a few seconds, the secretary got off the phone. "The Dean will see you now. He only has a few minutes."

Danny appeared tired, but relieved. He felt his ordeal was almost over, and then stared at the intimidating entrance to the Dean's office. Was it the gate to Hell?

The secretary smiled at Danny. "He's really a nice man... once you get to know him."

Oh sure, and grizzlies do not bite, he thought to himself. Danny inhaled a few deep breaths and slipped into the Dean's office.

Dean Mansbach peered up from his work. He had a huge stack of folders sitting on his desk. The desk was meticulous in its arrangement. He eyed Danny with that steely, penetrating look that wilted even the strongest faculty member. "You are...?" He fixed Danny with a frosty glare.

"Danny Watkins, sophomore." Danny's voice grew dry and raspy as he faced the imperious Mansbach. He felt like the orphan in the movie, *Oliver*, in which the hungry orphan begs the master for more food.

"Well, Danny Watkins, sophomore. What is it that you want?" thundered the impatient Dean.

"I was the reporter from the *Targum* the night of the faculty meeting. It was my fault that the story proved under par, and I'd like to personally apologize."

Mansbach stared up at him for a moment. He dealt with many people during the busy workday. He nodded his head as he recognized the hapless Danny. "Yes, now I remember. The reporter who came in late and then yawned openly."

"Guilty," choked Danny, his voice reduced to a whisper. Blood drained from his face. Mansbach glared down at Danny. "I have no excuse... I'm working at the paper... doing my studies and..."

Mansbach cut him off with a withering expression. "College is as close to the real world as you're going to get for a while. People make mistakes. They must pay the consequences. Good day."

Danny realized that their status was worlds apart. "I've already paid for my mistake, sir. I was fired from the paper, which is fine. I deserved it, but the issue is my scholarship."

Mansbach waved his hand, dismissing Danny.

"But, sir," Danny whined. "I'm an excellent student and student advisor—I just need someone other than Morris to sign off on my behalf."

"Good day, Mr. Watkins," he said, with an act of finality. The Dean resumed his work. His gaze fixed upon his pile of folders.

Danny struggled to think of a retort, but his mind went blank. Defeated, Danny slinked out of the room.

A few minutes later, Danny trudged back to the dorm and slammed the oak door to his room. "Goddamn, goddamn it!" Danny bellowed.

The slamming sound reverberated throughout the dorm section like a rockslide. Several students peeked their heads out of the door to discover the cause of the disturbance. In his room, Danny bent over the bed and packed his belongings into a cloth backpack. Danny stared blankly at the walls. He pulled a trunk from out of his closet and pulled his prized newspaper plaques from the wall and slowly packed them into the bottom of the trunk. He had held out a faint hope that the Dean would be understanding and listen to his story. He had been swallowed up by the fiercest beast of prey on campus. Danny had entered the beast's lair and had become the next meal. Danny collapsed on his bed and lay immobile for the next hour. He was a vision of total defeat.

36

Military Recruiter

That night at dinner, Danny related his unsuccessful experience with Dean Mansbach to Ryan. Danny was glum and certain that he might have to leave school. Ryan did his best to cheer him up, but the cold hard truth was that it was a difficult problem to solve. He offered him a pep talk and told him that leaving the paper was not the end of the world. Danny listened and smiled. "I knew that I could count on you to cheer me up," Danny uttered with a smile.

"You haven't told your parents about this have you?" Ryan questioned.

"Are you shitting me?" Danny replied in a low tone of voice. "My father will disown me, even if he gets exactly what he wants," said Danny.

"Forget your old man, I'll disown you, you dumb bastard," said Ryan. "Besides, I need you to help me with the music," said Ryan. "Who else can I get to sing backup vocals for me?" quipped Ryan. "There's got to be another way around this!" Ryan insisted.

The next morning, Lieutenant De Vincenzo, wearing starched green fatigues topped off with a green military cap, emerged from his battered purple Ford Mustang in the ROTC parking lot. His chest sported several gold medals pinned on his chest. He was not above flaunting his medals for everyone to see and strode like a proud peacock into the ROTC building. He walked with the aura of a man on a mission. He was someone willing to take any possible negative reception in stride. He carried a bulging black briefcase as he mounted the steps into the building. He saluted the young cadet on duty occupying the front desk. He smiled with his piercing, no-nonsense expression. "I'm here to see Colonel O'Neill," he said firmly.

The cadet saluted back and escorted the military recruiter to the office of the commanding officer. O'Neill sat at his desk immersed in paperwork. He looked up from the stack of files to see the military recruiter stride into the office as if he owned the place. He rose from his desk and grasped his hand in welcome. He motioned for De Vincenzo to sit down in the chair adjacent to O Neill's desk. "Glad to see you're on time," said the Colonel.

"My duty is to be on time," said De Vincenzo without missing a beat.

"You've come at a difficult period for us here at Rutgers," said a sorrowful Colonel O'Neill.

De Vincenzo noticed the vast book collection. He walked up to inspect the collection. He admired the photos and maps mounted on the wall. Several of them included General Patton and Eisenhower from World War Two and Westmoreland from the current struggle in Vietnam. He inspected a copy of a book on guerilla warfare by Mao-Tse Tung, the aging dictator of Communist China. "I see you're an admirer of Mao," he said in a huff. He was clearly not an admirer.

"Important to know your enemy," quipped O'Neill without skipping a beat.

De Vincenzo sensed that he had to switch to more pressing issues. He gazed at the colonel. "You'll set up a desk for me in the Student Center as we planned?"

The Colonel cleared his throat. He pulled a yellowed telegram from his desk. "You're certain that you're up for this?" quizzed the Colonel.

De Vincenzo was aware of the numerous anti-war protests on college campuses. It saddened him to see such a fever-pitch of anti-military fervor in recent years. He recalled the pride he had taken in joining the ROTC when he was a young student at college.

"You're going to be very unpopular on campus," O'Neill warned. "Might get ugly."

"I am expecting a rough reception. I eat hurricanes for lunch." He did not blink an eye. "Business as usual," he added. He slapped his worn black leather briefcase on the desk and pulled out numerous potential recruiting brochures. "I've handled tougher assignments." He held up a hand, missing two fingers. "I led our troops in the Central Highlands and was in Saigon during the Tet Offensive." O'Neill shook his head. "Can't be any worse than facing down the Viet Cong," said De Vincenzo.

Within the next few hours, De Vincenzo had set up a table in a booth near the auditorium. On the first day no one approached him and he sat reading the newspaper. He received many hostile stares from the passing students. One of the long-haired students snickered and uttered his knowledgeably bland comment, "Dig it, not for me, man."

Another student grabbed the recruitment brochure, then tossed it into the trash with a swift contemptuous motion. Another student spat on the brochure but again, the military recruiter stood firm under enemy fire.

Word quickly spread across campus to Bennett and his group. Danny, among them, had been at an earlier meeting and enjoyed sitting in as an observer, but had started participating as well.

"Everyone in agreement about the military guy sitting in the Student Center?" said Bennett.

"I think the recruiter crossed the line," said Danny.

Danny was not fully committed to being part of the radical group. He still disapproved of some of the principles of the group, but his sympathies were moving in that direction. He would read articles given to him by Barry and analyze them. The two men would vigorously discuss them and still found much to disagree about. He even pointed out sections of the book that Errol gave him. Barry was intrigued at Danny's gradual transformation. However, Danny kept politics a demilitarized zone with Ryan. He had made a tentative truce with Ryan over the politics and was determined not to let political issues undermine their friendship. They were only deadly rivals at darts and pinball machines.

"They are trying to provoke us." said one of the members. A murmur of agreement rose from the crowd.

"So, what should we do?" Bennett asked, as if he had not already made up his mind.

"Protest, march, show the administration that we will not stand for this," shouted Klonsky.

"Maybe that's what they want us to do? Let us wait and see how things shake out," said Danny.

"Let's close down the fucking Student Center," roared Klonsky.

Danny's voice of caution was drowned out by the desire to take some sort of action. Klonsky's comment met with an instant roar of approval from the group. They discussed how to carry signs and march in protest.

At the end of the meeting, Bennett approached Danny and shook his hand. "Welcome to the movement." Bennett smiled.

Danny smiled in return. "I just wish I were still working for the paper; this would be a great story."

"Danny, this meeting cannot go beyond these walls. You understand, don't you?" warned Bennett.

Danny nodded. His enthusiasm had gotten the better of him.

The next day, several protesters including Barry stood in front of the Student Center. They waved angry wooden placards loaded with anti-war messages. Other volunteers posted fliers at different places around the campus and passed them out. Some of the students were curious and examined the fliers; others were too busy to even look. Danny passed by the crowd. Barry handed him a flyer. Danny thanked him and told him that he had a class but would be back in an hour to check on the progress of the group. "I'll be here in spirit," uttered Danny. "Got to run."

Later that afternoon, Barry and another volunteer stood in front of the student center passing out fliers to students. Barry was not a fan of standing on his feet for any length of time. He felt like a used car salesman trying to sell a product. He felt better when a student would examine a flier and offer a positive response. It tore him up to see students read the flier and toss it into the garbage.

"Any hot chicks at the meeting?" a student passing by asked with a smirk on his face as he took a flyer.

Barry restrained himself from laughing, turned his back and addressed another student.

"Check it out. It will raise your consciousness." Barry promoted his cause with his most enthusiastic salesmanship. "Hey, we need you to attend, prove to the Dean that we are serious."

The fliers dwindled quickly as they passed out fliers to the final number of copies.

"Come to the demonstration, it will change your life," proclaimed Barry.

"Heard some of the kids from the jock houses want to kick your ass," chuckled one of the young students. This annoyed Barry. He did not want to waste his time arguing with students. He stood in the middle of the sidewalk so that others moving past him would be compelled to take a flier.

Across the courtyard was the ROTC building. Inside the building, several cadets watched the volunteers. Most of the cadets were satisfied to ignore the protesters. It had become such a daily event that many cadets felt it not worth their time to respond. Other cadets with buzz-cut hair and powder-blue uniforms stared at the protesters with malice on their faces.

"You see that bunch of punks," said one of the more acerbic cadets to his fellow cadets. "Let's shut them down." Several of the other cadets acknowledged their disdain and rushed out of the building to confront the young protesters. The cadets walked directly toward Barry and another volunteer. Their mood was clearly confrontational. The main cadet assumed that Barry's thin physique made him a pushover. He felt that he could easily intimidate Barry.

"You one of those fucking Communists?" he said, in a voice dripping with contempt.

Barry attempted to ignore the hostile cadet. "You're interfering with my handing out the fliers," said an irritated Barry.

The other cadet's mincing voice mocked Barry. "You're interfering in my handing out fliers." The other cadets snickered.

Barry was undeterred and turned away from the cadet. The cadet attempted to stare down Barry. He was puzzled by the fact that Barry was not easily intimidated. The cadet seemed determined to start some sort of confrontation. Finally, the two men were practically in each other's face. "Are you deaf? Can you hear me?"

"I can hear you perfectly, dipshit," said Barry.

"My brother's fighting over in Vietnam," said the cadet. "If we do not fight them in Vietnam, they will be in California in a few years. We must stop them. He's a hero, defending his country for dumb punks like you."

"My condolences," said Barry, without taking a breath. Barry shrugged and continued to pass out fliers to willing students.

"You're not listening to me, punk," uttered the belligerent cadet.

"I don't pay attention to assholes," retorted a belligerent Barry.

The cadet knocked the fliers out of Barry's hands. The fliers tumbled to the ground and Barry stooped to pick them up, then rose and shoved the cadet.

"What did you say, you wish he were dead?" the cadet roared.

"Fuck you!" Barry countered.

"My father says that you guys are a bunch of Commies," said the cadet in defiance.

"Tell your father he's a goddamn warmonger," retorted Barry.

Danny emerged from the nearby building and witnessed the confrontation. He rushed to the aid of his friend. "Hey man, leave him alone," he said to the cadet. "He's one of my students in my dorm."

The cadet sneered and remained undeterred by Danny's presence. The cadet shoved Danny to the ground. Danny rose from the ground and prepared to fight the belligerent cadet. Danny placed his hand on Barry's shoulders. He motioned to Barry. "Let's get out of here. It's not worth the trouble."

"No way in hell." Barry was firm. He was not going to leave his position.

The cadet's face grew flushed. He also had no intention of backing down. "Why don't you go back to Russia? Steal all the money from the peasants," he said defiantly. Barry and the cadet faced off and appeared ready to exchange death-defying blows.

Inside the ROTC building, Ryan was observing the brewing confrontation. He saw that his cadet was about to continue to escalate an already volatile situation and didn't like seeing Danny involved either. Angry crowds had begun to gather. He dropped his work and raced out of the building toward the combatants. He rushed over to Danny and asked if he was okay. Danny was grateful for the help but reassured him that he was fine. Ryan was incensed. Ryan didn't like Barry, but he felt the situation was escalating out of control.

"At ease, Cadet," said Ryan, approaching the two cadets

"He's a fucking Commie," said the other cadet, his face flushed in anger.

Ryan shouted at his fellow cadet. "I said stand down," he bellowed in a no-nonsense voice.

The other cadet swung at Barry but missed. Ryan stepped between the two men and took the punch. The air was temporarily knocked out of Ryan. The other cadet was mortified and reached down toward Ryan. "Are you okay, sir?"

Ryan got off the ground and dusted himself off. "Drop it, leave them alone," said Ryan with a stern demeanor.

The other cadet took a step back. He respected Ryan and listened to him.

"Get back to the ROTC building, immediately!"

The other cadets saluted and obeyed the order. Barry stood on the sidelines catching his breath, thankful the situation had resolved itself. Barry dusted himself off and mumbled an apology to Ryan for his help. "Thanks for the help. I'll buy you a beer the next time we go to the bar," muttered a grateful Barry.

"No big deal, just another day at the office." Ryan accepted their thanks and then headed back into the building to continue his work.

"Let's go to the cafeteria and calm down over their wonderful imitation beef." Barry smiled and followed Danny across the street. "Perfect end to a perfect day," said Barry.

Later that afternoon, after hearing about the confrontation, Mansbach discussed the matter with O'Neill. He fumed that this incident had nearly set off more unrest on his beloved campus. He offered O'Neill his total confidence and decided that the protesters were not going to run the ROTC off the campus. Neither side was happy about the confrontation. The incident was a match to an already incendiary situation. He needed to stop the brewing war on campus. It launched bad feelings on both sides and would soon escalate to a more combative stage.

37

The Dean and the Sound Truck

That morning, Danny and Ryan finished an early breakfast. They discussed yesterday's confrontation between the ROTC and protesters. "I know that it was Barry's fliers that started the confrontation, but I had a long talk with the cadet," said Ryan. "I told him to apologize to you."

Danny appeared skeptical. "He's never going to do it; you know it and I know it. What about apologizing to Barry?" questioned Danny.

Ryan remained silent for a moment. "Barry is a jerk. I hate his politics, but I don't want people beating each other up over politics. I don't care for his attempting to run us off campus, but violence is not cool."

"So, I guess the answer is—what's the expression? 'When hell freezes over.'" Danny laughed.

"I just hate that one of my guys acted like an asshole," said Ryan.

"Pretty uncalled for. Both sides must keep their cool when it comes to politics," said Danny.

They dropped the empty trays in the depository. Danny changed the subject. "I heard a rumor that Professor Curtis was having a guest speaker," said Danny.

"Got to be better than listening to Curtis attempt to be hip and be cool with the students," said Ryan. "That will be good, his class can get boring when he launches into one of his boring lectures about US imperialism," said Ryan.

"I like Professor Curtis, but he does try too hard at times," replied Danny.

"Do we know who?" replied Ryan. Both men headed toward the academic building.

Minutes later, Danny and Ryan entered Professor Curtis's crowded lecture hall. Danny was surprised to see Errol standing by the lectern wearing his army jacket. Danny waved to Errol, but Errol was studying his notes and did not see Danny. Curtis walked up to the lectern and explained that he had asked Errol Anderson to make a short presentation. "He came here to explain his opposition to the war," said Curtis.

Ryan rolled his eyes, but Danny shot him a look of displeasure.

Errol stepped up to the podium. He carried his notes but put them down. He would speak based on his own feelings and memories. "As many of you know, I served my country during the current Vietnam War. I was wounded but came home in one piece. For that I am grateful. I just want to give you my perspective on the war. You don't have to agree with me, but I'm putting my thoughts out there," he said in a somber manner.

"I was a young kid from Camden, New Jersey. I was gung-ho to join the Army and serve my country. I felt that way until we landed in Da Nang, one of the major ports in South Vietnam. I remember one day we were ordered to enter the village of Quang Dong. When we entered, there was a sniper hiding in a rice paddy, who fired at us. No one was hit, but the sergeant got pissed off and ordered several of the men to find the sniper, but he had vanished into the nearby jungle. The squad was angry and began to torch some of the huts," said Errol.

Ryan raised his hand to object. "'Our troops do not fight that way.

It's not the American way to fight." The room grew still until one of the students made a loud and obscene noise in response.

Everyone laughed and Errol continued his narrative. "So, you've been to Vietnam, son?" questioned Errol. His tone was blunt. Ryan sputtered and went silent. Errol continued his story about life as a soldier in Vietnam.

"We didn't get too close to our fellow soldiers. You had to protect yourself from getting too close. We never knew if our friend might be the next one to get killed by some VC sniper or landmine. We became sort of numb to the whole thing." Errol lowered his eyes and grew regretful. "When I think now on all our fine men, young and old, it just... I can no longer reckon why it's got to be like this." Errol choked up with emotion and wiped a tear from his eyes and then took a seat by the lectern.

There was total silence in the room as Errol recounted his story. The students were spellbound as he continued his speech. When he ended, the entire class erupted in thunderous applause. Even Ryan was deeply moved by the stories.

Danny walked up to Errol and shook his hand. "I'm sure my brother would be proud of you."

"Thank you, my brother," replied Errol.

"I'm deeply moved by your stories," said Danny.

Danny returned and joined Ryan leaving the lecture hall. Both men left the lecture hall, silent and lost in their thoughts.

"I'm headed to my Calculus class. I'll see you on the flip side," said Ryan.

Both men shared a fist pump and went their separate ways. After class, Danny stopped by the newspaper kiosk and purchased a copy of the latest newspaper. He scoured the front page for stories about Vietnam. Danny's view on the war was beginning to change. He had started school being a vocal supporter of the war. After all, his brother was fighting a life-or-death struggle. He began to have doubts about the thing. He read about the use of napalm and the indiscriminate torching of villages. He read about *Operation Rolling Thunder*, the air campaign against North Vietnam. How many innocent peasants were killed by US bombers? He felt that he could not speak to his parents and admit his doubts about the war. He felt strongly that his father would probably disown him. Danny went to his room in the dorm. He clutched a copy of the New York Times under his arm. He began to read the paper to take his mind off things. He went to the local section and spotted an interesting article on Abbie Hoffman signing a book deal. This was confirmation of the dialogue between Abbie Hoffman and Dick Cavett. The article indicated that he would be in the area and making the rounds of colleges. Danny clipped the article and inserted it into his back pocket. He decided that he would save it for further reading.

The previous week's candlelight protest outside Mansbach's home had been a rousing success. Mansbach had successfully resisted the demands after the unsuccessful meeting between him and Bennett, but it had significantly raised Bennett's profile. Bennett was planning a larger, more powerful massive march to the Student Center that would force the Dean to remove ROTC from the campus. This would strike a final, decisive blow for the movement. He would use the sound truck in mobilizing the students. In addition, he had already contacted the school gymnasium. He booked the gym to make what he hoped would be a victory speech following the march. The members nodded their approval for the plan.

The SDS members increased the production of fliers and announced a campus-wide strike for the following day. They demanded that the administration suspend classes during the day, so that students could be free to attend the massive demonstration.

In response, Mansbach granted them the time off from their classes and notified the Campus Patrol to prepare counter measures for the massive march and prevent any potential violence. He warned them that blocking traffic or anything besides a peaceful protest would be met with force.

The Rutgers protest began with the students mobilizing on the open field near the Henry Rutgers statue. The mob of students marched up College Avenue. Klonsky and his lieutenants moved with the precision of a military unit. Leading the procession was Bennett, who sat in the rented sound truck that moved to the front of the protesters. The protesting students marched down the street. He basked in the power of his voice projected from the speakers. He barked out commands for the group over the sound equipment in the truck. "Take your positions across the Student Center," he commanded.

The protesters marched in single file down the street. They finished their march upon reaching the front of the Student Center. They formed a blockade across the main street, preventing administrators and students alike from crossing the de-facto picket line. Buses were stalled at locations far from their destinations. Traffic became backed up and many drivers simply abandoned their vehicles. The streets leading to the Student Center became a virtual parking lot.

The crowd grew in intensity until it covered most of the area between the Student Center and the cafeteria. They chanted slogans. Many took their work seriously. For others, it was simply a good time; they were able to skip classes and meet friends without feeling guilty.

Danny leaned out of his window in the Tinsley dorm, watching the marchers surge up the street towards the Student Center. After listening to Errol's moving stories, he was deeply troubled by his support for the war. The arrival of the military recruiter had been a tactical mistake on the part of the administration. Students like Danny, who were initially neutral about the war, became angry with the recruiter's presence. He was also angry that the campus had become such a hostile place to both sides of the debate. He reflected on the confrontation between Barry and the cadet. Danny felt that the military recruiter was the last straw. He decided that schoolwork could wait for a few hours. He put his books on the desk and grabbed his jacket. He raced out of the dorm to join the protest. He had made up his mind to join the protest and make his voice heard.

At the head of the crowd was cheerleader Bennett perched in his sound truck. He alternated broadcasting speeches from militant speakers such as Abbie Hoffman and music from hip groups like *Crosby, Stills and Nash*. The somber hit song *Four Dead in Ohio* from Crosby, Stills and Nash was a sobering reminder of the disaster of Kent State University. Four students had been shot and killed by poorly trained

National Guard troops. It had become a rallying cry for the protest movement. It kept the protesters motivated. They even mouthed the words and sang along to the protest anthem.

The crowd increased and grew more vocal as the morning advanced. Danny had decided to join the protest and moved to the outskirts of the crowd. He spotted Barry in the middle of the crowd. Barry moved closer to him and offered him a Black Power salute. Danny reluctantly returned the gesture. Today, Barry and Danny had become reluctant comrades-in-arms.

In minutes, the blockade of the Student Center was complete. No one could enter or leave. Even Jim Morris was forced to become a reluctant bystander to the spectacle. The activities of the newspaper would have to be suspended until the end of the protest.

At the other end of the street, groups of ROTC officers, including Ryan and the fraternity jocks, gathered to witness the protest. They formed a counter-protest. Some of them carried signs denouncing the protesters. Others voiced catcalls and derision. They appeared helpless to alter the course of the protest. The battle lines had been drawn and Danny and Ryan would find themselves on opposing sides of the protest.

Dean Mansbach and several frustrated administrators emerged from adjacent buildings. They took turns pleading for the students to return to their classes.

"Go back to your classes," shouted the Dean through a bullhorn. The pleas were met with derision. Some of the protesters roared back at the Dean, "The campus belongs to us!"

Danny had joined the crowd. His sympathies had gone over to the protesters. He began shouting slogans and demands at the police and the administrators. The students waved their arms and shouted down the administrators. They swarmed into the first floor of the Student Center. It was only a matter of time before they went inside and occupied the entire building.

"Now is not the time to get weak," Klonsky bellowed. Bennett sat in the helm of his sound truck. He was the head cheerleader. He continued to blast music and vocal directives from the seat of the truck.

It was a great motivator, and he was enjoying controlling the energy of the protest.

The Dean retreated into an adjacent building. Inside the conference room, he set up an emergency meeting with the officers of the Campus Patrol. Dean Mansbach stared out the window at the noisy sound truck. He sat and contemplated his options for a few seconds. Suddenly, the solution flashed to him. He had an inspiration. He would mount the truck and silence the speakers.

The Commander was aghast at the idea, but the Dean was adamant. "I was a combat officer, and I am still in good physical shape."

The Commander scratched his head but was not about to deny the Dean his moment of fame. "We'll be right behind you," the commanding officer insisted.

"Just get me up there, I'll do the rest," he insisted.

The Campus Patrol quickly advanced on the sound truck. They surrounded Mansbach as he advanced on the vehicle. Bennett watched as the Campus Patrol advanced on the vehicle. He stopped the vehicle to observe the actions of the officers. They shielded the stalwart Dean as he advanced on the truck. In a bold move, they hoisted the Dean onto the very top of the truck. He was followed by two officers who climbed up for support. The maneuver caught everyone by surprise, even Bennett. Bennett stared, unsure of how to handle this unexpected wrinkle. The two men stared at each other. Mansbach carried in his hands a pair of bolt-cutters. The two men stared at each other. The Dean's bold move had violated the sacred space of the truck.

"What are you going to do?" warned an incredulous Bennett.

"What I should have done the first time," the Dean declared, with a wink and a touch of glee. The Dean snipped the wires connecting the sound system of the sound truck. The truck went silent. Bennett and the protesters were stunned. The wheels had abruptly fallen off the protest wagon.

As the sound truck went silent, a rousing cheer erupted from the ROTC and fraternity men gathered at the opposite end of the street. The students had witnessed the altercation between the fearless Dean and Bennett. Wild cheering and catcalls erupted from the ROTC crowd as the protesters dispersed from the Student Center area. For the counter-protesters it was July Fourth and Bastille Day all in one demoralizing package.

The Campus Patrol moved in to forcibly evict the protesters from clogging the Student Center and streets. They even lobbed a few tear-gas grenades into the crowd.

Danny motioned to Barry. "We better get out of here!"

The words were lost on Barry who continued to shout his defiance. Within seconds, billowing clouds erupted and drifted toward the protesters. They began coughing and clutching their hands to their faces. To the Dean's pleasure, they simply scattered and offered no resistance. Soon, the entire area had been swept clear of the protesters by the Campus Patrol officers. Wild cheering and whistles erupted from the ROTC crowd as the protesters dispersed.

The administration had won a significant victory in record time. Dean Mansbach was immediately hailed as a hero in the local conservative newspapers. Some even offered him interviews on local stations and suggested that he run for political office.

Danny and several other protesters made their way into the bathroom of the nearest dorm. Coughing, they splashed water on their faces to counter the effects of the tear gas. Soon, the effects of the gas began to wear off. Barry and Danny retreated to the comfort of Danny's room. The two men sat in silence as the effects of the tear gas wore off. They sat on the furniture and just gazed at the walls. "We're done," moaned Barry.

Danny sighed and nodded. "Nothing to do but watch some television and try and forget it." Danny said, as he flicked on the television. The two were mesmerized by a movie playing on the television. It was playing a military movie about Romans versus Barbarians. The defeated Roman army began to retreat. The leader of the Romans stood his ground, attempting to rally his stampeding, demoralized troops. He hoisted his sword in the air and proclaimed some fierce battle cry. The demoralized Romans rallied upon hearing the battle cry. They turned and advanced toward their enemy. The Barbarians were caught by surprise by the reenergized Roman force. Barry and Danny finished watching the movie.

Danny turned to Barry. "We need a rallying cry," said Danny. "You got a big sword to rally the troops?" questioned Barry.

Barry seemed mystified. Danny scoured a pile of newspapers on the floor. He sat in his favorite recliner and scanned the copies of the newspaper. He looked through several pages without finding the article that he was looking for. In frustration, he grabbed another newspaper off the floor. After a few minutes, Danny realized that he had stuffed the article in his pants pocket. He pulled the article from his pocket: *Abbie Hoffman Signs Book Deal.* He read it and underlined several sentences in the article. He smiled to himself and began to formulate his plan.

That night, Bennett returned to his apartment with some of the members of his organization. The room was silent. No one spoke for an eternity. All the members sat deep in thought. Finally, Bennett broke the silence. "Okay, we got beat today. We'll find a way to come back." The words sank into the crowded room. They were cheered by Bennett's unflappable resilience.

The doorbell rang. Bennett answered the doorbell. He was surprised to find Barry and Danny standing there. Each one had a big smile on their faces. He welcomed the pair into his apartment. Danny sat down in a chair, smiled, and waved the article in front of Bennett. It read *Abbie Hoffman to sign book deal in New York.* Bennett and the protesters were puzzled, but he was happy to see Danny.

"Don't you see? We need a bigger sword," crowed Danny.

"Bigger sword?" asked a puzzled Bennett.

"The Romans needed a symbol or reason to rally the troops," said Danny. "If we could get Abbie to the campus, he could do it. Turn defeat into victory."

"Sure, just like that," scoffed Klonsky. "Are you on some acid trip?"

Danny explained to the skeptical crowd that he would bring Hoffman to the campus. Nearly everyone scoffed. The plan sounded farfetched and unrealistic, and the odds of success were against him.

Bennett chewed on the idea and began to smile. "You have a great imagination. Hey man, go for it," suggested Bennett. He smiled and patted Danny on the back.

The group members shrugged, but they were willing to consider that this outsider might have found a way to return from a crushing defeat. Danny smiled, but it began to fade as he contemplated how to begin.

38

Pawnship and Errol

The next morning, Danny scooped out some traveling money from his hiding spot in a drawer. He winced as he counted his money. He deposited a few wrinkled bills and some coins on the table. It was not enough for the trip he had in mind. He cursed his luck. For a few seconds, he was inconsolable. He felt too proud to beg for money from the other students on the floor. He stared at his beloved guitar. It was among his prize possessions, but right now he needed to find something of value. He fondled it lovingly. It would be a tough choice giving up something that he cherished. However, he realized that he needed to get the extra money and it was the only thing of value that he had in his possession. He slung the guitar over his shoulder and grabbed his newspaper ID and slipped it into his back pocket. He might not need the ID after today, but for one last time he hoped it might be useful. Armed with a faded copy of the New Jersey Transit train schedule, he paused and took a long last inspection of the room, then threw open the door. He walked out of the dorm and headed toward the edge of the campus.

At the same time, Tracy was on her way to the office of the *Targum* to surprise Danny. She had bought some chocolate chip cookies. She entered the newspaper office looking for Danny. Several reporters looked up and ogled the attractive young woman as she passed by their desks. She carried a little tray of cookies in her hands. She smiled to introduce herself as she absorbed the admiring stares of the young reporters. "I'm looking for Danny. I know that he works here."

The reporters raised their heads. They hesitated to be the one to break the bad news about Danny's tenure with the paper. "Better speak to Morris," said one of the reporters with caution in his voice. He pointed to Morris sitting in the corner, chain smoking.

She approached Morris with the cookies in her hand.

Morris smiled at Tracy as she approached. "How can I help you, offer you a cup of coffee?" Morris was in the process of reaching for a cookie.

"I'm looking for Danny," she said.

"He didn't tell you?" Morris frowned; his manner changed. "Are you serious, or are you delirious?"

A look of annoyance pasted on her face. She was stunned by his blustery manner. "Excuse me?" said Tracy.

"I fired the son of a bitch; he's not working here anymore."

Tracy screwed up all her courage. "He's a good guy, can you give him another shot?"

Morris scowled; he was blunt, bordering on the rude. "I'm very busy, if you don't mind, I have a newspaper to run." Morris motioned to a reporter. "Show this young woman out."

The reporter stood up from his desk.

Contemptuously, she dumped the cookies in the garbage. "I can show myself out, thank you." Tracy stormed out of the office. She was visibly shaken by the experience,

Along the way, Danny walked down the street on his way to the train station. In the distance, he spotted Tracy. She was upset, on the verge of tears. "What's wrong?" Danny asked. He comforted her and wrapped his arms around her shoulders.

"I just came back from the newspaper office," said Tracy, fighting off tears.

Danny appeared exasperated. "Why did you do that?" questioned Danny.

"I wanted to surprise you, but I ran into that bastard, Morris."

Danny frowned; his expression hardened. "What did the prick say?"

Tracy broke into a smirk, relieved to hear Danny's reaction. "He was a dick. A cold-hearted bastard."

"That's Morris for you. Sorry you had to witness that," he said.

She noticed the guitar strung over his shoulders. "On your way to a gig?"

Danny leaned over and gave her a kiss. He checked his watch. "Don't have time to explain, I'll tell you later."

Tracy leaned over to offer him a peck on the cheek. Danny sighed and reluctantly pulled away. He was wistful.

She did not give him a chance to finish his sentence but kissed him again. "You know my dorm room, please stop by."

Danny returned the kiss and then resumed his trek to the railroad station. He waved to her as he plunged back down the street.

Danny walked down to the local pawn shop on Baldwin Street on the edge of town. The shop was on a side street off George Street, the main street in the city. The owner of the pawn shop, a pot-bellied, grey-haired man, inspected Danny as he entered his shop. He was used to dealing with students coming into his shop and pawning an old item for a few bucks. It was not hard to determine that Danny looked desperate for extra cash. He squinted as he inspected the instrument from different angles. He had decided how much to offer the student but pretended that he was giving it a serious thought. "I'll give you ten bucks for it," said the owner of the pawn shop.

Danny eyed the owner. He knew it was worth more but did not want to haggle with the owner. The owner had offered him a fraction of the value of the guitar. Danny frowned; his eyes narrowed. The more he thought about it, the more he realized that the pawnshop owner was not offering him anything close to the full value for the item.

"I want thirty-five, minimum." He eyed the owner and his precious guitar. He attempted to look resolute, but the owner of the shop was an old hand at obtaining the items at rock-bottom prices. The pawnshop owner shook his head and counted out ten dollars from the cash register drawer and shoved it in Danny's direction. "Ten bucks and I'm being generous."

Danny sighed. He was about to give in when he caught the owner displaying a devious smile.

"Look, I'm a busy man. Take it or leave it." The owner recognized a cash-starved student when he saw one.

Danny grew angry and rejected the offer. "If that is the best you can do, it's a no-go. It's worth more," said Danny with conviction. He had grown a steel spine following his confrontation with his father.

He turned down the owner's second-hand offer and grabbed his musical treasure. The owner made him a slightly better second offer, but Danny still refused. He grabbed the prized guitar and exited the shop. He stood outside the pawn shop for a few seconds and another idea popped into his head. He walked down the next few blocks and headed over to Errol's bookstore.

Errol was moving around the store stacking books on the shelf when he saw Danny enter with the guitar. "Playing a gig tonight?" Errol asked.

Danny shook his head and put the guitar down on the table. He explained to Errol the nature of his dilemma. "I'm going recruit Abbie Hoffman to speak at the school."

Errol was skeptical, but he did not want to discourage his friend. "You sure you can get him?" asked Errol. "Just walk in there and demand he speak?" Errol wanted to laugh, but he saw the determined look on Danny's face.

Danny scratched the back of his head. He exuded as much confidence as he could muster. In other words, he lied through his teeth. Errol reassured him that his word was good enough for him. He felt that Danny was undergoing a challenging moment for a good purpose. Besides, he was feeling generous. He popped open the cash register and handed Danny the money that he needed. Danny counted the money and smiled. He had enough to make his historic trek into the wilds of the big city. Errol was delighted to lend Danny the money. He trusted Danny and reassured him that he would hold the guitar for him.

Danny hoped that he would have enough for the round-trip train ticket and maybe something to eat in the big bad city. He crossed his fingers and hoped that this foolhardy mission would pay off and help redeem himself from his troubles.

39

Danny Arrives in New York

A short time later, Danny arrived at the train station in New Brunswick. It was located on the edge of the campus. At midday, it was nearly empty. It had been built at this location to make it easier for Rutgers students to travel back and forth from their homes. The wooden benches that held the middle-aged morning commuters were empty. The station had a musty, lived-in odor of a building that had seen few repairs or attempts to modernize it over the years. It might have been a scene from the late post-Second World War era. There were a few newsstands and pizza-stands dotting the terrain of the station. Most of the vendors appeared to be stoop-shouldered, elderly men who had opened shops at the end of the Second World War. New Brunswick had once been a thriving metropolis and it had seemed a good way to make a living for your family.

Danny was excited about his trip into the city. He was also a bit nervous. He had seen pictures of the city but had never been there in person. He was wondering if it were as overwhelming as he imagined it. There were no big cities in his part of Pennsylvania, so this visit promised to be memorable.

Danny stopped at a pizza-stand and ordered a slice of sausage pizza and a cold cup of Dr. Pepper. This was a popular, sugary soft drink. It contained mostly sugar but had a bold invigorating taste that gave the drinker a burst of energy. After finishing, he jogged toward the ticket counter. Danny stood in front of an elderly African American ticket agent. The ticket agent wore a red blazer with a badge that identified him as an employee of the railroad. Danny stood nearby and grabbed the accordion-folded paper schedule and tried to analyze it. He rocked back and forth for a few seconds trying to decipher the arcane symbols on the train schedule. The ticket agent grew impatient waiting for Danny to make up his mind.

"C'mon son, we don't have all day," groused the old man, who was probably anxious to get back to analyzing the racing forms and crossword puzzle littering his booth. Danny slid a few crumpled dollars across the transom and purchased a round trip ticket. "That's six fifty." Danny dug into his pocket to dig for the extra cash. He handed it to the agent. The agent counted the money and generated a round-trip ticket to New York. He glided the tickets into Danny's waiting hands. "Going sightseeing, are you?" the agent asked.

"Going hunting," was Danny's cryptic reply.

" Just another smart-aleck college kid." the ticket agent thought to himself .

"I'm going to invite Abbie Hoffman to come to Rutgers to speak."

The agent shrugged and seemed placated. He had no interest in Abbie Hoffman.

An anxious Danny stood on the windy train platform awaiting the train headed to New York. The wind buffeted him around. In the distance, he spotted a commuter train racing toward the station. The train slowed down and stopped as it reached the station. The chubby train conductor jumped from the train onto the platform. He stared at the lone passenger leaning against the railing on the platform. "All aboard," he called out.

Danny hesitated for a few seconds and hung onto the railing. Danny waged a last-minute doubt offensive with himself. Was he going to take the plunge? Take the chance that he would come back empty-handed?

After a few seconds, the train conductor motioned to him. "We're going to New York. Better get on board," said the impatient conductor, inspecting his watch to make sure that they were on schedule. The conductor leaped aboard the train. The train began to power up. The wheels rotated and powered out of the station. At the last minute, Danny hopped on board. He walked into the nearly empty commuter car and took a seat. Danny stared out at the speeding scenery. The urban landscape seemed to whizz by in a blur.

He was amazed at the enticing mixture of homes and large buildings. The size of the buildings seemed to increase as they got closer to the city. He was amazed at the contrast between the fast-paced life in the city and the more tranquil area of Pennsylvania that he called home. Danny saw an abandoned copy of the *Daily News* on an adjacent seat. He reached over and grabbed the newspaper. He began to scour the news and sports section. He was happy to have something to occupy his time and thoughts as the train sped along the tracks toward the big city.

Slowly, the skyline of New York jutted into view. Its magnificent landscape was dominated by the majestic sight of the Empire State Building. The tall building overshadowed all other buildings. The train ducked into the tunnel that connected New Jersey with New York City. The tunnel ran underneath the Hudson River. After a few moments, the darkness of the river tunnel gave way to the sight of the multiple sets of tracks leading toward Penn Station. The train slowed as it made its final maneuvers onto the inbound tracks. The train crawled to a stop. The conductor announced that the train had reached its destination. Everyone in the car grabbed their belongings and began to leave. Danny emerged from the commuter train. He was happy that the train trip was over. He stared at the darkened passageway leading up to the fabled railroad station. Danny walked along the platform and read some of the billboards advertising a host of products.

He mounted the stairs that took him into the heart of the train station. The sights and the sounds of the city fascinated him. He was just a kid from a rural town in Pennsylvania. If New Brunswick had been a bit of a culture shock, New York was an eye opener. He passed numerous mom-and-pop newsstands and several pizza stands. Rotund young men with pizza-stained aprons massaged dough and made pizza for waiting customers. He walked over to a newspaper vendor and scoured the day's headlines.

He opened his article and showed it to the vendor. "Where is Avenue of the Americas?" Danny questioned the vendor.

The vendor responded in brusque New Yorker manner. "Sixth Avenue, right after Seventh." Danny frowned. The vendor could see that Danny was from out of town. He examined Danny's article. "Oh, you're looking for the big publishers. Most of them are on Sixth Avenue. I had a cousin who worked for one of those guys," said the vendor.

"How do I get there?' Danny said.

"Take the Number 2 uptown." The vendor frowned at the naïve rube from out of town. The vendor leaned over and pointed to a subway entrance.

Danny followed the brightly colored signs for the subway station that would transport him uptown. Danny stood in front of the token booth.

The clerk examined Danny. "That will be thirty-five cents," said the clerk.

Danny hesitated.

The clerk began to scowl as people began to stand in line for tokens. "We don't have all day."

"Uptown to Avenue of the Americas," said Danny.

The clerk nodded. "Kid, you look lost. Here is a token. Go to the Uptown platform and take it two stops."

Danny plunged into the darkness of the subway station. A traveler pointed Danny toward the Number One subway line. Danny thanked the man and continued his odyssey toward the Number One train. He teetered on the edge of the platform and gawked as the subway train emerged from the darkened subway tunnel. It stopped at the edge of the station. He had never seen anything like it at his rural home. The door slid open and several people exited the train. He hopped on the subway train and hung on as it sped him toward his destination.

Danny emerged from the gleaming subway exit on Avenue of the Americas. The sun engulfed the crowded sidewalks. For a few seconds, Danny collected his bearings. He had seen pictures of the city but had never been there in person. It felt totally alien to a hick from the sticks.

He approached a well-dressed New Yorker wearing a shirt and tie, walking briskly in his direction. "I'm looking for Avenue of the Americas," he said. The New Yorker stared at him as if he were a Martian. He shook his head and walked away. Danny was stung by the rudeness of the citizen. He approached another citizen. He had a hopeful expression on his face. "I'm looking for Avenue of the Americas."

The citizen chuckled. "This is it. You're on the Avenue."

Sheepishly, Danny thanked the stranger and wandered off down the street. "'Of course; I knew that" he muttered to himself as he ambled down the avenue. He glanced up at the glistening office buildings. He cupped his hand over his eyes to shade his eyes from the glare. The buildings were taller and more magnificent than anything in his hometown or surrounding areas. Of course, this was New York City, the Big Apple. He noted that the buildings were neatly numbered with bold numbers popping off the outside of the buildings. This city was so different from any large town or city that he was familiar with. The streets were laid out in a logical pattern and most businesses had signs that proclaimed the nature of their business. He was also intimidated by the sheer volume of large office buildings. He thought that maybe someday he could work in a place like that.

He spotted his destination in the distance. He mustered up all his courage and, like an urban pioneer, strutted toward the intimidating glass structure in the distance which held so much of his fate now. He wondered if he would have a good experience or return home disappointed. Approaching a celebrity was a big risk. Danny knew that Hoffman was probably approached by numerous strangers daily. However, Danny felt that his mission was a good one and he decided to cross the Rubicon.

40

Danny at Grossett & Dunlap

Danny stepped into the lobby of the intimidating glass and marble office building. The rotating glass door made him a bit dizzy as it spun around. It finally stopped, depositing Danny in the middle of the enormous lobby. The lobby consisted of a few welcoming kiosks and more gleaming steel and marble. Several banks of elevators divided the building into different sectors. He was struck by the vast quantities of information that visitors needed to navigate the large number of offices located in the buildings. How did New Yorkers handle it? He absorbed the unfamiliar sights and proceeded toward the information desk in the center of the concourse. The information desk was situated in the middle of the lobby floor. It was a steel-framed structure with a sign that proclaimed, 'Information Desk.'

At the desk was an elderly woman who sat in a leather swivel chair. She was a large-boned woman with a bored, seen-it-all expression. She wore a blue blazer with a white shirt and a tie, with the name of the building in bold red letters sewn on her jacket pocket. On her head was a pair of stylish, black-framed glasses. She filed her nails as she browsed the news from the paper in front of her. The remains of a cup of coffee with lipstick stains and a Danish were tucked away in the corner of the desk. A neat pile of papers was stacked in the cubbyholes of the desk.

Danny smiled at the woman. She evaluated the young student, then smiled at him. She pointed to a large glowing sign that indicated 'Messenger Center.' The sign indicated that the messenger center was in the basement. He knew that the messenger center was not his correct destination. He wanted to scream at her that he was not a messenger. "I'm not a messenger. I am looking for—"

She cut him off before he could finish his sentence. She lowered her glasses and shot him a disapproving look. "Where are you going? " she inquired in a flat, official tone.

"Grosset and Dunlap, the publishers."

The woman cut him off and pointed to a second bank of elevators. She answered in a rapid-fire New York manner. "Second Bank, 23rd floor. Walk to the end of the corridor and make a left," she said, almost robotically. She dismissed Danny and returned to work.

Danny thanked her and politely backed off. Danny walked over to the elevator bank and jumped in. The elevator was half-full of people returning from lunch or late shopping expeditions. The door closed and soon it went zooming up to the chosen floor. The other people in the elevator were dressed for work and kept their distance from the young stranger. They treated him like he had some strange disease or was some hippie weirdo that their mother had warned them to avoid. The elevator stopped with a thud. It opened and all the passengers flowed out of the elevator and returned to their jobs.

At the far end of the hall, he saw a welcoming sign. It read *GROS-SET & DUNLAP, PUBLISHERS*. Danny walked down the hallway on the plush pink carpeting. He entered the office through the frosted glass doors. The room was crowded with celebrities, security officers and editorial staff members.

Danny walked past the security desk. The security guard leaned over and observed Danny. Without hesitation, he had Danny pegged for a messenger. Obviously, he was not dressed to fit into the décor of the business. "Deliveries go to the mail room," said the security guard without looking up.

"I'm not a messenger," Danny retorted. He was offended that he was being typecast. The security officer glared at him. To him, Danny was just another long-haired kid. Worse yet, it screamed that he did not belong in the high-end environment. He motioned Danny toward a large door leading to the basement. "You look like one, kid."

Danny hesitated and stood his ground. "I'm here to speak to Mr. Hoffman."

The security guard seemed unmoved by Danny's explanation. Danny pushed his way toward the main office. He brushed off the security officer and headed toward the front desk. "You're not listening to me, kid," growled the officer.

Danny was stopped by a second security officer. The officer motioned for him to stop. He threw up his hands in a stop motion. "Where the hell do you think you're going?" he asked, with a large amount of pumped-up authority. Danny repeated his request and got the same response. "You got a pass?" he uttered, crassly.

Danny shrugged. He had no official paperwork, only the desire to meet the famous speaker. "I'm here to see Abbie Hoffman."

The security guy was weary of Danny's statement and moved from behind his desk. He sneered and grabbed Danny's hand in a vice-like grip.

"I work for a college newspaper," he insisted.

The security officer was not responsive and tightened his grip.

"Please take your hands off me," Danny said firmly, but remained polite and non-confrontational.

"Son, you're not good at listening."

Danny was unshakable in his mission. He stood his ground.

"Only authorized personnel can enter the office."

Danny brushed the security officer's hands from his body. The guard was not pleased. He was deciding what course of action he would take against the intruder.

"My name is Danny Watkins. I am with the press. *Daily Targum.*" He reached into his hip pocket and flashed his college press pass.

The security officer stared at it for a remote moment and burst out laughing. "Is this for real?"

Danny was not amused at the ID being dismissed in this manner.

"You buy that at Woolworth's?" the guard sneered.

Woolworth was the Walmart of its day. A chain of five-and-dime stores that sold cheap, affordable household and personal items.

"*Daily* what?" The security guard's voice grew impatient.

The second security guard advanced on Danny. Danny did not look like the typical hippie, but long hair was the style in those days. "Throw his mangy, long-haired, marijuana-smoking ass out the door."

Danny struggled to make himself heard and repeated his request. "I am a reporter for the Rutgers *Daily Targum*. I want to invite Abbie Hoffman to speak at Rutgers."

The security guard remained impassive. The two just exchanged stares. Finally, the security guard rolled his eyes, without any sense of amusement. He returned to his desk. He pressed a button to summon reinforcements. Several other security guards emerged from another room. The security officer nodded toward his fellow security guards.

"You want me to beat the kid up?" said the second security guard.

"Nah, he'd just cause trouble. Let us escort him out of the place quietly."

They grabbed Danny and dragged him protesting toward the door. Danny scuffled with the brawny officers but soon realized he was over-matched. The noise percolated into the main office. Several workers peeked their heads out of the door to see what the commotion was all about. A tall, bearded editor from the next office was talking to several workers. He heard the commotion and walked out of the office to observe the commotion. He spotted the men dragging Danny out of the office complex. He motioned for security to release the young journalist.

"What's the commotion?" asked the editor.

"Sorry to bother you. We'll have him removed in a few minutes."

The editor nodded his approval but something sincere reeked out of Danny. He motioned for the guards to stop.

"This punk kid wants to see Abbie Hoffman."

The editor was semi-amused. He analyzed the young journalist, equally dismissive. "Sorry, no one gets to see Abbie." The editor evaluated Danny. He could see that Danny meant no harm. His earnestness and serious demeanor demanded that the editor at least hear him out.

Danny approached the book editor. "I want to invite him to speak at Rutgers." Danny could not believe that he was saying these things.

The editor remained unmoved by Danny's bold request. "Abbie Hoffman's schedule is booked." He said that with a firmness that a hurricane could not move. "He's going to Yale and Harvard. No time for a small campus like Rutgers."

Danny pumped himself up with fake bravado. He brushed himself off and stood face-to-face with the editor. "Well, maybe you read that the protest at Rutgers went national," said Danny.

"Yes, I recall something like that, so what?" The editor shrugged and remained unimpressed. He was used to people pleading their cases. The editor was expert at defusing their false enthusiasm.

"I guarantee he will get ten thousand students to hear him." The words exploded out of Danny's mouth. Danny reached into his pockets and handed him a crumpled copy of the *Daily Targum.*

The editor scanned the paper. It appeared genuine but he appeared unimpressed and shook his head in disdain. "Harvard will be twenty thousand at the very least," sniffed the book editor.

Danny upped the ante. "Ten thousand copies of the new book and I'll have a special party for him at the Student Center." Danny realized that he had made up the numbers and the party, but it sounded good and he went for broke. He almost believed it himself.

The editor smiled at the perplexed Danny and shook his head. "Small potatoes, nice try, kid."

"He's the voice of our generation. He will not be silenced. We will not be silenced." The words spilled out of Danny. He repeated the line that he had heard during the Cavett interview with Hoffman.

"That is a nice slogan, kid. I'll have to remember that" chided the book editor.

Danny appeared certain that he had impressed the book editor. However, his hope appeared short-lived. The editor was not moved. Danny appeared deflated. He had run out of ideas and decided that he had lost.

Abbie Hoffman, frizzy-haired prominent protest leader of the era, sat in the small nearby glass-enclosed conference room. He watched the confrontation between Danny and the staff with a sort of streetfighter fascination. "Kid's got balls. I'll give him that." His chest heaved with amazement. Hoffman exited the conference room and walked toward Danny and the editor.

"Don't worry, Mr. Hoffman, we have the situation under control."

Abbie Hoffman nodded and offered Danny a small smile. "Kid, you got a lot of balls, I'll give you that."

Danny was star-struck. He blurted out his invitation. "I want to invite you to speak at Rutgers. I'm a reporter for the *Daily Targum*. We will have ten thousand people listening to you."

"Nice try, kid, I'm going to Harvard tonight. They'll have twenty thousand students."

Danny had an inspiration. He had one final card to play. "Errol Anderson says hi."

Abbie was about to turn around and walk back to the office when he heard Danny. Abbie was caught off-guard. Danny explained that he and Errol were sort of friends. He related the tale of his brother's letter. He explained that Errol ran the bookstore in New Brunswick and Danny had been told of his being Abbie's friend. Abbie solicited more information. Danny recounted the fight between the young Abbie and the teacher. Abbie was amused that the story was still being told.

"He wanted to know are you serious or are you delirious?"

Abbie started to laugh. He could not believe it. "A bit of both," he said cheerfully.

Danny recounted that Abbie had tried to talk Errol out of going to Vietnam. Abbie recognized it as the truth. "Nice to hear from him. Send him my regards. Better yet, I will send him a postcard from Cambridge. What is his address?"

Danny gave him the street address and phone number for the store.

"Have a nice trip back to Rutgers or wherever." He turned his back on Danny and returned to the office.

41

Abbie Spots Danny

W hen Abbie and the editor returned to the conference room, they gazed at the maps mounted on the wall and the galley version of his new book. The editor joked, "The kid said that you were a voice that could not be silenced. Did you really say that?"

Hoffman scratched his head and thought for a second. "I don't remember, but that's a hell of a slogan. I want it on the next edition of the book."

"Good, now let us get on with it. We have a limo picking you up from Logan Airport around four p.m."

A short time later, Danny found himself back at Penn Station. He trudged into the airy but forbidding train station. He passed the illuminated pizza and donut shops. Several pizza makers hawked their wares, but Danny was discouraged and not hungry. He passed the aromatic pizza stand without even looking or satisfying his desire for the tasty snack. In fact, his appetite had been killed for the day. Danny stood out in the crowd. The waiting room was filled with dozens of conservatively dressed and perspired commuters making their way home. Many of the men wore jackets and ties despite the heat. Some of the commuters gave a double take as they stared at Danny's hippie attire. Danny sat down on a bench and waited for his train to New Brunswick to be announced. He was too downbeat to worry about how he looked to the other commuters. He pulled the round-trip ticket from his pocket.

A booming voice emerged from the loudspeaker, announcing, "Northeast Corridor train to Trenton boarding on track ten. Making stops in Newark, Elizabeth, Edison, New Brunswick and Trenton."

Danny headed for his train located on the number ten train track. He grasped the ticket and walked down the stairs with the other commuters and headed for his homeward-bound track. He spotted the track number and descended to the train waiting below to carry him home. He felt defeated, like the baserunner who gets tagged before making it to home plate. He was alone in his misery.

A dejected Danny walked toward the idling train on the sooty platform. The trip appeared to have been for nothing. He wondered how he would convince Errol to return his precious guitar. Maybe Errol would feel sympathy for his effort. For a moment, he stared up ahead into the long platform. A long, multi-car commuter train started its engine. He hopped on board the train bound for New Brunswick. In disgust, he pulled the Abbie Hoffman article from his back pocket and tossed it into the nearby cluttered trash bin. He hoped that he could forget the afternoon's adventure and return to face the music.

On board the train, Danny huddled onto his hard leather seat corner, lost in his thoughts. The other commuters stared at him. He appeared oblivious to his surroundings. He wondered to himself how he was going to explain his grandiose but failed adventure. Maybe the subject would not come up. Either way, the afternoon would not go down in his future memoirs as part of his finest hour. Maybe he could pretend that he never went. His reverie was broken by the conductor in his blue jacket and cap who approached him. "Tickets, tickets" the conductor shouted. Danny handed the conductor his paper ticket. The conductor scanned the ticket, determined that it was genuine and punched it. He placed a ticket stub on the top of the seat. Danny returned his gaze and observed the speeding countryside as it flashed before his eyes.

Danny stared out at the surrounding countryside as the train went past numerous smaller towns. The countryside whizzed by in an indistinct blur. The empty countryside of the Secaucus area quickly transformed itself into small towns and then metamorphosed into large metropolitan cities like Newark and Elizabeth. They flew by in a blur as the commuter train sped down the parallel silver band of tracks.

Danny decided to take a brief snooze. He was no longer absorbed by the scenery. He woke when he heard the conductor announce that New Brunswick was one of the next stops. He did not want to miss his stop. He spotted a sign in the distance that read 'New Brunswick.' The conductor walked down the aisle. He called out, "New Brunswick, New Brunswick is our next stop."

The announcement broke Danny's concentration and he snapped out of his dream state. The train began to slow down as it pulled into the station at New Brunswick. Danny jumped up from his seat and walked down the aisle toward the exit. He alighted onto the New Brunswick platform. He spotted some of the familiar sights of the Rutgers campus in the distance. He decided that he would hold off visiting Errol till the next morning.

That evening, Alex and Ryan shared dinner together in the cafeteria. Ryan filled her in on Danny's attempted visit to New York. They had enjoyed each other's company at the frat party and had begun to see each other on a regular basis.

"Errol told me what Danny was planning," said Ryan.

"He's not really going to do that, "Alex exclaimed.

"He's not normally crazy but I think losing his scholarship drove him to make the attempt," said Ryan. He shook his head sadly.

She took a deep breath and sighed. "Well, I wish him luck, but I'm sure that he's going to return empty-handed," she noted.

"I guess when he comes back, we'll find out," said Ryan. "He asked me to bail him out if he ever got arrested." Ryan smiled as he contemplated the image of Danny sitting in a New York prison cell.

"At least you haven't gotten the phone call yet, so I guess he's okay," said Alex. Alex resumed drawing a caricature of Ryan. She sketched Ryan as George S. Patton, the famous World War Two general.

Ryan admired the likeness. "I don't think Patton had a ponytail," he said.

Alex frowned. She attempted to grab it back. Ryan smiled and admitted that he liked the drawing. At that moment, over the radio the booming voice of a DJ announced that Abbie Hoffman was speaking at the Rutgers Campus. A cheer erupted from the crowd. Ryan listened wide-eyed in amazement. The only thing he could utter was "Fucking Danny did it." No one understood what Ryan meant. Ryan apologized to Alex and rushed out of the cafeteria.

After leaving the station, Danny walked a few blocks. He was back on the main street on the Rutgers Campus and walked along the tree-lined streets of College Avenue. He stopped off at the Greasy Truck and ordered a cheesesteak.

Danny turned and spotted Ryan standing behind him. "How did I know you would be here?" said Ryan. Danny said nothing. He stuffed the cheesesteak in his mouth. His appetite had returned, and he wolfed down the cheesesteak as if it were his last meal on earth.

Ryan waited for him to finish. "You went, didn't you?" Danny remained blank. Ryan was the DA interrogating his witness.

"What are you, my fuckin' mother?" Danny retorted, acting defensively.

"I was looking for you all afternoon. I went down to Errol's. He told me what you had done."

"I owe him some money. Not sure when I could pay him back."

"Errol said it was for a good cause. He said that you can pay him back another time."

Finally, Danny could not control himself anymore and blurted out, "Yeah, I did go, it was a waste of time." Danny was still feeling the sting of defeat and did not want to talk about it. "Can we change the subject? I was this close to him. I saw him in the other office talking to some people, but they wouldn't let me near him," he said, dejected.

Ryan stared at him, dumbfounded. "You don't know?"

"Know what?" Danny questioned Ryan. Danny looked down at his feet. "You mean Danny Watkins made a fool of himself trying to get Abbie Hoffman to speak."

Ryan seemed dubious. "You don't know? It is the biggest news of the evening. I was eating at the Commons and the news came over the loudspeaker. You dumb bastard. He is coming. And you must have had something to do with it. Abbie Hoffman will be stopping off at our campus in about an hour."

Danny was flabbergasted. The news had indeed spread like wildfire. Dean Mansbach had initially tried to stop the speech. However, it was too late: the gym had been booked for a speech. Upon hearing the news, Bennett voluntarily gave up the position as speaker of the night and handed the reins over to the visiting guest. He was a little miffed about being upstaged but he felt that the chance to bring a nationally known speaker like Abbie Hoffman to the campus might reinvigorate the movement.

Danny broke into a huge smile that stretched for a mile. "I guess Rutgers beat Harvard."

Ryan was confused. What did he mean?

A stunned Danny hugged Ryan. A triumphant look crossed his face.

"Do you know what you've done?" asked Ryan. Danny was unsure of the meaning. "You have singlehandedly revived the protest. When Abbie Hoffman speaks, he will reignite the protest. Bennett failed and you are about to reignite it," Ryan continued.

Danny smiled. He had not thought of the long-term consequences.

"I hate what he says and what he stands for, but man, to hear him. Something I can tell my grandkids." Ryan stood wide-eyed at the possibility, even if he disapproved of the politics.

"He's coming. I told you he would."

Ryan did not want to be a killjoy or spoil Danny's happiness, but he felt that he needed to be a realist. He did not want Danny to be too disappointed in the outcome. Ryan spoke in measured words so as not to hurt Danny. He spoke haltingly. "Danny, if anyone speaks to him, it'll be Kevin."

Danny refused to come down off his emotional high. He pondered the words and tried to make sense of it. Slowly it dawned on him, and he realized that perhaps Ryan was correct. He formulated a plan. "Maybe if I spot Kevin first, I can knock him unconscious, stuff him in a closet and pretend to be him," said Danny with a laugh.

"That's a dumb idea," joked Ryan.

"He'll talk to me. I'll find a way," responded Danny.

Ryan shook his head. Would he ever learn? Despite his early negative opinions, he remained an optimist. Probably that was the thing that endeared him most about Danny. He refused to look at the negative side of life. He always wanted to move forward.

It had gotten dark early, and the pair continued walking down the street toward the well-lit gym. A large crowd gathered outside the gym. Boys and girls from all the dorms and the fraternities crowded the sidewalk outside the gym. The crowd buzzed with excitement. It was a great event and a chance for the guys to meet the girls that might be standing on the line near them. It was a giant social event. Danny and Ryan evaluated the crowd. It was exceptionally large and growing, like water being released from a dam. Danny and Ryan walked up to the door of the gym. A few muscular students appeared at the doorway. They were working as bouncers. They tried to regulate who would get in the gym.

"We're full up, we might try and set up speakers outside the gym," the bouncer said.

A groan of disappointment rose from the crowd. "Sorry guys, the gym is near capacity."

Danny had an inspiration. He flashed his ID from *Targum*. "I have to get in. I am going to get an interview with Abbie."

The bouncer sneered at him with a skeptical look. He started to laugh. "Right, and I'm Joe Namath," said the haughty bouncer.

He started to move the crowd away. Danny looked defeated. He put his hands in his pocket. The two started to leave the gym property. *Miracle denied*, he thought. He had come so close.

Ryan suddenly had an inspiration. He reached into his pocket and pulled out a small key. It was the key to the downstairs door to the boxing gym. He had forgotten to return it and motioned for Danny to follow him. The two dashed down the stairs to the small door that led to the boxing gym. Ryan turned the key, and the pair entered the bowels of the gym. "The keys to the kingdom," Ryan uttered.

In the darkened basement, Ryan and Danny were lost. The area was poorly lit and both men had trouble finding their way. In the distance, they heard a loud rumbling sound. "Follow the noise," Ryan noted. He motioned for Danny to follow him. After walking a few yards, they discovered a flight of stairs that led up to the main gym area. He saw a pathway that was illuminated, and the pair walked up the steps.

At the top of the stairs, Danny and Ryan followed the large herd of students moving into the main gym. It was packed wall-to-wall with students and onlookers. The room was buzzing with excitement. Danny and Ryan followed the crowd into the gym. It was wall-to-wall people, barely enough room to breathe. In the distance, Danny spotted Pamela, Alex, and several other freshmen from the dorm. He was too preoccupied to go over to greet them. Everyone was excited about the evening's guest speaker. They moved toward the big open area in front of some large, black, mounted stereo speakers.

The room buzzed with excitement. It was a big event and one that kids would remember for a lifetime. Abbie Hoffman was a rock star in the protest world. He had also earned a reputation of being a fantastic speaker. They followed the crowd into the packed gym and moved toward the big open area of the gymnasium. Janitors hustled as they set up impromptu bleachers.

Several minutes earlier, a large black van drove up to the rear of the gym. Abbie Hoffman jumped out of the van and entered the gym through the rear delivery bay. He motioned to another man sitting in the darkened van. "I'll get you an escort once I'm in the building and set up for the speech." The hidden man nodded.

Hoffman was surrounded by a group of Rutgers staffers and advance men from the publishing company. They pulled up to a stage door. It was marked with impromptu signs welcoming the celebrity *du jour*.

"Thanks for coming on such short notice." The administrator

smiled. He was a bit starstruck. Abbie Hoffman was indeed a star in the protest world and the biggest name to honor the campus since Melanie, the famous folk singer, had been to the school. "Can I have your autograph?" the star-struck administrator asked.

Hoffman happily obliged. "I wouldn't miss this for the world. How many people can this place hold?"

"Five to ten thousand if we pack 'em in," said the administrator.

Abbie Hoffman walked toward the door to the stage. The man from the van joined the group. It was the bookstore owner, Errol Anderson. When Abbie appeared in the press section, he was mobbed by a crowd of reporters. They were all waving their arms and shouting Abbie's name. They were all clamoring for an interview. It was loud and nerve-wracking. He was peppered with questions such as, "What are your plans? Are you planning a reunion with the Chicago Seven? When will your book be released?" Abbie Hoffman smiled and took it all in good humor. He basked in the sunshine of the attention. He grew more expressive and engaging. The attention of the reporters was life-giving, like pollen to a bee. After a few minutes, he broke free from the crowd.

Hoffman and Errol conferred. "Don't forget the reason you're here," Errol whispered.

Abbie smiled and leaned over to a nearby college official. He whispered in the man's ears. "Page this kid, Watkins."

The college official was puzzled. He was unclear who 'Watkins' was supposed to be. Was it some college official?

Hoffman realized that Danny Watkins was not known to them. He replied, "He's a kid working for your newspaper." Hoffman jotted down the name on a slip of paper and handed it to the college official.

"Okay, Abbie," the official said as he moved away from the group. Within a few minutes, an announcement blared over the loudspeaker. "Danny Watkins, come to the main office. Danny Watkins of the *Targum* come to the main office."

Danny stood in the middle of the crowded gym with Ryan. He looked puzzled and alarmed by someone calling his name over the loudspeaker down to the main office. Danny headed from the front of the gym to the main office. The sound reverberated throughout the building. Danny milled with the rest of the crowd. *Got to be a mistake,* he thought to himself. For a second Danny hesitated and then the feeling that it might be him warmed over him. He grew excited.

The booming announcement repeated itself. "Danny Watkins from the *Daily Targum* please report to the administrator's office."

It began to sink in: the notice was for him. Danny puffed up with pride and headed forward.

Backstage, the reporters cornered Abbie Hoffman as he prepared his notes. A crowded press section consisting of over a dozen reporters from different newspapers peppered him with questions. "How does it feel to be in New Brunswick? Do you want a rematch with Judge Julius Hoffman?"

Hoffman smiled at that remark. The cranky old judge had been the presiding judge at the infamous trial for the Chicago Seven. The judge had been his nemesis in the *Chicago Seven* case. The two men were not related at all. Hoffman scanned the room.

Kevin and other reporters pressed him in the close quarters. Kevin held up his pad. "Kevin Wheeler, *Daily Targum,*" he said proudly.

Abbie stared at him. "I'm looking for this Watkins kid. That isn't you."

A deflated Kevin was taken aback. He had been chosen to be the lead reporter for the unfolding event of the evening. Any story would feature his byline. Kevin wondered why Danny of all people was getting the attention of this world class celebrity. "He's not a good reporter. Jim Morris fired him a few days ago." Abbie stared at Kevin with disdain. "I am the kid—I mean, the reporter from the *Daily Targum.* Could you tell us if you plan to protest next week in New Haven?"

Abbie ignored the question and continued to scan the room for signs of Danny. "I'm going to talk to the other kid, the one that I saw this afternoon."

Kevin was confused. He waved his press pass, but it made little impact.

"Where's Danny Watkins, the kid from *Targum?* The kid that nearly got himself arrested this afternoon. He's the one that I want to speak with."

Kevin recoiled; he was upset that his arch-rival Danny was getting the story. The door flung open and a hopeful Danny entered. Hoffman spotted Danny from a distance. Hoffman hailed him. "Hey, you, *Targum* kid with the big balls." Danny pointed to himself. Hoffman nodded and motioned him to join him.

Errol stepped out from the crowd and welcomed Danny. "I told him that he had to come to Rutgers for the night," exclaimed Errol. Errol patted Danny on the shoulder in congratulations. Errol explained that Abbie had called him at the store. He told him about Danny's visit to the publisher.

Hoffman barked, "This is all your fault, kid. I cannot pass up ten thousand adoring fans."

Danny absorbed everything and suddenly grew excited. This was the big break that he had hoped for. He could not believe it. Neither could Kevin, as he realized that he was not the *Targum* reporter to get the story. He waved the other reporters away. Abbie smiled. "Just hang on. We can talk once the speech is over."

The lights had gone out in the gym. The students drew candles from their pockets or shirts and began to light them to illuminate the gym. There was a hushed silence as everyone waited for their guest speaker. Suddenly a cheer erupted, and the room was filled with the sound of everyone chanting "Abbie, Abbie."

Abbie gave Danny a big high-five. "Meet me backstage after my talk. You're the man," said the ebullient Hoffman. Hoffman headed for the stage.

Danny grinned from ear to ear. He saw a stunned Kevin staring enviously, with eyes boiling with hate. Danny could not resist giving him the middle finger of contempt.

The gym was packed wall-to-wall with eager students. Hoffman stood at the podium delivering his speech. He was a charismatic speaker. "Today, I am asking you to join our movement. We are a million young people demanding change. We are taking on the Establishment!" he shouted so that even the students in the back of the gym would hear him.

The speech went on for another half an hour as he regaled the crowd with war stories of his days as a leader of the protest movement. He told the story of his humble beginnings and rise to prominence. As he wrapped up the speech, he uttered the phrase that had inspired him to make the trip. "I am a voice of this generation. We are the voices of this generation. We will never be silenced!" The audience drank in the audacity of the line. There was silence for a moment and then the entire gymnasium erupted in a loud cheer and applause that rattled the foundations of the building. It would be a line that would become a battle cry for the movement.

Later that night, Abbie sat on a chair in the guest lounge. His voice was hoarse from the lengthy speech. He drank some water and rested for a few minutes and then invited Danny downstairs to take notes. Hoffman talked non-stop. He loved an audience. Danny wrote notes as fast as his hand could move. He was suffering writer's cramp, but it did not matter. He wanted to get every great word or thought on paper.

"We were in Lincoln Park in Chicago in the dead of summer. Thousands of us. We marched through the streets toward the Democratic Convention. We hoped to get into the Convention, but the police were waiting for us."

Danny paused. "You got tear-gassed?"

Abbie nodded, "And hit by a policeman's baton. Nothing could stop the protest." Abbie Hoffman displayed a faint scar. Danny looked closely and whistled. Finally, he began to talk about the infamous Chicago Seven trial. "And old Judge Julius Hoffman had me bound and gagged. The Chicago Seven, man... what a group."

Danny continued, "I watched the entire Chicago Convention from my hospital room. I had pneumonia that summer."

Hoffman was impressed with Danny's style and grasp of the situation. Danny had finally found his groove. He was born to do this interview. After an hour had passed, Hoffman yawned. "I got to call it a night."

"Of course, I have to get this to my editor." The sound of the word 'editor' touched a nerve. Danny smiled at the sound of the word.

Abbie Hoffman patted him on the back and reassured him. "You're probably a hell of a reporter. I will have the security guys give you my phone number. If you want some more details," he said with a bold smile.

Hoffman flashed the peace sign and walked down the hall to his waiting van. He turned around and spoke. "Hey man, you want to join us? We are going over to Harvard tomorrow."

Danny forced himself to conceal his large smile and offered his sincere apologies. He told him that he had studies to catch up on.

"I'll have my editor call your editor tomorrow. I will make sure you get any other exclusives from me."

Danny was giddy with excitement. He still felt as if he were imagining the entire event, but it was very real. Danny was about to become famous. He trotted out of the gym in a bit of a daze. The students flooded out of the gym. Some of them hung around the gym drinking and celebrating. Occasionally, he heard someone shout, "We will not be silent." Danny smiled to himself. It was the experience of his young lifetime. He was intoxicated with the evening's events. He could not wait to see Morris's face. He broke into a run.

"Hold the presses, Morris, Watkins is coming back... in style," he chimed and broke into a little victory dance. Danny could not wait to get Morris's reaction to his triumph. Would he be humble or make the man eat crow for the sense of humiliation from being fired from the paper? Danny was not the vindictive type, so he decided not to rub it into his former editor's face. He was in too good a mood to say anything that would start a fight. He entered the semi-darkened room of the news office.

Dejected, Morris sat alone in the newsroom. Danny entered quietly. It was a few moments before Morris looked up from his seat. "We're closed," Morris said, dejected.

"Not after you see what I got," crowed Danny. Danny dragged his notebook from his hip pocket and showed him his worn-out notebook.

Morris's eyes widened. He did a double take. He could not believe it was Danny that had brought in the scoop. He thumbed through the contents of the interview, forcing himself to conceal his smile of delight. "An exclusive from Abbie Hoffman? How did you get it? Never mind. Just type it up and give it to me." He practically ripped it out of Danny's surprised hands. Morris rushed to the phone and dialed. He waved the notepad in the air as if he had discovered the greatest literary masterpiece. "Stop everything. I have tomorrow's lead," he boasted to the voice on the other end.

Danny sat down at the typewriter and pounded out the article. When he was finished, he handed it to a giddy Morris. Morris smiled and gave him the thumbs-up gesture. It meant that the article passed muster with the fickle editor.

The next morning, a tired Danny walked down the stairs of the cafeteria. As he made his way to his usual table, he spotted several members of his dorm reading the article with Danny's byline splashed all over the front page.

"Way to go, Danny, way to go," cheered Ryan. Alex rushed up and kissed him on the cheek. Danny blushed; the praise was intoxicating.

"You the man," cheered Fred.

Ryan handed Danny a note from Tracy; Danny quickly read the note: *I knew you could do it. See you soon, Love Tracy.* Danny smiled and placed it in his shirt pocket. Of all the heart-felt comments, the note from Tracy hit home with Danny. He felt that a strong relationship with her was blooming.

Barry beamed and smiled at Danny. "Welcome to the movement, bro." They gave him the high sign and chanted. "We will not be silent. We will not be silent." The room erupted with the loud chant, and everything stopped as the crowd picked up the chant. It was the moment of triumph. Danny had reignited the movement.

Everyone crowded around him and cheered. Danny was embarrassed by the outpouring of praise and wiped a tear from his eye. Later that day, Danny sat in front and watched as other students thumbed through the paper. Danny had redeemed himself in grand style. He was certain that the future would be bright. He would call up his father and tell him that his future was at Rutgers and not back on the farm. Danny watched from a distance and smiled.

Acknowledgments

RON PETERSON for giving me the idea for creating the TV project in 2013, Larry Brody of TV Writer.com for suggesting that the TV script would make a good novel and Judy Hammett for being a world-class development editor for helping me develop the project through several drafts of the novel.

About The Author

LEW RITTER is a retired teacher from Bergen County, New Jersey. He has had many careers including working in the Air Courier industry before FedEx took over the field, graduated from DeVry College as a Unix Network Operations person and finally as a Social Studies and Library Media Specialist Teacher. He has been married for twenty-three years to Bonnie Mitchel.

His interest in writing began in college with a series of correspondence with the legendary producer of M*A*S*H, Larry Gelbart. He wrote an impassioned letter to CBS protesting the potential cancellation of M*A*S*H in its freshmen year. Gelbart was so impressed with the letter that they corresponded for several months. He sent him actual scripts and even gave Lew a chance to pitch story ideas for the series.

In 1975, Lew joined Mystery Writers of America and tried his hands at writing mystery short stories for the Ellery Queens Mystery Magazine.

He became enthusiastic about becoming a Copywriter for advertising agencies in NYC in the early 80s. This led him to taking classes at the School of Visual Arts in NYC. He took classes with Copywriters and Art Directors from such legendary agencies such as Ally & Gargano and Doyle Dane and Birnbach.

His decision to become a screenwriter began in 1985 when he attended a Screenwriting class led by Ron Peterson. He wrote several entry level screenplays but reached his level in 2011 when he was a Finalist in the Wild Sound Film Festivals Classic Spec script contest for a Magnum P.I. script. It received a Table Read by actors at the same Film Festival in 2015.

He worked with Ron Peterson and fellows from Crossroads Entertainment in Los Angeles on several projects including Disclosure, a Sci-Fi script. *Turbulence* has undergone several major changes since its creation in 2013. Since then, it has developed into a potential

Netflix streaming series with a five-year worth of story ideas. He currently works with Joe Rosario, an acting coach, writer and stage director on versions of *Turbulence* and Mr. Zak, a series about a wounded Veteran who works in an inner-city school. In 2018, Lew decided to turn the television script into a novel.

Hidden in Plain Sight

Turbulence Book #2

S ometimes, it just doesn't pay to pick up the phone. The news may exhilarate you, or leave you totally depressed. It is rare that the conversation even with close relatives would be of both varieties.

Danny sat in the brown phone booth in the corner on the floor of his dormitory. He grasped the phone and listened to Sarah, his mother, report the latest news and gossip from his hometown of Jersey Shore Pennsylvania. She seemed to enjoy being the town gossip and reporting on all the newsworthy events of her neighbors. He listened with half an ear to the local gossip. It made his mother happy, so he pretended to be interested.

Danny was shy by nature. He avoided confrontation whenever possible. Growing up, he had listened to the loud and endless bickering arguments between Matthew, his father and Kenny, his brother. Danny preferred to remain neutral and not get involved.

However, Danny had grown as a person since the last visit by his parents. He smiled to himself as he recalled the events of the dinner at the fancy restaurant. Sarah and Matthew had driven all the way from rural Pennsylvania to visit their him. He recalled that his mother Sarah was an attractive matronly woman and Matthew was a burly retired marine who ran the family farm foe decades. They had come to visit and ate at a fancy restaurant called the Hearth. It was a fancy restaurant with white linen tablecloths and waiters dressed in suits. Matthew and Danny spent the evening arguing over the Danny's changing attitude toward the Vietnam War.

"They are a bunch of Communists," Matthew roared. His manner bellicose.

"The protests are legitimate. The war is simply wrong," declared Danny.

Both men eyed each other and refused to give ground on the issue. Sarah sat across from the two men hoping for an end to the argument in order that they spend the rest of the evening enjoying a quiet family dinner.

"You are not the son that I raised," Matthew declared.

"I am my own person and I'll make my own decisions," declared Danny.

A few minutes later, the meal arrived and both men grew tired of bickering and settled down to enjoying the sizzling steak dinner sitting in front of them. The rest of the dinner went quietly as both sides declared a ceasefire in order to enjoy the fine décor and the steak dinner. After a few moments, Danny decided to ask the inevitable question.

"How is Dad doing?"

Sarah answered, but her voice quivered as she related the numerous trips to the Emergency Room. She recalled sitting by her husband's bedside in the Emergency Room as Matthew lay on the table being examined by a young doctor. His father had been a retired Marine and felt that made him invincible. However, even marines get old, and Matthew was no exception. The strain of the physical work and the effort to manage it had taken a toll.

Danny sighed as he listened. He was doubtful that his father could recover, but he kept his doubts to himself. Sarah's voice was half – hearted that indicated that she instinctively knew Matthew's best days were behind him.

After listening for a while, Danny was about to hang up. "Oh, last thing before I let you go. I have bad news about your friend Phillip." Sarah inhaled and took a deep breath. She hesitated and informed

Danny that his old friend Phillip's body had been found in his house in Jersey Shore.

Danny had not thought about his old friend for a long time. They had been friends growing up but had gone their separate ways during high school. Danny had made many new friends at Rutgers and memories of high school were light years away. Many of the people that he went to school had graduated and moved on with their lives. Danny assumed that Phillip would do the same with his life.

"He committed suicide," replied Sarah in a hushed tone. Danny felt that he had been sucker punched. He gasped as he listened to the disturbing news.

"But how, why?" Danny asked with a puzzled expression.

Danny recalled that he and Phil had been friends since the early grades, but Phil's lack of social skills made it difficult to maintain their friendship. Phil had been a lost soul since his days at the Jersey Shore high school. He was smart, overweight, wore glasses and lacked the social skills necessary to navigate the treacherous waters of high school social life. He recalled with sadness Phil's failed attempts to speak with girls. He would stutter and blush and then walk away humiliated. Danny remembered walking into Phil's room and marveling at the shelves crammed with comic books and toy soldiers.

"I actually have a copy of Sgt. Fury and his Howling Commandos #1," declared Phil

Danny sighed. He felt remorse because he felt that he had left his friend down. On several occasions he had failed to come to the aid of his former friend as he was harassed by Roland the school bully. Roland was the type of kid who liked to pick on the weaker kids and called them names or beat them up and steal their lunch. Phil was unable to defend himself and was constantly a target for other bullies. Danny tried to encourage his friend to stand up for himself.

"Stand up for yourself."

Phil would shake and grow defensive. "I can't fight."

However, Danny wanted to be part of the in-crowd and never come directly to the aid of his hapless friend. Phil was a lost soul, and no one felt the need to befriend him, or stick-up form him. He had heard from some classmates that Phil had held down a menial job as a cashier at a local supermarket. Phil had turned to alcohol and hard drugs to bind his wounds. It was obvious that he was drifting and have a rough road moving ahead in life.

After hanging up the phone, Danny plucked a shelf worn a copy of his high school yearbook from his newly pained bookcase. He opened to a page with a picture of Phillip. Phil had signed his yearbook. Danny read the comments written by Phil. "To my best friend. I enjoyed showing you my comic book collection." He deduced that many of the fellow students had not signed Phil's yearbook. At that moment, Danny made a silent vow to himself that he would never let a friend down again. He regretted not keeping in touch with the boy, but their lives had gone in different directions.

Danny was also a former dorm advisor of Tinsley dormitory. He had grown tired of the responsibilities. His role was that of a young Sigmund Freud providing guidance to a confused young freshmen students. Danny had attempted to intervene in the affairs of his young students when they got into fistfights or demanded new roommates. The last straw was the death of a young, troubled student named Stefan. That final night, he had a repeat offender sitting in front of him. Stefan had a bad case of acne; oily hair fashioned into a ponytail and unfashionable clothing. He rarely smiled and seemed to be a loner who enjoyed his own company.

That last night, he had met with Stefan to try and help the troubled young man. Stefan reminded Danny of the famous cartoon character who had a rain cloud constantly hovering over her head even in the bright sunshine. The two men met in Danny's room. It was a messy student's dorm room filled with books and papers stacked in haphazard fashion around the room and piles of laundry waiting for its date with the laundromat. Danny sighed as he rocked back and forth in the chair. He leaned forward to address the troubled young man.

"You don't have to do it." pleaded Danny.

"I just want to fit in," explained Stefan.

"Drugs like LSD are not something you should mess with," warned Danny.

Stefan tried to reassure Danny or perhaps just to reassure himself. "All my friends tell me that it's a great experience. It will be okay." Danny shook his head and motioned to Stefan.

"I just don't think it's a good idea." warned Danny.

Stefan jumped up from his chair and headed out the door. He offered Danny a fake smile and the thumbs up gesture.

The next morning, Danny received a call from the Campus Patrol. He went over to their office. Danny sat across from the officer as he displayed pictures of the body of the dead student. Danny shook his head and confirmed the identity of the victim. Stefan had been hallucinating after ingesting the LSD tablets. It induced into his mind the illusion of invulnerability. He had leaped across barriers onto a busy highway despite warning from other students and was hit by a car careening down the road. A few seconds before, Stefan had stood in the middle of the highway smiling, oblivious to the dangers.

"The driver tried to swerve, but the kid just refused to budge," said the Patrolman. "He was hurled to the side of the road and died within a few minutes."

Shaken, Danny trudged out of the building feeling depressed. He knew that he had done his best to help the young man but felt that he had enough responsibilities without feeling responsible for every misguided students like Stefan. A few days later, he offered his resignation to the Dean of Students.

After a semester, he found that between classes and working at the newspaper, he was too busy to keep tabs on his former freshmen. He had remained friends with a few like Barry Lipkin and Alex Doherty. Sometimes, he regretted his decision. However, these doubts were becoming fewer and farther between as the weeks went past. He had rented a small apartment with his friend Ryan Marshott. He was happy pursing his ambitions as a reporter without being responsible for the well-being of the freshmen in the dormitory.

Danny stared at the clock, he recalled that he had a meeting of the Daily Targum, the school newspaper. He was reluctant to go. Despite his love of the work, he was always afraid that there would be new challenges. It always provided challenges to Danny.

Mr. Lewis Ritter
215 Pond Tier
Twp Washinton, NJ 07676

Made in the USA
Middletown, DE
13 October 2022